## Also by Sasha Summers

KINGS OF COUNTRY
*Jace*
*Song for a Cowboy*
*Country Music Cowboy*

DISCARD

# COUNTRY
## MUSIC
## COWBOY

### SASHA
### SUMMERS

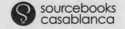
sourcebooks
casablanca

Published by Sourcebooks Casablanca, an imprint of Sourcebooks
P.O. Box 4410, Naperville, Illinois 60567–4410
(630) 961-3900
sourcebooks.com

Printed and bound in Canada.
MBP 10 9 8 7 6 5 4 3 2 1

*Dedicated to Deb Werksman.*
*Thank you for giving the Kings a home and introducing*
*them to readers. It's been a joy working with you!*

# Chapter 1

"IF WHEELHOUSE RECORDS THINKS ONE PRACTICE SESSION IS going to change the way I feel about Travis King, they have another think coming." Loretta Gram adjusted the wireless earpiece—well enough to clearly hear her manager's heavy sigh.

"Loretta, please remember you're a professional," Margot Reed said, near pleading. "This is important."

*Tell me something I don't know.* Today was important. *Very important.* Margot had made sure to drive that point home.

"When have I ever been anything less?" Loretta pushed through the front doors of the recording studio, the sting of Margot's words sharp. "I get it, okay?" Her career was on the line. "I won't let you down." *I won't let myself down.* "I'll give one hundred percent. Charm them. And go." *Before I say or do something I'll regret.*

"I know, Lori, I know you will." Another sigh. "This year has been…a nightmare."

Nightmare? *Hell was more like it.* The year had started with Margot's breast cancer diagnosis, then Johnny, then her father's ongoing pleas for money, and now Wheelhouse Records expressing concerns over Loretta trying to go solo when the label "really needed more duos and groups."

"Look at today as your chance to turn things around," Margot went on. "I know you're not exactly a fan of Travis King—"

Loretta couldn't hold back a snort.

"But this isn't about him. This is about you. I'm not giving up, you hear me? You can go solo. I believe it. Now you need to start believing it, too, all right?" Margot had a knack for getting herself all fired up by her own pep talk.

Loretta smiled. "All right." A solo career had *never* been part of the plan. But without Johnny… Well, she *was* on her own now.

"Rehearse, perform, and you're done. That easy," Margot reminded her. "Then we'll go back to Wheelhouse to see what they're thinking. If we need to look for a new record label then that's what we will do. I don't care how important Wheelhouse Records thinks they are, they're not the only recording label in the world."

But they both knew Wheelhouse Records was one of the best record labels in the country music industry. Loretta ignored the bitter taste in her mouth, smoothed a hand over her hair, and scanned the lobby of the Kings' lavish recording studio. All golden and shiny and privilege. *Just like the man I'm singing with.*

"If I could be there, I would." There was no missing the snap to Margot's words.

"I know. But you are where you need to be. Concentrate on resting, on your chemo, and taking care of yourself." Loretta didn't need to tell the woman she was pretty much the only person she had left in the whole world. *I need you.*

"I'm fine. Who needs boobs anyway?" Margot chuckled. "I'm keeping my phone nearby. I expect a full report when you're done."

"Will do." Loretta forced as much enthusiasm as she could muster.

"That's my Lori." Margot chuckled again. "Head up, girlie."

"You know it. You keep kicking cancer's ass." After their goodbyes, Loretta was left to her thoughts. And her frustration. Everything about this rubbed her the wrong way. From Wheelhouse Records CEO Ethan Powell's sympathy phone call that turned into a "the future of your career" call to the fact that her opinions and objections about this duo with Travis King didn't matter. All Ethan Powell had said was, "Travis King is a changed man, Loretta. I have every confidence that this performance will be unforgettable."

Unforgettable as in Travis King would humiliate himself, and her, and the whole thing would be a catastrophe? Or, less likely, they'd manage to pull off some sort of miracle performance that wasn't a total embarrassment. *A changed man, my ass.*

Mr. Powell was *wrong*. Plain and simple. She didn't need to spend five minutes with the Comeback King to know a leopard didn't change its spots. Travis King lived a gilded and entitled life, had more good looks that common sense, and fans who'd defended him even after that damning video had taken over every social media outlet on the planet. If he could still be loved after that, why change? *He wouldn't.* People like him didn't have to. The fact that she was standing here, eyeing the Kings' wall of success with Wheelhouse Records in preparation for this disaster-in-the-making performance, proved that.

Margot had an infinite wealth of wisdom she'd dispense at appropriate intervals—something Loretta could sorely use at the moment. Likely Margot would use one of her go-to sayings like, "Never let a bad situation bring out the worst in you." Or, another favorite, "Learn to pick your battles."

Bottom line, Travis King wasn't worth the fight.

"Loretta? Glad you could make time to meet with us." Hank King was headed her way, all smiles.

*Hank King.* "Of course." Her throat had gone bone-dry. Because…well…this was *the* Hank King. She didn't want to get starstruck but… *Hank King.* Growing up, his albums had become the soundtrack of her life. There wasn't a Hank King song she couldn't play or a lyric she didn't know by heart. "Thank you for this opportunity."

Hank cleared his throat. "I'm pretty sure we should be thanking you," he said, stepping aside…for his son.

*The Comeback King himself.*

Travis King, in person, was ridiculously good-looking. It was fact. *Everyone* knew it. Including Travis King.

*Be nice. Be charming. Smile.* For Margot. *Show them what you're made of. Show* him *what it means to be a serious musician.*

"Loretta. It's good to see you," Travis said. "I am sincerely sorry about Johnny."

The familiar lump, cold and hard and jagged, wedged itself in her throat. "Thank you." Two months of anger and frustration, sadness and grief so crushing that getting out of bed on some days was a challenge. But hiding under the covers, eaten up with useless emotion, carrying on and crying buckets of tears wasn't her way. It's not like it helped. *It damn sure didn't change a thing.*

"We were at the Oasis together." Several of Travis's trademark tousled dirty-blond curls fell forward onto his forehead as he spoke. "Last year."

The Oasis. Johnny's home away from home. The Malibu California addiction treatment center catered to the very rich and famous. It had worked, sort of. Johnny always came home clear-minded and determined to stay clean and healthy…but it never lasted for long. This last time, he'd barely made it two months.

"He was a good guy," Travis added.

"He was," she agreed. Good and beautiful and gentle and too broken for this world.

"You need anything?" Hank asked.

"No, I'm ready to get started." The sooner this rehearsal was under way, the sooner it was over.

"Come on, then." Hank waved her forward, then turned to head back the direction he and Travis had come from.

She followed, glancing at the man walking alongside her.

The Golden King. The Casanova of Country Music. The Heartbreak King. King of Smiles. King Charming. Over the years, that tabloids had given him an impressively long laundry list of nicknames. To be fair, she had never seen a bad picture of him. Even in *the video*, he'd looked pretty perfect. And yes, up close, he did have a blindingly perfect—almost Photoshopped—appearance.

The hair. The blue-green eyes. The body. But his beauty was skin deep.

"Here you go." Hank opened the door for them. "I was hoping we could have this out at our place today." He broke off, coughing. "Excuse me. My wife built a studio out there, we're calling it the Music Barn, and it's something." Hank shook his head. "Saves time, back and forth from home and Austin."

"Another studio?" She scrambled to recover. "This isn't... I mean, this isn't yours?"

"As of next week, Wheelhouse Records is the owner." Travis stood with his hands shoved deep into the pockets of his faded jeans, looking more than a little uncomfortable.

*What was that about?*

"Made a lot of good memories in here. And some damn good music too." Hank inspected the room. "But times change and you gotta learn to change with it." With a smile, he added, "Y'all get set up and we'll run a sound check. They sent the music?"

She nodded. The music had popped into her inbox seconds after her frustrating phone call with Ethan Powell. "It looks good."

"It does." Hank cleared his throat again. "I'll give you a minute to get settled?"

"Thank you." Loretta turned, slowly, to take in the Kings' private recording studio.

That was when she saw Travis King pull a prescription pill bottle from his jeans pocket. He opened it, shook a pill into his hand, popped it into his mouth, and closed the bottle. Seconds later, it was back in his pocket and he was taking a drink.

A drink—from a whiskey glass. A now empty whiskey glass.

It was so surreal she wondered if she was seeing things. Surely that's what it was. Surely Travis King hadn't just taken a pill with a whiskey chaser? That hadn't really happened. When had he started using pills? She glanced around, looking for other witnesses—hoping for confirmation that she was seeing things.

Only she wasn't. And, honestly, she was surprised. She'd known Travis wouldn't stay sober for long… But that didn't stop her anger, hot and fast, from damn near choking her.

Ever since the news had broken that the duet for the International Music Awards "In Memoria" performance would be Travis King's big return to the stage, the anticipation and buildup was *everywhere*. Unavoidable. Inescapable. All the hype and media were about him, his recovery—his comeback. The Comeback King.

It was a lie. All of it. The proof was literally staring her in the face.

*Sonofabitch.*

How was she supposed to do this? This year's "In Memoria" would include Johnny. Her best friend. Her singing partner of eight years. Whether or not they shared DNA or blood, he'd been her brother. He was gone.

Professional. Cool, calm, and collected. One song.

"Ready?" Hank King's voice echoed in the live room, waving through the glass that separated the live room with the control room.

*No.*

"Side preference?" Travis asked, smiling, those blue-green eyes giving her a quick head-to-toe inventory of her, setting her blood to boil.

"What?" she snapped.

His smile dimmed, a crease forming between his brows as he asked, "Which stool?" He pointed at the stools arranged, mics at the ready, surrounded by the floating walls used for optimal acoustics. "Lady's choice."

*Choice?* That was a joke. Her *choice* was to walk out. Or take all the anger she'd been boxing up inside and let *him* have it. Yelling. A few select curse words. Lots of finger pointing—a few solid jabs square in the middle of the well-sculpted chest his skin-tight grey

T-shirt clung to. She'd put him in his place and wipe that smile from his too handsome face and, maybe—hopefully, finally—feel some relief.

"You okay?" His voice was low and concerned. Or was that sympathy?

*No. Not really.* But she wasn't about to let him know he'd gotten under her skin. He already thought the world revolved around him—she wasn't going to feed his ego. "Fine." She would be fine. All she had to do was get through the awards show. "Left," she said, crossing the hardwood floor. She picked up the waiting headset, took her seat, and waited for him to take his spot.

*The sooner this is done, the faster she could leave.*

Travis took his seat opposite and put his headset on. Eyes glued to the music, he flipped through the pages, took a deep breath, and ran his fingers through his hair. Another deep breath and he pressed his hands against the tops of his thighs, agitated.

*The pills were kicking in.*

"Ready?" Hank's voice echoed in her ears.

At their nod, the rising swell of music demanded one hundred percent of her attention.

It was split, the verses split—two lines for Loretta, two lines for Travis. The chorus, they sang together.

> *Day breaks, the sun rising in the sky.*
> *At work, my life is one big damn lie.*

Loretta resisted the urge to look at her singing partner. She knew how magical collaborating could be... But this wasn't Johnny. The sharp twist of her heart reminded her of that.

> *Hours pass, and there's still no end in sight.*
> *Promised you, not to give up on the fight.*

Travis King might be an alcohol-addicted pretty boy set firmly on the road to self-destruction, but he could sing.

*But all your words are now the song left in my head.*
*And all your smiles are brightest when I'm in our bed.*

Loretta closed her eyes, hoping to blot out a memory of Johnny's smile.

*I get up and go out and live each day.*
*Couldn't know losing you would hurt this way.*

The rasp in Travis's voice rolled over the words, the last three gruff and thick and laden with emotion so pure no one could manufacture it.

Somehow, they were singing together now. Somehow, she'd made the mistake of looking his way. And now, the words became a melody—all while his blue-green eyes held her gaze.

*So, I'll hold you closer.*
*Keep you warm in my heart.*
*Your name is a whisper.*
*Until we're not apart.*

She tore her gaze from his before the next verse picked up. Maybe this wouldn't be a train wreck of a performance after all. As long as he sang from the heart, as long as she kept her cool, they might just be able to pull it off. And then? She'd move on and Travis King and each and every one of his bad mistakes would go back to being tomorrow's scandalous headline for the entertainment tabloids.

Travis had taken one look at Loretta Gram and known this was a mistake. The tension had been so much he'd resorted to taking one of his anxiety pills. *Not that it helped.* Since the studio was mostly packed up and ready for the move to the home studio, cup options were limited. After a quick search, he'd found only the whiskey glasses his father and Ethan Powell had used to toast the sale of the recording studio. Not exactly appropriate but he had no other options. Still, the ice rattling around in the cut crystal tumbler had him reaching for the guitar pick he kept in his pocket. It was a focal point. Something tangible meant to help him pause and process. When things pressed in on him, stringing him so tight he might break, rubbing the smooth surface between his thumb and forefingers helped him focus. It was also a tangible reminder that life was about the choices he made.

Like now. He didn't *want* any of it.

It had been a year since he'd been on a stage. A year. A lifetime. Now Three Kings had a tour coming up, a tour that was supposed to be his return to the stage. That was something he'd done hundreds of times, safe and sound, with his sisters front and center while he played and sang from the periphery of their spotlights. But even after years of touring under his belt, he worried about screwing something up.

Singing? A duet? Bearing the weight of a spotlight?

If his daddy hadn't asked him to step in, he'd have offered up an alternative—*any* alternative. But his father had asked, something he never did. It had been his choice, but there was no way Travis could say no.

*Maybe I should have.*

He already felt like a damn imposter—filling in for Hank King. It was a fucking joke. *He* was a fucking joke. He'd grown up in his father's shadow knowing he'd never be his father. His father was a country music legend for a reason. The charisma. The voice. The energy and confidence.

Travis was a backup singer.

To make matters worse, Loretta Gram showed up, all narrow-eyed hostility. He got it. She was anything but pleased with the situation. *That makes two of us.*

The only time she hadn't looked ready to tear off his head was when they'd been singing. Music did that. It was powerful. It smoothed off the rough edges, filled an empty ache, triggered memory or longing… Singing the chorus together, the first time, had been the only time those amber-topaz eyes of hers hadn't been shooting daggers his way.

Now they sat, silent and awkward, while his father played back the recording of the session. A recording. Not exactly standard practice protocol. But the recording wasn't for them. It was for Wheelhouse Records. Because his own record label didn't trust him either. Nope. They'd needed verifiable proof that he was capable of pulling this off.

Apparently, his father was the only one who believed he could do it.

Since his release from the Oasis, he'd been working out daily. The physical exertion helped work out the stresses of the day. Tonight, he'd need one hell of a workout.

Travis's phone vibrated from the recesses of his pocket.

He ignored it. According to Momma, playing on your phone while keeping company with others was rude. Considering how popular he already was with Loretta, he figured he'd avoid adding fuel to that fire.

Still, Loretta was studying her fingernails like they were the most interesting damn thing in the world. She had been since they'd stopped singing. Her long, dark hair hung forward over one shoulder, a glossy curtain hiding most of her face from view. *There is no way her nails are that interesting.* But her nail-gazing was better than her glaring hostility.

His phone vibrated again. *Screw it.* He pulled it from his pocket and swiped it open.

A picture—from his sister Krystal. A very flattering picture of Loretta Gram. Long brown hair. A mischievous smile on red lips. A pale blue sweater that hugged curves he'd been hard-pressed not to acknowledge since the moment he'd spied her waiting for them this morning. It was a good picture. Of course, the Sonic Blue Fender Jazzmaster guitar in her lap helped.

*Damn fine guitar.*

Three little blue dots bounced on the screen until Krystal's text popped up. Is she madly in love with you yet?

He glanced at the woman sitting opposite him. No smile. No eye contact. Hell, he wasn't even sure she was breathing. About the only thing he was certain of? She did *not* like him—not one teeny-tiny bit.

His response was short. No.

Three little dots started bouncing again. Emmy Lou says you should tell her you've stopped being a man-whore.

Travis burst out laughing. His twin little sisters were as different as night and day. He knew damn well Emmy Lou would *never* say man-whore. But Krystal? She wouldn't think twice. She was likely laughing as she typed the text.

His laughter had temporarily halted Loretta's all-encompassing nail inspection. Now, those big tawny eyes were waiting. Actual eye contact.

He smiled, holding up his phone in explanation.

*There it was. The death glare.*

Loretta turned her attention to the sheet music now. She lifted the pages from the stand, reading over each one as if it was the first time she'd lain eyes on the notes and lyrics she'd been singing so sweetly for the last thirty minutes.

His phone vibrated in his hand.

Krystal's text popped up. Okay, fine. I said man-whore.

I figured as much, he responded. Thanks for the vote of confidence.

What? Am I wrong? I said no longer, didn't I? Never mind. How'd it go? Knowing Krystal, she was rolling her eyes right about now. I've been sucked up inside Emmy Lou's wedding vortex all morning. When are you coming to save me?

Travis smiled. *Wedding vortex?* Emmy Lou's wedding was the best thing that had happened to the family in recent years. But Krystal wasn't one for making a fuss out of things and just about everything involved in Emmy Lou's wedding had fuss involved.

Wrapping things up here now. If there's cake involved, save me some. He hit send, then followed it up with, Session went well. He thought. He hoped. *The musical part anyway.* But he was no Johnny Hawkins. Johnny had been a rare artistic soul. A musical pioneer. How he'd found a way to blend folk, rock, classical, or rap into hit songs was a mystery. Most die-hard old-school country music fans didn't take too kindly to their country sounding like anything other than country. But Johnny had made it work. He and Loretta together? They'd had the sort of connection that made their music soulful and true.

Losing Johnny Hawkins had been a blow to the industry.

He risked a glance Loretta's way. It would have been a hell of a blow to her. She'd worked with one of the best and now, this? She'd lost her long-term partner and been saddled with a backup singer to honor his memory. Was it any wonder she was so resentful? No. *Hell no.* He owed her an explanation—if not an apology.

"Thank you, for this. I know I'm a piss-poor stand-in for my father." Travis waited for her to respond. At this point, any acknowledgment that he'd spoken was fine.

Her wide-eyed surprise wasn't exactly the response he'd expected. "Stand-in?" Her voice sounded brittle. "You mean..."

*Shit.* "You didn't know?" She honestly thought their record company would put him up as a first choice for this? That they'd put her with someone like him? *Guess I get why she's so pissed off.*

Now that he'd made her good and worked up, he didn't have much hope he'd be able to smooth her ruffled feathers. Still, he tried. Maybe now that she knew he was the stand-in she'd cut him a break and turn down the hostility. "Daddy wanted to but, well, I'm sure you've read about my parents?" Everyone had heard about it—the radio, television, and every damn tabloid had run a piece on the downfall of the long-standing power couple.

She went back to studying the music she still held. "I've heard things are strained."

"I guess that's one way to put it." He ran his fingers through his hair. His parents might not be officially separated yet, but that wasn't stopping his mother from acting like they'd finalized their divorce. "Daddy heard she was coming to the awards show—with a date. He's not taking the news well."

She glanced his way. "No. That's…no."

"Yeah." He nodded. "Daddy worried the attention over more King family drama might overshadow the performance. So, you're stuck with me."

Loretta stiffened, her full lips pressed flat and her eyes narrowing just enough to suggest she was holding something back.

*Don't ask. You don't want to know.* "If you've got something to say, go ahead." He leaned back and braced himself. Whatever she had to say wouldn't be pretty.

She hesitated briefly, took a deep breath, and said, "You…" She swallowed. "You think making the 'In Memoria' your return to the stage doesn't do just that?" There was a not-so-subtle hint of accusation to her tone.

"Now? Yes. But that's not why I'm doing this." If he could go back… No, he'd do the same. "At the time, I was doing a favor for my father. He doesn't ask very often."

Her posture eased just a bit. "I'm sorry your family is going through this."

"It's been coming for a long time." Which was true. As far as families went, he was pretty sure the Kings won when it came to the most emotional baggage. "Maybe they'll be happier this way."

This time, she didn't hide behind her nails or the music. She wasn't even trying to hide that fact that she was studying him now. He figured he had the right to do the same.

He'd seen dozens of pictures of her—videos too. A country girl. Unlike his sisters, Loretta wasn't one for sparkles and bling. She looked every bit the country girl, sitting here in some frilly red top with a tie and little blue flowers or dots all over it. Red earrings— he'd noticed them swaying when she was singing. Faded jeans that fit just right and hand-tooled leather boots. A country girl, through and through.

But Loretta Gram the person? He was having a hard time figuring her out. She was something to look at. Thick and wavy hair, a mix of deep browns and reds and warmth that fell down her back. He'd already experienced the power of those eyes… They were something. The hint of gloss tinting her full lips was just enough to draw attention. She wasn't smiling like she was in the picture Krystal had sent, but she was just as beautiful. Beautiful and angry.

"That'll do it." His father came out of the control room, nodding. "You two made some mighty pretty music today."

"We're done?" Loretta asked, slipping from her stool and offering his father the only authentic smile he'd seen her make all day. "Then I'd best be on my way."

Travis stood too. "I'll walk you out." Things might have started out rocky, but maybe they could finish out the day on a more positive note.

"You don't need to," she argued, her smile going flat.

"I don't mind." He held the door open and followed her into the hall.

As soon the studio door closed behind them, she spun to face him. "As much as I appreciate what you're doing for your father, I think it's important that you know exactly where I stand on this… arrangement." Her cheeks flushed deep pink.

*So much for being positive.* "I think I got the gist of it." He shoved his hands into his pockets.

"I'd rather there was no confusion." Her brows rose. "We are not friends. We will never be friends. Both of us are doing this for our career—period. You don't need to walk me to my car or give me first pick of the stools or act cordial or even talk, really, since the two of us have nothing in common."

"Considering how uneventful this recording session has been, this seems like an awfully strong reaction." As far as he knew, he'd never done wrong by Loretta Gram. Overall, he was a likeable enough guy. Maybe less fun now that he wasn't drinking, but still. This speech didn't add up. "Did I do or say something to piss you off?"

"This isn't about today." She sighed, impatient. "This is about… you. To be frank, I just don't like you. Period." With that, she brushed past him, headed down the hall, and went out the door.

Travis stared after her, wondering what the hell had just happened.

# Chapter 2

LORETTA SAT CROSS-LEGGED ON THE SIDE OF THE STAGE, watching the director and the choreographer argue. All around them was a flurry of activity, the stagehands, designers, and sound techs a coordinated team doing their jobs with efficiency—regardless of the drama unfolding on the stage itself. Right about now, she envied them. They could get their work done. She could not. Not until the director said they were good to go. Gabriel Luna, the awards show director, had yet to recognize her presence, let alone give her the thumbs-up to rehearse.

She was too far away to hear what the argument was about, but their body language stopped her from finding out. Not exactly riveting stuff, but she watched, devouring her snack-size bag of candy-coated peanuts. The alternative was acknowledging Travis King's presence—something she was trying very hard not to do.

Luckily, Travis hadn't tried to make small talk. After his initial nod of greeting, he'd flopped onto the stage with a well-worn paperback novel in his hand. He lay flat on his back, holding his book above him, and was seemingly engrossed in the pages in a matter of minutes.

They'd been slated to have the stage for thirty minutes. That was forty minutes ago. Forty minutes of the crinkle of her wrapper as she crunched away on candy-coated peanuts and the flip-slide of Travis turning the pages of his book and running his thumb down the side to smooth it in place. She knew the cause of the flip-slide sound because, after its fourth occurrence, she'd covertly managed to assess the situation from the corner of her eye…under the cover of reading the back of her candy-coated peanut wrapper.

For reasons unknown, her curiosity hadn't been satisfied by determining the cause of the sound. Like it or not, her attention lingered on the man lying on the stage. He was too good-looking. Until now, Loretta hadn't known that was possible. But it was. Even slumming it in ripped jeans, a faded heavy metal band T-shirt, and boots that had seen better days, he looked like something out of *GQ. That hair though…* He probably rolled out of bed that way. Careless and irreverent and, honestly, beautiful. It bothered her. A lot.

She didn't want to be bothered by him. She didn't want anything to do with him.

What had Johnny seen in Travis?

Once, she'd gone off on the Kings—Travis especially—and Johnny had been quick to come to the other man's defense. He'd said Travis King had been dealt a shit hand and was doing his best with what he had. But Johnny had always found a way to see the good in a person. Always. Even when they didn't deserve it. Especially when it came to those he considered a friend. Their time together at the Oasis had made them friends. At least, Johnny had thought so. Johnny's last stint at rehab before his death. As far as she knew, Travis never reached out to Johnny once he'd left rehab. *Not such a good friend after all.*

She sighed and pushed off the edge of the stage, anger coursing through her veins. *Not the most productive train of thought right now.* Twenty-six hours from now, she could shoot Travis King the finger and walk away. *And that's just what I'll do.* The image made her smile.

A burst of sound, a garbled yell, snapped her back to the confrontation still unfolding in the midst of her scheduled rehearsal time. The director's clipboard went flying. The choreographer laughed.

Loretta glanced Travis's way. He'd propped himself up on his elbow, causing the muscles in his arm to bulge, to watch the conflict. Eyebrow raised, curls falling onto his forehead, blue-green eyes wide, and the corner of his mouth cocked up. If she took his picture and posted it on Instagram right now, his fangirls would begin a snowstorm of likes and reposts so frenzied they'd probably break the internet.

*Whatever.*

Irritation renewed, she crumpled up her candy wrapper and shoved it in the pocket of her blue chambray dress. With her snack gone, all she could think about was getting back to her hotel room. Tomorrow would be nonstop. In the morning, she'd have her final fitting for the two gowns selected for her, hair and makeup, and on to the endless red carpet and then the dreaded performance itself.

Tonight, she needed a little decompress time for herself. Las Vegas wasn't her scene; growing up with her father had removed all interest in gambling or drinking. Her night would be more of the eating-room-service-cheesy-fries in her fluffy white bathrobe while watching her favorite British baking show marathon. To her, that sounded pretty close to perfect. Way better than this, anyway.

Waiting. And waiting.

Travis's page turning.

The now elevated voices still bickering.

The low roar of conversation and movement as the stage workers prepped all the bells and whistles for tomorrow night.

She walked along the edge of the stage, slowly—like a tight rope. Back and forth, then stared up to count the can lights mounted on the catwalk overhead.

"Miss Gram, Mr. King." The director, Gabriel Luna, approached. "Please forgive the delay. We are ready now."

"Oh good." She didn't bother hiding her relief.

That was when she realized Travis was watching her. Smiling. Why was he smiling? The smile was irritating. Almost goading—whether or not he knew it. What was his problem? Really? And why didn't he own a shirt that wasn't vacuum sealed to his chest?

What did he put in his hair to make it look so…so perfect all the time?

*The sooner I get back to my room, the better.*

"Ready?" Travis asked. "We can wait, if you're not done doing whatever you were doing."

She ignored him. *Go use all your…charm on someone else.*

"With or without music?" Gabriel asked. "We're a bit behind."

As far as choreography went, they didn't really have any. She walked in from one side of the stage, he walked in from the other side, and they met in the middle to finish the song.

"I'm fine just walking through our marks?" Loretta asked, glancing Travis's way. No singing. No dragging this out. Just run through their blocking, pausing on the little taped "x" marks for the right amount of time, then moving on to the next. That would wind things up nice and quick.

Travis ran his fingers through his hair, the muscle in his jaw twitching. "Fine by me."

The hair, the jaw twitch, the shift of his arm muscle… She had to admit there was a certain mesmerizingly virile quality about Travis King. He was ripped. Distractingly so. If she hadn't seen him popping pills with a whiskey chaser, she'd have thought he was some health nut that worked out all the time.

Travis's blue-green gaze bounced her way—and held.

Even knowing he was all the things she despised most didn't dampen the rush of warmth that filled her belly. The sudden tightness in her chest only compounded her frustration. She was only vaguely aware of Gabriel saying, "Wonderful."

*Wonderful?* This was not wonderful. *No, it's fine.* She was in control of this situation. A pretty face and an incredible body were not going to cloud her judgment. *I refuse to be distracted by you.* With an impatient sigh, she ended the over-long look with a pointed glare and all but stomped off the stage to wait for Gabriel's count.

Altogether, it took less than three minutes and they were standing awkwardly in the middle of the stage.

A smattering of applause broke out from the back of the dimly lit theater.

"Bravo!" A woman's voice echoed from the shadows. "I'm pretty sure there was supposed to be a song, though."

Travis groaned.

"Behave." Another woman's voice. "You two look good together. I can't wait to hear how you sound."

Travis groaned again. "You've met my sisters? I'd hoped they wouldn't come after I explained things to them. But they didn't believe me." He shook his head. "I'll go ahead and apologize now."

"What?" Loretta was still scrambling to understand what he'd said. She'd managed to glean his sisters were here, but that was it.

"You. Not liking me." He shrugged. "They don't believe you— No, I guess they don't believe *I* was telling the truth about you *not* liking me." He shook his head, the corner of his mouth kicking up. "Most people like me. I'm a likable kind of guy. Try it, you'll see."

He'd told his sisters what she'd said? And now they were here? Loretta was horrified. But before she had time to make a quick exit, the beloved twins of country music, Krystal and Emmy Lou King, were walking across the stage toward her.

Loretta had nothing but respect for the sisters. As musicians and advocates for several worthwhile charities, they understood the difference they could make—beyond their music. They might be twins, but they were as different as night and day. While she didn't know them all that well, the Kings were media and tabloid staples.

The midnight black stripe that had been added to one twin's signature long honey-blond locks was a dead giveaway as to which twin was Krystal. But, even without the hair, Krystal's resting bitch face and confident "Fuck you" vibe was unmistakable. What Loretta admired most was the woman's refusal to explain or apologize for who she was. And who Krystal King was, was one hell of a performer—and one hell of a survivor.

Emmy Lou King had some sort of inner glow thing happening. She was like a fairy-tale princess come to life. From her megawatt smile to her genuine warmth, Emmy Lou King oozed "*it.*" Star power. Like millions of Instagram and Twitter followers and record sales and ridiculously loyal and adoring fans sort of star power. And yet, somehow, she'd managed not to lose her down-to-earth accessibility and, by all appearances, kindness.

"Loretta." Emmy Lou drew her into a hug. "My heart hurts for you. I am so sorry about Johnny. He was a gentle soul."

Between the emotion lacing Emmy Lou's words and the ferocity of her unexpected embrace, Loretta nearly crumpled. There were times she ached for this—for support. Just as quickly, Emmy Lou stepped back and Loretta did her best to recover.

"I didn't know him all that well, but I loved every single one of his songs. His lyrics said a lot about who he was, I think," Krystal said, her green eyes assessing. "I am sorry. I can't imagine how hard this has been for you."

The ache in Loretta's chest turned painful, but she did manage to say, "Thank you." She could leave now, couldn't she? The sting on her eyes was telling; so was the lump in her throat. She really needed to leave. "Well, it was nice to see you."

"We thought, maybe, you'd like to have dinner?" Emmy Lou asked.

They wanted her to have dinner with them. She'd been thinking "Why?" but apparently, she'd said it too. And now they were all staring at her. *Because that was rude.* "I mean, that's kind of you, but—"

"That's Emmy Lou." Krystal smiled, nudging her twin. "She's kind. I'm not. But we are both nosy. Which is another reason we were hoping you'd come to dinner."

Which was a bit brash but Loretta appreciated the woman's honesty.

"Krystal." Emmy Lou looked and sounded mortified.

Travis mumbled, "And now you see why I apologized."

"You apologized?" Krystal's brows rose, shooting her brother a narrow-eyed glare. "For us? *Really?*"

"Oh wow." But Emmy Lou wasn't commenting on their increasingly bizarre conversation. She was looking up.

With all the commotion going on, Loretta hadn't noticed the large screens being lowered, let alone the images for tomorrow night's "In Memoria" performance. So many faces. So much talent. Groundbreakers and innovators. Producers, lyricists, and composers. Music Hall of Fame members and fledgling artists taken way too soon.

The moment Johnny's picture appeared, Loretta looked away. She had to. Seeing his smiling face tore at the still-raw wound. Every day, it was there. Every day, she missed Johnny. And every day she was tormented by the questions that would never be answered. She'd known it would be difficult but this…this ball of pain and anger wrapped up inside a ball of razor wire shredded her insides and left her bleeding.

But that was her problem and hers alone. She was not going to fall apart now—not publicly—and definitely not in front of the Kings.

*Keep it professional. Calm, cool, and collected.*

"I have dinner plans but thank you," she managed, taking care to avoid direct eye contact with the siblings. "Maybe next time. Have a good night." She was already walking, rapidly, backstage—and much-needed space. She dodged cords and workmen, wheeled wardrobe racks, and a group of dancers clustered together before pushing open a door and stumbling out into a mercifully quiet, mostly deserted, hallway.

A few of the stage crew workers had been taking a smoke break, but they took one look at her and jumped up, leaving a plastic cup with cigarette butts, an empty can of soda, and a newspaper on the box they'd turned upside down for a table.

Deep, cleansing breaths helped. So did leaning against the cool concrete wall and closing her eyes. She pushed off the wall and sat on one of the folding chairs. Eventually, it would get easier. Maybe not the grief part, but the anger part. *I hope.* When she thought about Johnny, she didn't want to think about his death—she wanted to think about *him*. Smiling, laughing, singing. His beautiful face.

"I miss you," she whispered, rubbing her palms against her thighs. But missing him didn't stop her from being angry with him. And she was oh so angry. "I miss you so much." Her words were a garbled mess and there were tears on her cheeks but, for a second, she didn't fight them.

"Loretta?"

She jumped, surprised by Travis King's sudden arrival.

"You left this." His voice was low and soft.

Her phone. Her purse. She blinked, beyond embarrassed. *That's what running away gets you.* "Thank you." Her hand was shaking when she reached for her things—making things ten times worse.

"Here." Travis dug in his pocket and pulled out a white cotton handkerchief. "It's clean. Wrinkled, but clean."

She sniffed, eyeing the white fabric.

"You can not like me and still take my handkerchief." He shook his head. "And, no, I'm not offering it because I'm trying to change your mind, either."

*It wouldn't work.* She sniffed again, her throat too tight to answer.

"You're crying." He cleared his throat, those blue-green eyes focused solely on her. "Please...take it."

She did, whispering, "Thank you."

"Someone called." He nodded at her phone.

She tapped her phone. Donnie Gram aka Deep Breath. Her father. Not that the reminder to take deep breaths before she answered ever help. *What do you want now?* Because that was why he was calling. That was the only reason he ever called her. It was enough to have her slam the phone down on the cardboard box, knocking the cup over and the newspaper to the ground.

Travis knelt, stacking the paper back together and placing it back on the box. "Everything okay?"

She twisted the handkerchief in her hands. "Yes." From the corner of her eyes, an image caught her eye. The paper.

Not a real newspaper—it was one of those shock-headline gossip rags.

With Johnny's picture.

And a headline that set her stomach churning and made the pulse in her temple throb.

JOHNNY HAWKINS'S DEATH: OVERDOSE OR SUICIDE.

———————————

*Fuck.* One look at her face was all he needed to know just how much that classless headline gutted her. If she hadn't made it clear she wanted nothing to do with him, he'd probably have hugged her. He'd caught sight of her face when Emmy Lou had hugged her.

The longing he'd seen… Add this fucking paper? Dammit. Loretta Gram needed hugging.

Instead, he grabbed the page and wadded it up. "People are assholes." He stared at the crumpled paper ball in his hands. "But the people that write this sort of shit? They make the assholes look like saints."

She hadn't moved. The page was gone, but she stared as if it was still there—as if the words had branded themselves into the pages beneath.

Johnny Hawkins's addiction and depression had been public knowledge; it wasn't a huge leap to assume the worst. In the three weeks Johnny had been at the Oasis with him, Travis had quickly learned that Johnny used humor to deflect or dodge questions that dug too deeply into his past. Since Travis tended to do the same thing, they'd gotten along well.

But there was no doubt Johnny had been haunted by something. After he'd been found dead in his bathtub, there'd been speculation. After all, a celebrity overdose offered up months of sales. Throw in some irrelevant but easily manipulated interviews, add some hard facts about Johnny's struggles, and toss in a real humdinger like some childhood trauma or recent heartbreak. It was all about making money and that sort of crap was solid gold. But every single time one of these bastards came up with a new hypothesis, Johnny would be stripped bare for loyal fans and tabloid readers alike.

And those closest to him? Like Loretta? It wasn't just words or a story to her... It was being dragged back through that hell all over again.

*Dammit all.*

She could hate him all she wanted, but he couldn't leave her. He sat in the other folding chair, not saying a word, and leaned forward to rest his elbows on his knees. Sometimes knowing someone was there was enough. For him, anyway. Hell, he had a full basketball team full of people there for him.

Who did she have?

Her phone started ringing, the words "Deep Breath" scrolling across her phone screen. He wasn't one to judge but, as far as nicknames went, that was weird.

Loretta sort of crumpled into herself. Hands, and his handkerchief, covering her face. He heard a muffled groan but couldn't come up with a thing to say before she reached for the phone.

"Hi." She swallowed. "Rehearsal." Another pause. "For tomorrow night, yes." She stood then, wrapping one arm around her waist as she walking to the far end of the hall. "No. No one. I'm going alone. I couldn't get an extra ticket, I told you that."

She glanced his way then, but her expression was mostly

shielded by the fall of her thick hair. He took comfort in one thing. *She's not glaring.* That was something.

His phone vibrated, but he didn't have to look to know who it was. Loretta's quick departure hadn't gone unnoticed. How could it? She'd all but bolted from the stage *and* left her phone and purse behind. Once her fight-or-flight instinct had been triggered, everything else had been forgotten.

Is she okay? Emmy Lou texted.

From the corner of his eye, he took inventory. *Was she?* Loretta's posture was ramrod stiff, the grip on her phone white-knuckled, but her face gave nothing away. I'm not sure. He responded.

We're going back to the suite. Join us when you can. Love you. The blue dots scrolled across the screen before Emmy Lou followed up with another text. She is welcome to join us, of course.

He smiled at the screen. His little sisters could be a huge pain in the ass, but he was damn lucky to have them. If he'd ever needed proof of their loyalty or love, the last year had done just that. Once he'd dried out and had his head straight, he'd vowed never to take them for granted again. Not that he'd ever stop teasing them.

Love you too. Travis sent his text and slid his phone back into his pocket.

"How much? I thought that was paid." Loretta's voice rose slightly. "When do you need it?"

Now that he could hear her conversation, he wasn't sure he should be listening.

"It's not that at all." She ran her hand over her hair, twirling one long strand around her fingers. "That's not fair." Her tone was brittle. "Why are you saying that?"

He tossed the wadded-up paper back and forth, debating what to do.

"I'll get it." She sighed. "Give me a couple of days and you'll get it." Another pause. "I have to go." Seconds later, the phone disappeared into the pocket of her dress.

He tried to give her a minute, tried to act like he was just hanging out—not making sure she was okay. But she saw him glance her way and she wasn't happy.

"It's rude to listen to people's private conversations." She didn't look at him. "What did you hear?"

"Me?" He held up his hands, the paper ball falling to the ground. "Nothing. I wasn't listening."

Her brows crinkled, a deep V creasing her forehead. "You were just…sitting here?"

He stood. "Yeah, pretty much." He dragged his fingers through his hair.

Her long hair swayed as she shook her head. "Travis, I—"

"You don't like me." He cut her off. "I'll leave. I just wanted to make sure you were okay."

"I am fine." Tawny eyes flashed and those rosy full lips pressed into a tight, flat line.

"I see that." His gaze snagged on her lips. Her mouth. Damn, but she was a fine-looking woman. "Now, anyway." Damn, but he liked looking at her.

She must have picked up on that, because she was back to glaring at him. "I know what you're trying to do and it won't work so you might as well save your energy."

"Okay." He shoved his hands in his pockets. "Just so I know, what am I trying to do?"

"What it is that Travis King always does." One eyebrow arched high. "I thought I'd made it clear I'm not interested."

*Oh, she'd made it clear, all right.* But he wasn't sure what the "What Travis King always does" comment meant.

Her cheeks went fire engine red. "So, you and your hair and your smile and your tight shirts and all your…your…*you* can just…stop."

She had his full attention now. For a woman so hell-bent on making sure he knew how much she didn't like him, she seemed awfully flustered by him. Good damn thing, because she got under his skin too. Her words, her blush, and the way her gaze fell away from his when the air between them grew charged.

But she rallied. With a toss of her head, she unloaded on him. "I know this whole comeback thing is a stunt. I hate being a part of it. I'll be glad when the awards show is over and done with and I can remove myself from the whole damn mess."

He wasn't sure which stunt she was talking about. His father's misguided attempt to build up his son's confidence by having Travis stand in for him? The shameless way Wheelhouse Records had capitalized on the performance as his comeback? Or maybe she recognized him for the overall imposter he was.

She kept going. "Tomorrow isn't about you—"

"You think I don't know that? Or that I want it to be?" Travis's laugh was forced. "I know you have a low opinion of me, Loretta, but I'd never do anything to sabotage our performance tomorrow night. You have my word."

Her expression hardened. "You might mean that. But we both know that you're not in control. As long as you're drinking, your word doesn't mean a thing." She pulled the door open, shot him a parting glare, and left before he had time to fully grasp what she'd just said.

*Are you kidding me? What the hell was she talking about?*

The whole stunt comment had been about his sobriety? This was bullshit. Her attitude was bullshit and her words left a bad taste in his mouth. She didn't know him, but that hadn't stopped her from judging him. And it pissed him off. Every day, he made the conscious decision to stay sober. Every day, he had to fight off the self-doubt he'd never quite silenced. Every fucking day, he had to overcome self-loathing for hurting those he loved.

He ran his fingers through his hair, the blood roaring in his ears, and left through the same door Loretta had used.

He didn't catch her—hell, he didn't see her. *Probably for the best.* She must have sprinted out of there. It wasn't like he wasn't going to see her tomorrow. And, whether she liked him or not, he was going to set her straight.

"We leaving?" Travis's bodyguard, Sawyer, was waiting just outside the door.

"Yeah." Travis slipped his sunglasses on, still agitated.

"Guess rehearsal went well?" Sawyer asked, his expression as deadpan as ever.

Travis laughed. "Sure."

"Next?" Sawyer asked, his gaze sweeping the distance between the side door and the waiting black SUV.

"Gym?" He didn't care that he'd already worked out this morning. After this, he was too worked up.

"Ready?" Sawyer shot him a quick look, then nodded. "There's not too many waiting."

*Fans.* Travis nodded. Not Three King–specific fans—they wouldn't know he was rehearsing. Not that it mattered. These were the sort of die-hard fans that stood under the Las Vegas sun hoping to get a selfie or autograph with someone famous. He rolled his head, pasted on his smile, and nodded. "Ready."

Sawyer opened the door, and his black King's Guard shirt caused a series of overlapping questions. "Who is it?" and "Is it Three Kings?" plus several "Is it Hank King?"

*Nope. It's just me.* He hesitated, steeling himself for the reaction to come. Once this new tour had been set, he'd been plagued by nightmares. All his fans turning on him, yelling insults or booing him... So far that hadn't happened, but it didn't stop him from bracing for just that. *You brought this on yourself. Now, grow a pair.*

There was a lull as the crowd outside waited to see who was emerging, but the moment he set foot on the blinding white concrete parking lot, the screams began.

"Travis. It's Travis!" The shriek set off a crescendo of screams.

*Smile, Trav.* He could hear Emmy Lou in his head. *They love you. Give them the best version of you.*

"How are y'all doing?" he drawled, sliding off his sunglasses and giving them his best smile.

"You're here." A teen with pink hair, a nose ring, and a brightly colored tattoo sleeve started sobbing. "You are really here."

Since there wasn't much to say to that, he winked and took the pen and notebook being shoved his way.

He posed for at least a dozen selfies. Sawyer handed over a second permanent marker when he'd made it halfway from the exit to the car. He scribbled his name on autograph books, shirts, a shoe, and several arms by the time he reached the car. With a final wave and smile, he climbed into the black suburban—to find both of his sisters sitting on the opposite seat.

"You made it." Krystal said, glancing through the darkly tinted windows. "For a minute there, I thought that soccer mom was taking you down."

Travis had to smile. "You know how partial I am to soccer moms."

Sawyer climbed into the front passenger side, his gaze flitting to the rearview mirror. Clearly, he hadn't expected to find the other two members of Three Kings aboard or he wouldn't be wearing that look. For Sawyer, the slight eye-narrow headshake combo was about as close to surprise as it came.

"Yeah. Surprise?" Travis sighed. "As my bodyguard, shouldn't this sort of thing not happen? Not without you knowing about it, anyway." He ran his fingers through his hair. "That way, I don't know, you could stop them?"

"Sawyer knows we're not dangerous." Emmy Lou leaned forward to pat Travis on the knee.

Sawyer's eyebrow shot up.

Travis laughed.

"What?" Emmy Lou asked.

"Nothing." Travis shook his head and stared out the window at the blinking lights and crowded sidewalks of the Las Vegas Strip. "Why, exactly, are you here?"

"We have a family dinner tonight, remember?" Emmy Lou answered quickly. "Brock should be here soon."

Travis and Krystal groaned in unison.

"Does that mean we'll be talking wedding talk?" Krystal slumped back against the black leather seat. "Don't get me wrong, Em, I'm super excited for you and Brock and the wedding. It's just…it's such a *thing*."

"Harsh." Travis shot Krystal a look. The "Wedding of the Decade" stuff was taxing, but it was worth it. Emmy Lou had never been this happy. He'd keep eating cake samples, offering his opinion on bridesmaid fabric, and look at pages and pages of potential place settings if it kept that joyful smile on Emmy Lou's face.

And, selfishly, this wedding couldn't have come at a better time. Emmy Lou had more followers than…anyone. Her wedding and every little thing related to her impending nuptials trended regularly on social media—taking the attention and pressure off of him and his parents' rapidly declining marriage. How could the third wheel of Three Kings's return to the stage or another celebrity divorce compete with the wedding of country music darling Emmy Lou King and football star Brock Watson?

"No." Emmy Lou smiled. "No wedding talk. I promise. We *all* need a break." She rested her head on Krystal's shoulder. "I'm just glad he'll be here. I miss him when we're apart."

Krystal took Emmy Lou's hand, her green gaze meeting his. Krystal wasn't the hard-ass she tried to be. She guarded her heart from the world—save a select few. At the top of that list was her twin. Hell, when it came to Emmy Lou, they were both fiercely protective. "You know you can still change your mind." Krystal said it at least once a day.

"I know. I won't. But I know." Emmy Lou glanced up at her

sister. "I also know that we're in Las Vegas and there are a million wedding chapels around and you and Jace—"

"Emmy." Krystal cut her off. "Let's take one wedding at a time, okay? Besides, we are now way off track."

Emmy Lou sat up and, together, his sisters turned all of their focus his way.

"I thought this was about dinner?" Travis asked.

"It is." Emmy Lou smiled. "Partly."

"How much longer is this car ride?" Travis ran a hand over his face. "If this is about Loretta Gram, I only have one thing to say. Her not liking me thing? Well now, the feeling is mutual." They had one other thing in common too: both of them couldn't wait for tomorrow night and their collaboration to be over.

# Chapter 3

"THE BRANDY FIRST? AND THE PEACOCK FOR THE PERFOR-mance?" Juliette Rousseau, her stylist for the awards show, asked. "Then again, the brandy color *is* more somber?"

Loretta nodded, staring at her reflection in the floor-to-ceiling mirror of her suite. "I agree. The brandy dress for the performance." The peacock gown was lovely, but not right for an "In Memoria" performance. Loretta prided herself on simple fashion, nothing over-the-top or too flashy. The peacock dress was a classic ballgown of near-weightless silk, sleeveless with a gentle V neckline that didn't reveal too much skin. But when she moved, the pleats of the skirt parted to reveal vivid jewel tone silk inserts with peacock feather embossing. "It's one of the most beautiful dresses I've ever worn, Juliette."

Juliette stood back, gave her head-to-toe assessment, and nodded. "You look elegant and feminine and every bit the country music star you are. Head up, shoulders back, and you will own the red carpet." She plucked a pin from the pincushion her assistant was holding. "One day, you'll let me put you in a real statement dress. You're so young, Loretta. With that figure and my magic, you'd make an entrance no one would ever forget."

Juliette and her assistant were both wearing the same hopeful expression, but Loretta shook her head. "I appreciate it but…this is me. This is perfect. I love it."

"Let me see," Margot sounded off.

Loretta had almost forgotten Margot was there. Well, not actu-ally *there*, but on FaceTime. She couldn't be there in person, but she was doing her best to be there virtually. And Loretta loved her all the more for the support.

"You're killing me here." Margot gave an extra-exaggerated sigh for good measure.

Loretta held the phone away from her. "Don't get too excited."

"I will promise no such thing." Margot twirled her finger. "Turn me around or flip your phone or something. Let me see."

Loretta smiled as she held up the phone so Margot could see. Over the years, Loretta had come to trust the older woman's instincts. She studied the industry, every detail. Branding was key and she'd made sure Loretta was always on brand. If Margot didn't like the dress, there would be a reason.

"Lori-girl, you look so…so…" Margot broke off.

"Lovely? Elegant? Classy?" Juliette offered. "Beautiful."

"All those things. I'm speechless." Margot nodded. "You need to stay away from Mickey Graham, you hear me. That man has too many hands and none of them are up to any good."

Loretta laughed. "I know."

"I guess I'm glad you're sitting with Hank King. The man can't stand Mickey Graham, either," Margot said. "Turn around."

Loretta turned, considering Margot's statement. If she was sitting with Hank, she'd be fine. Hank King was a gentleman. But she wasn't just sitting with him. She was sitting with the whole King entourage. And, after her hasty exit, she wasn't sure what sort of reception she'd get from Three Kings. Of course, Margot didn't know about any of that. As far as she knew, the rehearsal had gone off without a hitch—because that's what Loretta had told her.

"I love the laces down the back. And the extra fabric in the skirt. The patterns." Margot nodded. "You look like a princess."

"You approve?" It had been a long time since Loretta felt put together, let alone pretty. It was a nice feeling.

Juliette waved her hand dismissively. "Margot, you have to help me convince her to take a risk now and then. Something daring. Unique and…sexy. She has the figure for it. A plunging neckline and low-cut back too. Not too low. I remember dressing another celebrity and she requested her gown be cut so low in the back, you could see the top of her bum." She shrugged. "But her bum is insured for thirty-million dollars so I suppose it's worth showing off."

Loretta blinked.

"Imagine that? I doubt my ass is insurable." Margot laughed. "I don't think now is the time for Loretta to be taking risks."

"Next." Juliette sighed with disappointment and glanced at her phone. "No time to waste."

"Who else are you dressing today?" Margot asked.

Loretta put her phone back on the stand and raised her arms so Juliette could help her out of the dress.

"People." Juliette winked. "Bree, here, will come back to help you get ready for the evening." She nodded at the assistant holding the pins at the ready.

Next was the brandy-colored dress. Once it was on, she wasn't sure what to think.

"It looked more sedate on the hanger," Loretta murmured.

"Looks can be deceiving." Juliette winked and stepped back. "Turn, slowly."

Loretta did as she was told. The dress itself wasn't the problem. It was off the shoulder with three-quarter-length sleeves and a hip-hugging mermaid skirt, but it had sheer tulle overlay on the bodice and a skirt covered in hundreds of near-invisible tiny beads and crystals that caught the light and gave her a slight glow. "It's... not too much?"

"It's perfect," Margot said.

"Of course it is. As much as I'd like to put you in something more, I know Loretta Gram's style." Juliette pointed out. "A few beads, a little sparkle, it's not too much. Not even close."

Loretta ran her fingers over the beading and nodded.

"Good. There's not time to find anything else at this point, anyway," Juliette pointed out. She was slipping out of the dress when she heard Margot say, "I'm so mad I'm not there to hold your hand, Loretta. If there was ever one awards show not to miss, it's this one."

"Why do you say that?" Loretta accepted her white robe from Bree. "Thank you."

"Turn on *TNM*. Don't look at me like that; turn it on." Margot believed there was always some truth to what was reported. At least, that was the excuse she used.

Loretta turned on the television, putting on the closed captioning versus turning on the volume. She wasn't a fan of *TNM*. They'd been relentless in their coverage of Johnny—most of it had been fabricated and none of it had been nice.

"They're doing a greatest hits sort of thing. They've gone back through the last twelve months to see if any of tonight's nominees had a scandal," Margot said. "They're talking about Travis King now."

Travis King. Pictures of Travis playing pool, in boxer shorts, with a bunch of bikini-clad or naked women. Images of Travis King's various trashed hotel rooms. The transcript of his drunken drive-through visit where he ordered everything on the menu and left a two-hundred-dollar tip for the drive-through attendant. And his bizarre tackling of a Christmas tree because one of the bulbs was out.

The segment culminated with that night—*the* night—and the video that twisted his party-boy image into someone on the edge and threatening.

"I can't watch this again." Juliette frowned and turned away from the television. "I don't care what people say, I know this family and I know Travis. If he's going to have a fresh start, this sort of thing needs to stop."

He'd already blown the whole fresh start thing; Loretta had seen it herself. It was sad...but, more than that, it was infuriating. Why did Travis King get a *fresh start*? What made him more worthy than Johnny?

The moment the footage of that fateful night started, Loretta couldn't look away. She'd seen it before—you'd have to live on a deserted island not to have seen it before. The camera recording from someone there at a rodeo. They'd caught the large, in-your-face guy heckling Travis until the heckling got out of control. And the look on Travis's face when he was finally goaded into taking the first swing. The fight didn't last long and, honestly, Travis was getting his ass kicked, but security—Travis's bodyguard—managed to break it up. Cut to ten minutes later, this video from a phone in the gravel parking lot of the rodeo. A visibly stumbling Travis, baseball bat in hand, breaking headlights and denting the crap out of the body of a parked red pickup truck. A couple of young teens were laughing and filming—all sorts of expletives beeped out as Travis continued to decimate the truck. The kids were filming Travis—filming each other filming Travis—and having a great time. But one boy got too close, tripped, fell, and Travis spun around, baseball bat raised over his head.

The video ended there with the image of Travis, looking furious and ready to use the bat on the teen lying helpless on the ground.

Loretta wrapped her arms around her waist, putting herself in that kid's position long enough for her heart to lodge itself in her throat. He was terrifying... And totally out of control. For months afterward, that picture had been everywhere.

It was hard reconciling this image with the man who'd offered up his handkerchief to her. *But that was Travis King.* So handsome and charming it was hard to believe he was capable of doing something like this, even with the damning proof right in front of her.

But *TNM* wasn't done with the Kings yet.

Next up, Hank King. And CiCi King. Rumors of their impending divorce. CiCi's work as a guest judge on this year's season of *Next Top American Voice.* And the relationship between her and the show's runner-up, Kegan Scott.

"If they keep things going at this pace, there's no way this will last four hours long," Margot said.

"Four hours?" Loretta frowned and turned off the television. "Margot, you can't watch this for four hours." She couldn't stomach another five minutes.

"Why not? It's not like I have anything else to do. Might as well entertain myself up until the red carpet fashion show starts." Margot blew kisses. "Remember the label is sending you security for tonight; they insisted. I asked for Gina again. You liked her, didn't you? Now, you have fun tonight. Listen to Juliette on the whole posture thing. I'll be on the lookout for you. Not that I'll have to look that hard. That princess dress is a showstopper."

Juliette sighed, saying, "Princess," like it was the worst sort of insult.

Loretta smiled, her confidence more than rattled by *TNM*'s bit. "I'll blow you a kiss." The call ended.

"You look great," Bree offered.

Juliette glanced at her assistant. "Great? No. Fabulous? Yes."

Great was fine. Fabulous? A showstopper? Not words she was comfortable with.

Juliette glanced at her watch. "Hair and makeup are coming? In ten minutes?" She waited for Loretta's nod, packing up her pins, needles, thread, double-sided tape, and other bits into her large work tote.

"I'll leave a few pins," she said to Bree, pointing at Loretta's chest. "And use the tape to keep things in place. The dress is too sheer to wear undergarments."

Loretta eyed the tape. *Lovely.* Nothing like having to tape your boobs into place. But she didn't want to think about the alternative. She vaguely remembered a costume malfunction of a performer years back—during the halftime show of the Super Bowl. Not the sort of media attention she wanted tonight. Or any night, really. "Tape me up." She tried to sound enthusiastic.

Within an hour, her suite was overflowing with people. The expected hair and makeup crews were well-oiled machines.

Wheelhouse Records had sent a masseuse too—to help her relax. But being touched by a stranger, naked, wasn't exactly relaxing, so she politely declined.

And then the bodyguard arrived. So far, Loretta had managed to avoid hiring her own personal security detail. But maybe it was time to rethink that. The idea of having someone watching over her every second of every day was unnerving.

"It's nice to see you again, Gina. I'd get up…" Loretta trailed off. Here she sat, in her fluffy white robe, with hot rollers in her hair, several nail technicians working on her hands and feet, and a makeup artist unpacking a tote full of brushes and sponges and who knows what else. It was too much and, honestly, a little embarrassing. But if she wanted to stay in Wheelhouse's good graces, she'd play her part in this dog and pony show.

"No need." Gina didn't seem the least bit fazed by the flurry of activity underway. She'd worked with Gina a handful of times but she'd forgotten just how intimidating the woman was. From her steely-eyed assessing gaze to her well-muscled arms, crossed over her chest. Loretta was five foot eight, relatively tall for a woman, and she wasn't exactly a waif either, but she was comfortable with her curves. Next to Gina, Loretta seemed tiny.

"You can sit, if you'd like?" Loretta paused. "Or can you?"

"I can." Gina's glanced her way. "But I'm fine."

*That makes one of us.* The longer it took for Loretta's appearance to become "camera ready," the further away she was from fine. Between the extra eyelashes, bright red lips, intricate half-up, half-down mass of curls the hairstylist had spent close to an hour executing, and the peacock dress that had been steamed smooth and was ready and waiting for her, Loretta regretted not bringing someone with her—even her father. *No, no, that would only make things worse.*

"What do you think?" The makeup artist—whose name Loretta couldn't remember—stood aside so Loretta could see her reflection clearly.

What did she think? She didn't normally wear much makeup so she wasn't one to judge. But she was pretty sure that wasn't the right answer and since five women were all waiting for her opinion, she opted for the truth. "I'm speechless."

"Excellent." The makeup artist sighed, her smile relieved. "If you don't make the Best List tonight, it won't be my fault."

"She will." Bree carried the peacock dress forward. "She will be at the very top."

Putting on the dress was a production in and of itself. At least this part of the evening was done; she was officially one step closer to this night being over. Now all she had to do was smile her way through the evening. It wasn't like this was her first awards show—she'd been to a dozen. But this *was* the first time she was going solo.

No, that wasn't exactly true. Walking the red carpet on her own wouldn't be too trying since it was all about the photo ops and quick interviews lined up into the auditorium. Once she was inside, she'd be sitting next to the Kings. Lucky for her, she was seated by Hank King because the less time she spent with Travis King, the better.

---

Travis glanced at his sister, Krystal. She sat facing him in the rented black limousine, her arms crossed and a frown on her face. "What?"

Krystal pointed, indicating all of him. "Stop."

"I'm going to need more to go on." Travis tugged at the collar of his white dress shirt as if that would ease his anxiety.

"Stop getting in your head." Krystal leaned forward. "You have nothing to worry about. It's not like you can't sing. Or fans don't love you. Or you've suddenly stopped being the second-most attractive man on the planet." She lowered her voice and leaned closer to her beau, Jace, to whisper, "Because you're the most attractive man."

"Pretty sure he picked up on that." Travis shook his head. "He's not just a pretty face."

Jace chuckled and bent to kiss Krystal's cheek. "I'm glad you think so."

"I don't *think* so," she argued, all sass, "I know so."

Travis groaned. "Please." He turned his attention to the tourist-lined Las Vegas sidewalks outside, considering Krystal's words. She was right about one thing—he was definitely his own worst enemy right now. But there wasn't a damn thing he could do to stop the worry. Tonight wasn't just about proving himself to Wheelhouse Records; he needed to do this for himself. Which would be a hell of a lot easier if he hadn't been paired up with a woman who'd already written him off as a failure.

Krystal's phone pinged. "Emmy Lou." She shook her head, her fingers tapping out a response. "She said she's worried about Daddy." She frowned. "Have you noticed him coughing, Trav?"

"A little." Travis shrugged. "He said he was fighting a cold."

"Well, Emmy Lou thinks it's something more." She turned, looking out the window at the limo in front of them, where Emmy Lou was. "I wish we'd all ridden together."

"We'd have been packed in like sardines." Jace took her hand. "I think that's what you said."

"Your dress does take up a whole seat." Travis glanced at her. "But you look beautiful so I guess it's worth it."

"Damn straight." Jace smoothed a long, blond curl from her shoulder. "I'm a lucky bastard."

"Yes, you are." Travis agreed. He liked Jace Black, liked the way the man treated his sister. But if there was ever a time he thought Jace took his little sister for granted—Travis would make sure Jace would answer to him.

Krystal smiled at him. "You two clean up pretty well yourselves."

Krystal cocked her head, eyeing him. "I guess you and Sawyer living at the gym is what's turning you into a muscle-man."

Travis tugged at his shirt collar again. "Right."

"Um, right." Krystal rolled her green eyes, her tone dripping sarcasm. "Do you own a mirror?"

He had to laugh then.

The limo slowed as it pulled up in front of the MGM Grand Garden Arena. The traffic came to a stop a few feet from the red carpet. Limos, town cars, and larger SUVs were grouped together, being directed by the police who'd been tasked with managing tonight's production. The carpet had metal control barriers running down both sides, additional security placed at regular intervals between the barriers. Not that the fans cared. They were bunched together, screaming and waving and craning their necks to see who was coming next.

"Is that Loretta?" Krystal asked. "Holy shit. I mean, seriously. Wow. She looks incredible."

"Who?" Jace asked, leaning around Krystal. "In the blue?"

"Yes. Look at the skirt." Krystal wasn't easily impressed.

There was a knock on the passenger side window. Their father waved, gesturing to them to get out.

Travis had forgotten just how deafening the fans could be. Nothing was as humbling as hearing the way the fans reacted to them—Three Kings. Their loyalty was second to none. Emmy Lou did the lion's share of the work. She kept her millions of social media followers close, posting daily snapshots of whatever struck her fancy. Music she was listening to. What her cat, Watson, was up to. Lots of selfies of Three Kings together. She connected with the fans in a way he and Krystal hadn't mastered.

Emmy Lou went first. She and Brock Watson held hands and looked suitably smitten with each other. Fans ate it up.

Jace and Krystal followed, her arm tucked through his— keeping her tight against him.

"Guess we're bringing up the rear." His father clapped him on the back and smiled.

Travis nodded, sliding his hand into his pocket to rub the guitar pick inside. He'd held the anxiety and panic at bay all day but, here—now—all the tiny fears and insecurities felt magnified. The noise kept coming, rolling over each other in various pitches and tones. It was hard to make out actual words, but the energy of the crowd helped. Not enough to remove the fear that this whole enterprise had the potential to go horribly wrong—but at least now he was excited about it.

"That's for you too," his father murmured. "See that?" He nodded at a group of young women holding a poster board covered in large letters and glitter that read, "Travis King's #1 Fans!"

He'd been accused of being a cocky bastard, having a big ego, and thinking he was the center of the universe—mostly by exes or musical rivals. Up until a year ago, that was true. Still, he had to admit the cheers and excitement, all for him, had him feeling pretty damn good.

Travis grinned and ran his fingers through his hair—Krystal's advice. Then he smiled—Emmy Lou's reminder—and the resulting surge of near-frenzied yells and cries had his father chuckling.

"Feels pretty good, doesn't it?" Hank was studying his son closely. "You hold on to that and sing for them and you'll always give your best."

*We have a career because of our fans.* It was Emmy Lou's response every time he or Krystal gave her grief for how active she was on social media. She had a point though. So did his father. Maybe it was time to subscribe to the Emmy Lou and Hank King playbook—making this about the fans. And it would keep him out of his head.

"Is that Loretta?" his father asked. "Who is she here with?"

Bits and pieces of her phone conversation came back to him then. She'd said she couldn't get a ticket. For tonight? She'd rather come to a three-hour award show alone? He hadn't meant to search her out, but that's exactly what happened. His gaze caught and held. *Incredible?* Is that the word Krystal had used? *True.* More than true. Seeing her… Damn, she was something to look at. Those eyes. Her hair. That smile. For a second, he forgot how quick she'd been to write him off. Hell, for a second, he forgot to breathe. She was…beautiful. Blindingly so.

"Travis?" His father nudged him.

"What?" Had he missed something?

The corner of his father's mouth kicked up. "You should see if she wants to join us?"

"She won't." Besides he wasn't exactly pro-Loretta at the moment. So why did his gaze keep shifting her way—over and over? *Because she's beautiful.* Hostile and sanctimonious as hell, but beautiful nonetheless.

"Might be worth asking." His father's gaze tightened. "Call me old-fashioned, but I'd rather she wasn't left alone to deal with the likes of him."

Travis followed his father's gaze. *Shit.* Mickey fucking Graham and his smug-ass smile. He'd caught sight of Loretta, all right. It was the way the asshat was looking at Loretta that dictated he take the high road. He wouldn't wish Mickey Graham on his worst enemy.

But his father beat him to it.

"Hey, big brother. I didn't get a chance to tell you how hand-some you look tonight," Emmy Lou said once he'd reached her side. "But I think they beat me to it." She turned, smiling at the group still screaming his name.

Travis waved again—sparking another wave of enthusiastic fandom.

"What's Daddy doing?" Emmy Lou asked.

"What Daddy does. He saw Mickey closing in and…" Travis explained, continuing down the red carpet—still smiling, still waving.

"Rescue mission, eh?" Emmy Lou's nose wrinkled, the only outward sign of her agitation.

Travis nodded. Mickey was an asshole; he'd always been as asshole. The sort of asshole that treated women like second-class citizens, used his private life for press, and didn't even try keeping his hands to himself. He'd made the mistake of tangling with Krystal a few years back, but, from all reports, he hadn't learned his lesson.

That's why his father stood, waiting as Loretta had a thousand more pictures taken from every possible angle. Sure, his father was talking to reporters and entertainers and being his normal jovial self, but it was clear he—Hank King—was waiting for Loretta Gram. And it was drawing attention.

"Daddy and his big heart." Emmy Lou was Daddy's little girl. To her, their father could do no wrong.

"Speaking of which, any sign of your mother?" Brock Watson, Emmy's fiancé, asked.

Travis knew exactly what Brock was asking. He wasn't the only King facing potential humiliation and scandal. If his mother showed up with her reported boyfriend Kegan Scott, things were bound to get awkward as hell for his father—for all of them really.

Travis sought out his father. "No sign of Momma." His father was walking back to them, Loretta Gram on his arm. "Or Kegan Scott."

"No." Emmy Lou waved as they made their way, slowly, along the carpet. But she must have been thinking along the same lines because she said, "That's just talk, you know that. Momma thrives on drama, but our family has always come first. She wouldn't bring another man here tonight. She wouldn't."

Travis and Brock exchanged a look, but conversation came to a stop as they approached one of the night's red carpet emcees. A live two- to three-minute soundbite to give at-home viewers a better look at the musicians and celebrities in attendance.

When Travis saw their emcee, the knot in his throat eased—just a bit. Molly Harper was one of the few reporters that had never treated his family with anything but respect. And, for that, Travis was a fan. Krystal liked to tease him about it—she'd even bought him a coffee mug that read Molly Harper's #1 Fan.

Right before they stepped up onto the elevated stage where Molly waited, Loretta whispered something to his father and let go of his arm. Instinctively, Travis searched for signs of Mickey Graham.

For the first time that evening, his gaze collided with Loretta's. The smile on those red lips never wavered, but her topaz eyes flashed with hostility. She almost made him laugh. Why the hell did he think she needed protecting? All it would take was one of those looks and Mickey Graham wouldn't know what hit him.

It was a solid reminder. *She is not my problem or my responsibility.*

Travis stepped up on to the dais, holding out his hand to assist his sisters with navigating the steps without tripping over their voluminous skirts.

"We can all squeeze in," Molly said once they were crowded together on the small platform. It meant a great deal when Molly accepted his hug and whispered, "It's good to see you back, Travis. I believe in you."

Hugs all around and they waited for Molly to count down.

"I'm here, live, on the red carpet, and look who's here?" She turned. "The King family. Hank, Emmy Lou, Krystal, and Travis. It's so wonderful to see you here tonight. And, may I say, all four of you look smashing."

Travis tuned out as his sisters listed off the designers of their dresses and the cost of the jewelry they'd been loaned for the evening.

"Travis, you're wearing?" Molly asked, waiting.

Travis glanced down. "Armani." He resisted the urge to tug at his collar.

"I'm loving the exaggerated shawl label of the jacket. And, look at you, leaving your dress shirt unbuttoned. Very Travis King." Molly's smile was sincere.

"Thank you?" he asked, uncertain.

"You're welcome." She laughed. "I know I speak for many folks here tonight, especially your fans, when I say we are glad to see your return to the stage. You look like you're feeling well. You've been working out." She shrugged. "I, for one, didn't think it was possible for you to get more handsome. It seems I was wrong."

Travis blanked. Was he supposed to say something witty? *I got nothing.*

"What have you been doing to prepare for tonight?" Molly's question caught him off guard.

He cleared his throat, knowing all eyes were on him. "Rehearsing mostly. Lucky for me, I know some people willing to help with that." He paused, glancing Loretta Gram's way. "But seeing as I'm getting to perform with one of the most talented artists out there, I'm pretty sure no one will be paying much attention to me."

"Three Kings are up for Song of the Year and Hank, you're up for Album of the Year. Good luck tonight. I'll be rooting for you." Molly smiled into the camera until she turned. "All clear. Thank you so much."

Things wrapped up quickly. Jace helped Krystal, Emmy Lou took Brock's hand, and his daddy followed him down.

"Shit." Travis heard Krystal's whispered curse word. "Momma."

From the corner of his eye, he saw her. His mother. And she wasn't alone. So far, Daddy hadn't spied them... If he could steer them all inside, there was a chance the strained reunion wouldn't happen before several hundred cameras and reporters ready and waiting to pounce.

"Mr. King." Loretta's voice was soft. "I hate to hurry inside, but I think the sun is getting to me. Do you mind?"

"Not at all," his father assured her, patting her hand. "I'm not too partial to the Nevada sun, myself. You need something cold to drink, a little air conditioning, and some shade."

"I think you're right." Loretta sounded relieved. "Thank you."

"I'm glad you said something, Loretta." Emmy Lou flanked their father's other side. "My dress weighs a ton. I think I'm melting."

"Well, then, let's get you two inside." His father picked up the pace, steering Emmy Lou and Loretta through the crowd—and farther away from his wife.

Travis followed, doing his best not to stare at Loretta Gram's back. It was hard. The ribbons lacing up the back of Loretta's dress fluttered in the mild breeze, drawing his attention. Once he was looking at the ribbons, it wasn't like he could ignore the rest. That dress, on Loretta, had him caught. A fly in a spider's web. He'd try to look away but got tangled up in the sway of her hips or the way she smoothed her curls over her shoulder to expose the column of her neck.

A year ago, he'd have gone out of his way to wine her, dine her, and wear her out in bed—regardless of the tension between them. Hell, a little tension and fire made sex more fun. And while there was a part of him that was tempted by the dining and bed part, her accusations were like barbs sunk deep. Until he cleared the air between them, he couldn't get them out.

"Guess we can all be thankful your singing partner got over-heated just in time to dodge a bullet." Krystal squeezed his arm when they reached the lobby.

"You think she did it on purpose?" Jace asked, tilting his head so Krystal could adjust his collar. "Better?"

Krystal nodded, her gaze locking on Jace's mouth. "You look good enough to eat."

"No," Travis interrupted them. "I don't think she did it on purpose. Why would she care?"

But seconds later, Loretta was peering over her shoulder. Not at him, but beyond him—searching, a deep V between her brows.

As covertly as possible, he turned to see who or what she was look-ing at. The answer was there, in a bright red dress and blond hair piled high. His mother. He turned back just in time to see Loretta asking for help to find her seat. Of course, his daddy volunteered.

*She'd known exactly what she was doing.* She'd spared his father public humiliation and, likely, heartbreak too. It was decent. More than decent. *Dammit all.* Travis ran his fingers through his hair, then slipped his hand into his pocket—worrying the guitar pick between his fingers. *After* he'd set her straight about his recovery and *after* he'd accepted her apology for jumping to conclusions, he'd thank her.

He'd thank her, they'd sing their song, they'd go their separate ways, and Travis wouldn't have to deal with Loretta Gram or her beautiful, angry eyes ever again.

# Chapter 4

"I DON'T KNOW IF I CAN GO OUT THERE IN THIS." Loretta's reflection stared back at her, her eyes wide with terror.

"You look amazing," Bree said.

"Not to be rude but you have to say that, don't you? Since you're the one that put me together like this?" Loretta shook her head. "How do I look?" she asked Gina.

Gina looked her over with same intensity she used while sweeping a room. "Nice."

*Nice?* Loretta sank into the director's chair, ready to cover her face with her hands—

"Don't! No touching," the makeup assistant called out. "You don't want to smudge anything."

"Right." Loretta sat back. Not only had she changed dresses, they'd added some sparkle stuff to her cheeks and given her way dramatic smoky eyes. And tape—so much tape. She suspected removing the double-sided tape from her nipples would require substantial time in a steamy shower, but that was a small price to pay for her peace of mind. There was no way—*no way*—she'd have a wardrobe malfunction tonight.

The makeup assistant pointed at the television screen. "Country Song of the Year is up." Jace Black and relative newcomer, Becca Sinclair, were walking across the stage to the microphone. "LoveJoy is up for 'Rain Down,' right?" The makeup assistant started packing up her brushes. "It better win. I think it's y'all's best song ever."

*I love* "Rain Down" *too*. But it wasn't considered a serious contender for the award. "I'm pretty sure Three Kings has it. 'Blue' was a huge hit." It helped that Emmy Lou had written the song for her then soon-to-be fiancé. "It's a good song."

"It is." The makeup assistant nodded. "But 'Rain Down' is better." She pointed at the screen again. "Isn't your performance next? Shouldn't you get out there? And you don't just look nice. You look beautiful. Own it."

Loretta peeled her fingers from the arms of her chair, forced herself up, and marched to the door. *I can do this.* Gina held it open. "Thanks," Loretta mumbled, then hurried from the door. It wasn't about the dress or the makeup or the audience—it was about honoring Johnny in front of their peers.

*Own it.* If owning it meant avoiding eye contact and heading straight to the wings of the stage without interruption, then she was totally owning it. Her and Travis's performance was immediately after this award so, win or not, she was ready.

Onstage, Becca Sinclair looked exactly how Loretta felt—ready to bolt. But Jace and his easygoing smile gave the younger singer the encouragement she needed to finish their scripted banter prior to announcing the winner. They went back and forth, reading the nominees and pausing long enough for a sample of each song to be played. When Becca tore open the envelope, Loretta glanced into the audience. There, in the front row, sat Emmy Lou and Krystal King, their guys on either side of them, holding hands and looking excited.

"And the winner of Country Song of the Year is..." Becca waited for Jace to tear open the envelope. "'Rain Down' by LoveJoy."

Jace nodded, clapping hard, the envelope held in one hand.

But Loretta couldn't move. She couldn't.

"Loretta?" It was Travis.

Where had he come from? Why was he here? *Do something. Say something. Move.*

"They're calling you." He nodded toward the stage.

She shook her head. They were calling LoveJoy. LoveJoy was gone. Johnny was gone. She didn't want to do this alone.

"If you want…" Travis cleared his throat. "You need a hand?"

*No.* Not from him. He should be on the other side of the stage. Not here. She opened her mouth but her throat was so tight, she could barely breathe.

He stepped forward and held out his hand.

Was he serious? Was he after something or was she so pathetic that even he couldn't leave her to flounder by herself? She stared at his hand. Did it matter? *No.* The sad truth was, as much as she didn't want his help, she needed it. She stepped forward, gripped his hand in both of hers, and did her damndest to suck air into her lungs. *I hope I don't regret this.* "Okay," she murmured, letting him lead her out and onto the stage.

It took forever to get to the mic. If it felt like all eyes were on her, it's because they were. Jace and Becca. The cameras. The audience—all rising to their feet. Her hold tightened on Travis's hand.

"Congratulations." Becca handed over the crystal award, leaning forward to give her a one-armed hug.

The hug was awkward to begin with, but Loretta's hold on Travis didn't help. Not that she could let go. *Let go. Let go.* But her fingers did the exact opposite, gripping the sleeve of his designer tuxedo sleeve talon-style.

Travis's hand rested atop hers, warm and strong and—dammit—comforting.

As the clapping died down, Loretta scrambled for words—any words. "I'm in shock," she said, her voice wavering. "People always say that, I know, but I…I mean it. I knew 'Blue' would win. I just knew it." She glanced at Travis then. Travis—whose arm she had in a vice grip. "Sorry, I guess." Laughter rippled across the audience.

Travis winked.

*Looking at Travis was a bad idea.*

She stared down at the award. "This was… 'Rain Down' was the last song Johnny wrote. We never had the chance to perform it live..." She had to stop then, had to steady herself. "He said he wanted to write something that people could sing and be happy." Her voice was shaking now, dammit. "He liked making people happy. And I think this means he accomplished that. I hope so, anyway." She cradled the award against her. "I want to thank you. The fans. Our incredible manager, Margot Reed. And Wheelhouse Records. And Travis King for dragging me onstage." More laughs. "So, thank you."

As the audience applauded, she forced herself to let go of Travis. "I guess I'll let go now since you need to go that way and I'm this way."

"As long as you're sure." Those blue-green eyes swept over her face, a hint of a teasing smile on his mouth.

"I'm sure." She hadn't meant to snap. And, really, it wasn't even at him. She was mad at herself. She was the one noticing the smiles and the color of his eyes and the teasing. He was just being him.

"See you out there in sixty seconds." He was full on smiling then.

Travis King needed to wield that smile with more care. He might not know it, but it was dangerous. Even in her rattled state she felt the power of it. Why? Considering how much she disliked the man, it was more than a little infuriating that his smile made her ache. *Wait. No.* It had nothing to do with Travis and everything to do with what had just happened. The song. The award. The standing ovation. All of it. Travis was just...there. She hurried off the darkening stage, handed the award to one of the waiting attendants, and tried to get her head straight.

Positive thoughts. Eyes closed, she pressed her hands to her heart and tried to slow the thundering rhythm. This might be her first performance without Johnny, but it wouldn't be her last. She had to do this. All that mattered was doing her best. For her career. Her future. *And for you, Johnny.* Her skin prickled, her nerves stretched taut just beneath the surface. *I can do this.* When it was over, she'd give herself the night—just one—to let it all out. *After.* She took a deep breath and headed on stage.

Beneath the beam of the spotlight, she sang the opening verse with all the heart she could muster.

Travis's gruff and deep tone sent a ripple down her spine. "Hours pass, and there's still no end in sight. Promised you, not to give up on the fight."

The song kept going, the lyrics taking shape without thought. Which was good, because it was taking effort not to watch the slideshow. She couldn't. Not now, when she was so raw—so vulnerable...

It was the way the light hit Travis King that stopped her from spiraling. Better to focus on him than publicly lose it. After all, there was plenty to focus on. The just-right fall of his too-long curly hair. The perfect fit of his tuxedo, stretched taut over his broad shoulders. The hint of yearning in his voice that tore at her fragile control.

They kept singing, moving slowly, and moving closer—so close she could see the muscles working in his throat as he watched her sing. Focusing on him eased the hurt she'd been struggling with, but it did nothing to calm her nerves. Now that he was standing beside her, there was no space between them and nothing to stop the growing hunger she had for this man. Her breathing was unsteady and, honestly, she was panicking over her total lack of resistance to Travis King. Resisting him was the last thing she wanted to do.

She hadn't expected the brush of his fingertips against hers. If she had, she might have managed to hide her reaction. No such luck. He didn't miss her bone-deep shudder. She didn't miss the tick of his jaw muscle—or the slight flare of his nostrils.

*What is happening?*

The music rose, building and rising, until they sang the final chorus together.

*So, I'll hold you closer.*
*Keep you warm in my heart.*
*Your name is a whisper.*
*Until we're not apart.*

When the music ended, it was the audience's applause that jolted her back to the present. As in, on a stage, in front of hundreds of people, while being broadcast to millions of televisions worldwide.

*Don't freak out. No one noticed. It was nothing. It is nothing.*

She was the one who took his hand, smiling into the darkened auditorium, as they took their bow. Travis was the one who pulled her into his arms and pressed a kiss to her cheek. It was just a kiss. *On my cheek.* The slight stubble of his cheek against hers. The tantalizing scent of mint and leather. The brush of his breath against her temple. The press of his hand against her back. None of those things should register. But they did. And all those unnerving and delightful things were still registering when they left the stage to follow one of the stage assistants to the press room. As performers, they had one final appearance. A recap and final questions moment. Inside the room, a large IMA step-and-repeat would serve as the backdrop. The two of them would pose for a few pictures, answer a couple of questions, and they'd be done. As in, she would never have to deal with Travis King again done.

If only it could be that easy. Since pictures were being taken, bright lighting in the press room was a priority. And, after they'd each had a handful of pictures taken, the first reporter got right to the point.

"Miss Gram, let's talk style. Who dressed you this evening? First the blue dress was striking." The woman gestured at Loretta, her eyes round and her eyebrows high. "Now, this one. You normally shy away from sparkles."

Loretta wasn't sure whether she should be offended or flattered that this was the first question for her. "Both dresses are originals by Juliette Rousseau that she selected for me."

"You look incredible," Travis sounded off.

Loretta glanced his way. *Hilarious.*

But he wasn't teasing—and he wasn't staring at her with his patented Travis King charm. He was looking at her. And, now, he was smiling at her. That dangerous, lung-emptying, it's-pointless-to-resist smile she could not afford to get caught up in.

She stared blindly at the reporters, desperate to get this over and done with.

"Tonight's performance was emotional for you both, I'm sure." Another reporter jumped in. "How do you think Johnny would have felt about the win tonight?"

That lump was back, lodged in her throat and damn painful to swallow down. "He'd be pleased, of course. He said there was no greater compliment than having someone enjoy his music."

"You two have chemistry on the stage. That was an unforgettable tribute. What are the chances of you two working again?" asked another reporter.

"Oh, no. I don't see that happening," she answered quickly. Maybe a little too quickly.

"I'd be honored to work with Loretta again." Travis glanced down at her. "If the situation ever arose."

Which was a far more professional answer. Her gaze darted his way. Beneath the fluorescent lights, his eyes were shockingly aquamarine. *Which has zero relevance to what's happening right now.*

"How about we get a couple of pictures of you two together?" A photographer waved them closer.

With each new pose, her awareness of Travis King grew to an alarming level. Little details. The mole on the side of his neck. The scent of spearmint on his breath. One especially long curl that hung onto his forehead. *Like a blond Superman.* He had a slight bump in his nose. His hand was warm against her back. The gravel timbre of his voice. The more he smiled, the more she wanted to grab him and... *Push him far, far away.*

She didn't exactly push him, but she made sure to put space between them just as soon as the pictures wrapped up. With a smile and a wave, she was out of the press room. She wasn't exactly sure where she was going—only that she needed to get Travis out of her head.

She glanced at the sign on the wall, turned, and headed for the dressing rooms. If Bree was there, she'd change and attempt a quick exit.

"Loretta," Travis called out.

*No.* At this point, there was nothing left to say. *Don't look back.*

"Hold up." He was getting closer—his voice was getting closer.

*Pretend you don't hear him.* Keep moving. But she glanced back. *What are you doing?*

"Please." The corner of his mouth kicked up. Now, he was going to be charming? Why? *There is nothing left to say.* "It won't take long."

*Fine.* In spite of her worst fears, he hadn't let her down. If anything, he'd kept her on her own two feet. Even if his motivation was questionable, he had helped her do what needed to be done. A few more minutes wouldn't hurt anything. She slowed, then came to a stop, waiting for him to reach her before she asked, "What?"

He chuckled. "I wanted to make sure you were...okay?"

It wasn't an unreasonable question. Less than ten minutes ago, she'd nearly torn off the sleeve of his tuxedo. "I'm okay." Easy enough. "So, we're good?"

He shook his head. "No."

She waited, arms crossed, staring him down. Now he'd reveal his true colors, she could go back to hating him, and there be no loose ends.

But the minute she crossed her arms, his gaze shifted. To her dress. More specifically, her chest. With her arms crossed and the roll of tape securing her chest, she'd just presented him with an alarming amount of cleavage.

If he clenched his jaw any tighter, he might break a tooth.

She wanted to be angry—offended even. Instead, she felt empowered.

He cleared his throat. "I wanted to clear something up." He sounded angry.

She uncrossed her arms. *This should be interesting.* "Go ahead." She was curious in spite of herself.

His gaze locked with hers. Travis King *was* angry. "I don't know where you're getting your information, but I've been sober for eleven months and twenty-eight days." He broke off, stepping closer. "It's hard work. Work I take seriously. In this industry? *You* have no idea. I guess that's why I'm wondering what gives you the right to say otherwise?"

His declaration of sobriety had been a surprise. So had the very specific lie about the length of his sobriety. *What is he hoping to gain?* "I saw you." She lowered her voice, wondering why he'd choose to have this conversation here. "In the recording studio. Not just drinking but taking pills too."

"*That's* what you saw?" He ran his fingers through his hair and those blue-green eyes narrowed. "You don't know what you're talking about." His smile was tight.

"No? I *saw* you." She was beyond infuriated at this point. "You're denying it?" She'd expected him to lie about it—all of it. Why, then, was she so upset? Travis King was everything she'd expected. Charming, entitled, talented, deceitful, and more handsome than any man should be. It didn't make sense for her to be so…so disappointed.

Travis was at a loss. Pissed off, turned on, and generally frustrated. One minute she was holding onto him like her life depended on it, the next she was spitting fire and braced to fight—like now.

"You want me to deny what you *think* you saw? To explain myself to you?" He stepped closer, lowering his voice. "Someone who doesn't like me, doesn't know me, but is all too willing to accept the worst?" He shook his head. "Why the hell would I do that?" *Why the hell am I standing here, arguing with her?* His gaze swept over her face. Those topaz eyes were blazing—at him. But that's not what derailed him. It was her mouth. Full, red lips. Lips parted just enough to make him forget whatever else he'd planned to say.

Not that she'd offered up anything else. Instead, she kept staring at him—flushed and breathing hard and so damn beautiful he ached to touch her. To pull her close and taste that mouth...

Two sound techs hurried past them pushing a cart full of rattling cords and equipment.

*What the fuck?* This wasn't why he'd come after her. *Where the fuck did* this *even come from?* It had been a hell of a long time since he'd thought about sex, but here he was—in the middle of a goddamn public hallway—very definitely thinking about it. Not *just* sex. He was craving her. *Loretta.* The very woman hell-bent and determined to make him into a lying asshole.

He tore his gaze from hers, needing to think—needing to breathe. "You'd made up your mind about me long before you walked into the studio that day. You don't know me well enough to dislike me as much as you do. I get that your pissed off, but I didn't do a thing to you so save all the hostility for someone else." He sucked in a deep breath. "I'm not interested." *Which is a damn lie.* He was interested in Loretta Gram. Which made him a damn fool. He turned on his heel, heading to the dressing room.

His father was up for Best Country Album of the Year and his mother was bound and determined to keep the King family drama front and center in the tabloids, so Travis needed to get his shit together. Since his father was presenting an award, Travis hoped to catch up with him. He wasn't looking forward to being the bearer of bad news, but he couldn't send his father out there blind. His father needed him. So, no more thinking about Loretta, those soulful eyes, that damn dress, or her full red lips—

But Loretta caught up to him before he made it to the dressing room. "Travis?"

"Loretta." He ground out her name, doing his damndest not to look at her. He'd come in here hoping to clear his head and regroup, not battle temptation. And she was pure temptation. At this point, he wasn't sure which was worse: the hurt she caused or the want she stirred. "Unless you're apologizing, we're done."

"Give me a reason to." It was the waver in her voice that got to him.

He froze, meeting her gaze. Something more was going on here. Not that he had the foggiest idea what that might be. What did she want from him? He needed to know. "Why does it matter?"

She opened her mouth, then closed it, an impatient sound slipping through her lips. "I…I don't know." She glanced his way, then away. "But it does."

*Dammit all.* "It's Neurontin. For anxiety. And it helps with withdrawal too. I can pop up to three of those a day." He watched her. "The drink? Water." He ran his fingers through his hair, braced. "Those were the only damn cups not packed up for the move."

A sort of stare-down ensued. It was like she couldn't process what he'd said, like she was waiting for him to drop a punch line or brush her off. Her eyes never left his—searching. What got him the most was watching the struggle play out on her face.

"That's it?" she asked, still wary.

He nodded.

"And tonight? You were… Well, you were there. For me." The disbelief in her voice was a gut-punch.

His phone vibrated again. "The same way you were there for my father." He frowned. "What is it you think I'm after?"

She shook her head, then swallowed. "I'm sorry."

"Thanks." He hadn't meant to sound so dismissive.

"No, I mean it." She grabbed his arm. "I'm sorry. And thank you, for tonight."

He stared down at her hand. "You're welcome."

The dressing room swung open and Emmy Lou peered out. "I thought I heard you, big brother. Hi, Loretta. Congratulations on the award—and the performance. You two had me sobbing." She stepped aside, holding the door wide. "Come on in. I was just keeping Daddy company." For a split second, Emmy's smile faded. His little sister was worried.

"I could use a water." Travis winked at his sister, the only reassurance he could offer up at the moment. "You?" he asked Loretta. Now that a fragile peace had been established, he was in no hurry to see her go.

As expected, Loretta hesitated. But a tentative smile formed and she nodded. "Water would be great."

Inside the dressing room, things were crowded. Emmy Lou was hovering, doing her best to smile—even though she looked like she was close to tears.

"I'm sure Brock is missing you," Travis said, giving his sister a one-armed hug. "I got this," he whispered.

Their father was half-watching the television broadcast of the awards show, preoccupied by the care of his Stetson Diamante cowboy hat. It was his father's favorite hat—and worth a damn fortune.

"See you out there, Daddy." Emmy Lou pressed a kiss to their father's cheek and left.

"You ready?" Travis asked. "Make sure you read the right name. People don't like it when you call out the wrong one."

"I'll do my best." Daddy chuckled. "I'm proud of you. Both of you." His blue eyes shifted to Loretta. "I can't imagine that was easy."

"No, sir." Loretta shrugged, blushing from his father's praise. "I've never been so afraid of messing up onstage."

"Sometimes the only way to face our fears is head on." Hank smiled. "I'd say you did just that."

"Speaking of which." Travis cleared his throat. "Can we have a moment?" He spoke to the hair and makeup team and the stage assistant waiting to help as needed.

Loretta stood, her water bottle held close, and headed to the door.

"No, now, you can stay, Loretta. Let Travis or I take you back." It was clear, his father wasn't about to take no for an answer.

Because his father, the one and only Hank King, was a true gentleman. A man of his word. A family man. Loyal, to a fault.

"If you're sure?" Loretta asked, her gaze bouncing between them.

Travis nodded. She already knew what he had to tell his father anyway. She'd been the one to spare them all a red carpet nightmare.

"What's going on?" His father stood. "Your sister was nervous as a long-tail cat in a room full of rocking chairs."

Travis had to chuckle. "I guess we're all a little worried."

"About?" His father frowned.

"Momma's here." Travis had to force the words out.

The subtle shift in his father's features was telling. "Well… that's fine." But the words were thick, gruff. "I can't say I'm surprised. She loves this sort of thing."

"The attention?" Travis winced at the disapproving look his father shot him. He took a deep breath and said, "She is here with Kegan Scott." There was no keeping the hard edge from his voice.

There was a beat of silence.

"All right." His father did his best to put on a brave face, but his hand was shaking when he went to reach for his hat. "I appreciate the heads-up, son. Best to know now." He stared down at his hat, turning it in his hands. "How about you two go on out, find your seats. I'll be out in a minute or two."

There was no way he could leave his father now. "Dad—"

"I'm fine." His father clapped him on the back. "Go on, now."

*Bullshit.* He was anything but fine. Travis turned to Loretta, at a loss, his chest growing heavier with each passing second.

She didn't hesitate this time. Instead, she hugged his father. A fierce sort of hug. And then she slipped from the dressing room.

"Go on," his father repeated.

Every fucking step was a struggle. Leaving went against his every instinct. He may not have always seen eye-to-eye with his father, but this wasn't right. When the door clicked shut behind him, there a minute where Travis thought he was going to lose his shit. He shoved his hand in his pocket, but the smooth surface of the guitar pick didn't do a thing to ease him. He wanted to blow up. He wanted to punch something—to put his fist through a wall.

"Travis." Loretta stood just to the side of the dressing room door, one hand resting against the wall. "I'm so sorry. What can I do?"

He shook his head. *Nothing.* His mother had put him in a no-win situation. What other choice did he have? He'd just broken his father's heart, and there was nothing anyone could do to fix that. He flexed his hands, helpless and furious all at once. He paced down the hall, swallowing against the jagged lump in his throat. His fingers scraped through his hair, and he stared up at the ceiling overhead. *Fucking pointless.*

He was clear. He knew how to take care of himself. How to protect himself. It had been a long and bumpy road, but he was in a good place. But the weekly check-ins, all the classes and counseling sessions, and a whole library of recovery and self-help books wouldn't protect those he loved.

His phone vibrated, but he ignored it.

His father wanted Travis in the audience, so that's where Travis would be. He turned, the pulse in his temples throbbing, to find Loretta leaning against the wall hugging herself, waiting for him.

"Ready?" he asked, more growl that actual word.

She nodded, her eyes huge and her face pale.

He didn't pull away when her fingers threaded with his. Or when she tugged him toward her. "Are you?" She reached up, pressing her other hand to his heart.

His gaze was instantly tangled up in hers. His pain and betrayal and sadness were all there in her eyes, reflected back at him. Without a filter. She didn't shy away. There was comfort in that. He was caught and she was reeling him in, but he didn't want to fight her.

"This isn't your fault," she whispered.

He shut his eyes, wishing he could shut out the pain on his father's face too. "It sure as hell feels like it."

"It would have been so much worse if you hadn't told him."

Which was true. His father was a proud man. This was hard enough. Staring out over the audience and finding out that way?

Momma would love that. The drama. The reaction. There were times he wanted to shake his mother—to make her understand just how much her actions impacted the rest of the family. It was hard to believe she didn't know exactly what she was doing; she was too smart. But the alternative, that she knowingly inflicted hurt on the people she proclaimed to be her everything? That was a damn hard pill to swallow.

He drew in a deep breath, cleared all thoughts of his mother from his brain, and focused on what happened next. That was easy. Return to the auditorium and cheer on his father. That's what needed to happen. That's what he would do.

The brush of her hair against his nose surprised him. When he'd moved, he wasn't sure. But Loretta was pressed against the wall, he was pressed against her, and time came to a hard stop.

His reaction was instantaneous—desire all but grabbing him by the throat. She was...everywhere. Her breath was his. Her heartbeat matched his own. And the fire in those topaz eyes knocked the breath out of him. Hunger. Longing. Need. It would be so easy to give in to her, to this.

He leaned forward, then stopped himself. This wasn't right. Not here. Definitely not now. But her scent had him turning into her, running his nose along her throat. The curve of her ear and the spot just behind it—breathing her in until she filled his lungs.

Her fingers went tight around his hand, a broken gasp spilling from her lips. Those lips.

One kiss. One kiss and he'd stop this. He tore his gaze from her mouth and damn near groaned at the raw hunger on her face. Her eyes flashed as she gripped the front of his tuxedo jacket, pulling him in—impatient.

One kiss wouldn't be enough. No matter how much he wanted her, he couldn't do this. He reached up, smoothing the hair from her shoulder. "I want to kiss you." Her smile almost changed his mind. "But if I kiss you now, you'll always wonder if this was my angle the whole damn time. And I'll wonder if this is what you wanted or if I took advantage of you, because tonight... Well, tonight has been one hell of an emotional roller-coaster ride."

She didn't say a word.

"Loretta." He groaned. "I'm trying to take the high road here." He stepped back but rested his hand against her cheek.

She was having a hard time maintaining eye contact. "You're right."

"Just so we are clear, I plan on kissing you, Loretta Gram." His thumb traced her cheekbone. "At the right time and in the right place."

Now she couldn't stop looking at him, those brilliant eyes sweeping over his face a sudden intensity. "We should get to our seats."

It wasn't easy to put space between them. He'd made his

intentions known, but she hadn't done the same. She led the way back to the auditorium and, once inside, it was like nothing had happened between them. She cheered when Hank King won Best Country Album of the Year. Smiled and posed for pics with his father after the awards show. But right before she left—her bodyguard blocking any interference—she did pause to say goodnight.

"It's the right time and the right place," she said, standing on tiptoe to kiss him on the cheek. "Take care of yourself, Travis. Keep up the good work."

And, just like that, Loretta Gram walked away. But he couldn't shake the feeling she wasn't just saying goodnight—she was saying goodbye. And, dammit all to hell, here he'd thought they were just getting started.

# Chapter 5

TRAVIS HAD STUCK TO THE SAME ROUTINE SINCE HE'D LEFT the Oasis. Run five miles. Weight train for forty-five minutes. Shower. Breakfast. Monday, Wednesday, and Friday were rehearsing and endurance training and whatever else he could find to keep himself occupied. Tuesday was his weekly SMART recovery meeting and Thursday he'd check in with his sobriety coach, Archie. His recovery program did more than help him stay sober; it helped him stay accountable in all aspects of his life.

He had a card with the four points printed out and in his wallet, in case he ever needed reminding. Staying motivated to change, learning to cope with urges to use, managing thoughts, feelings, and behaviors effectively and without addictive behaviors, and living a healthy, positive, and balanced life. If he was doing those four things, he was staying on track.

Overall, he'd developed a solid routine since he'd moved back home. And since he and his father had the place to themselves and, for the most part, respected each other's privacy, life was orderly.

But in the week since the International Music Awards, privacy and order were in short supply. Every time he turned around, Krystal, Emmy Lou, and their significant others were dropping by for some reason or other. "I made too much food and didn't want it to go to waste," was one of Emmy Lou's excuses. "I think I left some music in my closet," Krystal had offered up another time. While he'd found his sisters' increasingly creative reasons for their presence amusing, he knew they meant well. And since having them all together made Daddy happy, he figured he didn't need his privacy all that much at the moment anyway.

This morning, he'd headed in for his regularly scheduled break-fast to a full table. His father and Sawyer sat, drinking coffee and reading the paper—like normal. But Emmy Lou and Brock and Krystal and Jace were all crowded around the large wooden farm table, talking over one another and being too loud for his liking. But since Emmy Lou had thought to bring two large boxes full of donuts, he wasn't complaining.

As soon as he sat, he stacked donuts on his plate, and settled into his chair with a sigh.

"I picked this up last night at the check-out register." Krystal waved an entertainment newspaper in the air.

"I don't know which is more shocking." Travis spoke around a mouthful of donut. "That you did your own grocery shopping or you actually bought a copy of the *Star Gazette*."

Krystal pretended to scratch her nose with her middle finger.

"Krystal," Emmy Lou chided. She'd always been the peace-keeper of the family.

"I love you too, little sister." Travis winked, then glanced at the paper in disgust. "Pretty sure they've made enough money off this family without you actually buying a copy."

"Which is what I said." After a slight headshake, Jace sipped his coffee.

"I'm sure there was a good reason," Emmy Lou said, defending her sister.

"I know, I know. But you said she didn't like you," Krystal said, tossing the gossip magazine on the table for everyone to see. "Turns out Loretta is sleeping with you and Daddy." Then she burst out laughing.

"Oh, Krystal." Emmy Lou shook her head. "Really?"

The donut Travis was eating stuck in his throat, forcing him to swig down his scalding hot coffee and burn his throat. He jumped up, filled a glass of water, and chugged down the contents. It had been over a week since the awards show, and he was still trying to figure out what the hell had happened. There was no denying *something* had happened between him and Loretta. But his *father* and Loretta? That was the sort of thing he didn't need in his head.

"You okay?" Brock asked.

Travis turned to find all eyes on him. His sisters. Brock and Jace. His father. Hell, even his bodyguard, Sawyer. "I'm good." He emptied the glass. "Donut. Coffee."

"Slow down, son. Chew a little." His father cleared his throat and peered over his newspaper, reading glasses perched on the tip of his nose. "As far as that…that horse crap? I'm not laughing, Krystal. She's your age." He coughed, shook out his paper, and went back to reading. "That sort of thing turns my stomach."

A crazy awkward silence followed. First, their father had all but cursed—a rarity. Second, because they all knew Kegan Scott was way younger than their mother. Unlike their father, she seemed delighted by her young boy toy.

"I think dating someone ten to twenty years younger than you is the norm for a midlife crisis, Daddy." Krystal patted her father's hand. "I'd say you're due a midlife crisis. Go for it."

Their father's heavy sigh came from behind his newspaper.

Travis didn't disagree with what his sister was saying, but he didn't want Loretta Gram involved in any way, shape, or form. He refilled his coffee, returned to his seat, and shoved another donut into his mouth.

Emmy Lou sat, sipping her tea, with her cat sprawled across her lap—stomach up. "Travis, you just choked. Are you sure eating a whole donut, all at once, is a good idea?" She leaned forward to peer into the pastry box on the table.

Travis shrugged. Maybe. Maybe not. But if he even mentioned Loretta by name, he'd regret it. He didn't want his family interfering with things he was still working through. It was safer to keep his mouth too full to talk.

"Might as well finish off the box. At the rate you and Sawyer are training out, you'll be able to compete for Mr. Universe." Krystal glanced at Jace. "Is there a Mr. Universe competition?"

Jace shrugged. "I have no idea."

"Are you talking about weight lifting?" Brock sounded off.

Krystal nodded.

Sawyer took a chocolate-covered donut. "Mr. Olympia? Isn't it?" he asked Brock.

"That's it," Brock agreed.

"Mr. Olympia, Mr. Universe… Whatever." Krystal sighed. "You get what I mean. You could probably eat your weight in donuts and burn it off like that." She snapped her fingers.

"All I'm asking is you try chewing them, okay?" Emmy Lou watched as Travis grabbed two more donuts.

"Will do." Travis smiled.

"There's a strawberry iced one." Brock leaned back, draping his arm around the back of Emmy Lou's chair.

"My hands are full." Emmy Lou smiled adoringly down at her cat, Watson.

"Mine aren't." Brock took the bright pink donut, tore a piece off, and held it up for her to eat.

"Aw." Emmy Lou leaned around the donut. "Kiss, first."

Brock was all too happy to oblige.

"It's great that y'all are here *all* the time now, but you've got to knock that shit off." Travis waved at Emmy Lou and Brock, then dropped the remainder of his donut onto his plate. "This is a bachelor pad now. Dad and I are living large." By living large, he meant eating lots of frozen dinner and junk food and not shaving.

Krystal rolled her eyes. "And dating the same woman, apparently." Her smile was all mischief.

From the corner of his eye, the picture of Loretta—in that blue dress—demanded his attention. And that smile? He wanted to make her smile that way. He wanted to make her laugh. An all too vivid memory of her, arching into him as his nose trailed up her neck... When it came to Loretta Gram, there was a hell of a lot he wanted to do.

He sipped his coffee, his gaze scanning over the paragraph beneath the picture.

"Krystal," their father grumbled. "Come on, now."

"I'm sorry, Daddy." Krystal was up, hurrying around the table, to hug their father.

But whatever else his sister said, Travis didn't hear it. He was rereading the absolute bullshit printed by whatever asshat had written the article.

> While tonight's performance was riveting, Loretta
> Gram's fate is uncertain. Johnny Hawkins, the duo's
> lyricist, will be unreplaceable. Does this make tonight's
> performance Loretta Gram's swan song?

Travis scanned the article until he found the name of the contributor. Evan Johnson. *Fuck you, Evan Johnson.* His hold tightened on his mug, preventing him from taking his frustration out on the newspaper.

"Travis?" Krystal's voice was louder than normal.

Too loud not to hear.

"What?" he asked, only half listening. Loretta didn't need a singing partner to have a career. Johnny's death sucked—there was no way around that. But she had the talent to make it on her own. If Wheelhouse backed her...

Krystal laughed. "See?"

"See what?" He ran his fingers through his hair and turned toward his sister.

"Just what happened between you and Loretta?" Krystal asked. "Because a little birdy told me you two were getting awfully chummy outside of the dressing room at the awards show."

"Sounds like this little birdy is seeing things." Travis sipped his coffee.

"This little birdy has 20/20 vision." Krystal crossed her arms over her chest.

"I think we'd best leave your brother's business to your brother." There was a finality to his father's words that stunned even Krystal into silence. "I know I'm old and anything I say will likely go in one ear and out the other, but I'm saying it anyway. Your gramma used to say a relationship is built on three things." He paused long enough to clear his throat. "Any relationship, mind you. Father, uncle, wife, or neighbor. The older I get, the more I agree with her."

"What three things, Daddy?" Emmy Lou asked, taking the hand Brock offered and leaning forward to hear what their father said next.

"Honesty, respect, and loyalty." He shook his head. "Honesty is a big word when you think about it. It includes things like trust, certainty, morality, confidence—it all means the same thing." He sat back in his chair. "Now when I say respect, it's not just respecting the other. It's about respecting the relationship too. Enough to honor, to preserve and protect and nurture the person or bond you share." His gaze fell to the paper he'd set aside, the muscle in his jaw tightening. "Loyalty isn't always easy. Your gramma used to say she went three years not liking my father once, but that didn't stop her from keeping her word." He cleared his throat. "Some might say it's easier to walk away when things get tough, but easy doesn't mean better. You give up, you'll be missing out on the good times as well as the not so good. It's loyalty that gets you through. It's peace of mind. It's faith. Devotion. The roots that ground you. Or oath to keep."

"What about love, Daddy?" Krystal had walked back around the table to sit in Jace's lap, wrapped around him as if it was the most natural thing in the world.

"Love?" Their father chuckled. "Well, baby girl, you put those things together and, to me, that's what love is."

Travis wasn't all that fond of the notion of love. Life had twisted and warped in the name of love too many times for the word to conjure anything but unease. Sitting here, it was obvious love wasn't always tainted that way. Jace had loved Krystal through some of the darkest times a couple could face. And Emmy Lou? She'd held on to the hope that somehow, someway, she and Brock would find their way to each other. Now the two of them would take their vows in what promised to be the most highly publicized wedding of the decade.

As happy as he was for his sisters, he knew he'd never risk opening himself up for that kind of damage. Love didn't always end well—his parents were proof enough of that.

His father glanced at his watch. "I've got a call coming." He stood, walked to the kitchen door, then paused. "You all sticking around?"

"We'll be here, Daddy," Emmy Lou answered for them all, her cheerful self.

But once the door closed, Travis ran his hands over his face and propped his elbows on the kitchen table. "Nothing like getting life lessons before you've had your second cup of coffee."

"You're not worried about him? You didn't hear his voice? All the coughing and throat clearing?" Emmy Lou asked, her gaze darting back to the door.

Travis nodded.

"It's worse today," Sawyer said, staring into his mug.

"He needs to go to the doctor." Jace shook his head. "He can't risk his voice."

"It's not like I can force him to go." But Sawyer and Jace were right. "But I'll do what I can. I can be just as stubborn as he can."

"Oh, we know." Krystal rolled her eyes.

"Not just his voice." Emmy Lou kept stroking her cat's belly. "The whole thing with Momma—"

"I'm glad." Krystal pushed out of Jace's arms, headed for the coffee, and carried the nearly full pot to the table. "Your second cup of coffee." She topped off Travis's cup. "Daddy is better off without her. Back me up on this, boys." She glanced at Jace, then Brock.

"I'm pleading the Fifth on this one." Brock held up his hands. "We might not be all that fond of each other, but she's still your mother. And, as such, I won't disrespect her."

Emmy Lou leaned forward. "I love you."

"I love you." Brock kissed her cheek. "But I do think your dad's been done wrong."

"Agreed." Jace nodded. "Not that it's our place to do anything about it. I get the feeling he'd say we need to let him handle his own business—same as Travis."

"Like that's going to happen." Krystal turned, her green eyes pinning his. "You know I love you so much it hurts, right? And, just like you want me and Emmy to be happy, *we* want *you* to be happy. We're worried."

"We are," Emmy Lou agreed.

Travis sighed, his gaze bouncing between his sisters. "Because?"

"You're not going out—at all." Krystal shrugged. "You haven't been on a date since you got home. Not one. Like, zero."

"Pretty sure that's what not one means." Jace laughed.

Brock chuckled.

"When I heard you were all tangled up in Loretta, I guess I was relieved." Krystal picked up the paper to stare at the picture.

Travis smiled in spite of himself. *Tangled up?* That was about right. He still was.

"She's talented and gorgeous and, I think, the sort of woman who could keep you in line," Emmy Lou added. "Once she decides to like you, of course."

"Look at you, being all sassy." But it was such a surprise, Travis had to laugh.

"You were sweet to her." Krystal was like a dog with a bone. "Above and beyond sweet to her."

"Like she was with Daddy." He shrugged. "Just returning the favor."

"Travis, you can't be happy spending all your time hanging out with Dad and Sawyer, no offense." Emmy Lou glanced at Sawyer.

"None taken," Sawyer answered, toasting her with his coffee cup.

"I'm not denying Loretta Gram is a fine-looking woman. And, I guess, you might say we had a *moment*. But that's all it was. A moment." He shrugged, doing his damndest to convince himself. "Maybe I like my freedom too much or maybe it's how fucked up our parents' marriage is, but I'm in no hurry to complicate my life. Especially with a woman as complicated as Loretta Gram. I thank you but...no thank you." He smiled. "Now, Jace, did you finish that song yet? If not, I've got a few ideas I thought we could try."

As distractions went, it worked. He'd meant what he said— Loretta was complicated. But if he ever got a second chance, and if she was willing, he'd sure as hell like to finish what they started.

---

The Wheelhouse Records headquarters were housed in downtown Austin. They'd bought out several floors of a mostly glass skyscraper that had been featured in a handful of movies. As she walked down the concrete sidewalk leading to the giant glass double doors, Loretta couldn't help but think about one of the movies filmed here. It involved the end of the world, a spaceship, and a very convincing and climactic scene of this building being blown to pieces. *Not helping.* Sure, Ethan Powell, CEO of Wheelhouse Records, had called her himself to schedule this meeting, but that didn't mean it was something bad, did it? *No. Of course not.* So, what was with the sense of dread twisting up her stomach? "You're sure you're up for this?" Loretta asked, holding the front door wide for Margot.

"I'm terrific. I'm having a hell of a good hair day too. Look." Margot turned her head left, then right. "I'm taking it as an omen of all the good things to come."

"Your hair is on point." Loretta was grateful her manager was here with her. If there was a person who could go toe-to-toe with Ethan Powell, it was Margot.

"Wasn't that movie made here?" Margot asked, her heels clicking on the marble floor as they headed to the bank of elevators. "The one where—"

"The building explodes?" Loretta nodded, waiting for the elevator doors to open.

"What? No?" Margot followed her into the elevator and pressed the button. "The one with the superrich guy and the whips and all the sex."

Loretta was in shock.

"Lori-girl, your eyes look like they're about to bug out of your head." Margot laughed. "What's wrong with watching a movie with some BDSM and dirty talk if it helps distract a woman from chemo-induced nausea?"

"Nothing." Loretta's cheeks were on fire, but that didn't stop her from apologizing. "I'm sorry, Margot. You can watch all the BDSM and whips and dirty talk sex movies you want."

"I feel like we should take the next elevator." A male voice—gruff and a bit raspy—came from behind her.

"Hank King, you get yourself in here and give me a hug." Margot laughed.

If Loretta had been embarrassed before, she was mortified now. To the point she couldn't bring herself to look Hank King in the eye. It was easier to stare at the ground until the previous comments were forgotten or the elevator ride was over—whichever came first.

But, according to her view of the ground, it wasn't just one pair of cowboy boots that had joined them in the elevator. Two. Two pairs of high-end, custom ostrich skin boots. Meaning it wasn't just Hank King who'd heard her.

"You get better every time I see you, Hank," Margot said. "What's your secret? And don't tell me it's clean living, because I know better." She paused. "I'm thinking you sold your soul to the Devil." Margot laughed. "Land sakes, look at you. A chip off the old block. You can tell you're his son. I don't know what sorcery is in the King genes, but it's mighty powerful."

Hank's son. His one and only son. *No. Please, no.*

"You're quite the sweet talker, Margot."

*That voice.* Loretta knew that gravel and velvet voice. That voice had pulled her from her sleep more than once since the IMAs. Travis. Travis was here. *Right next to me. Right now.* With his sapphire eyes and his just-right mussed hair and that smile.

The elevator dinged, the doors closed, and a moment's silence ensued.

*Just so we are clear, I plan on kissing you, Loretta Gram.*

How many times had she replayed that? Not by choice. It just happened. She could be washing dishes or doing her morning yoga routine or knitting blankets for the local animal shelter. Out of nowhere, she'd hear his words and wind up aching and distracted for an hour or more.

She'd done the right thing. She'd do it again. Because kissing Travis King would lead to more than kissing and that would be a colossal mistake. But maybe… *A mistake worth making.*

Thankfully, Margot seemed to have been carrying on a conversation the whole time. "Congratulations on the win. If I was a betting woman, I'd have bet every cent I had on that album. One of the best albums in years."

"I appreciate that, Margot." There was an odd rasp to Hank's voice. "It was quite a night."

*Quite.* She toyed with a strand of hair, focused on calming her heart, and managed to acknowledge Hank—and Travis—with a sort of smile. At least, she hoped it was a smile. From the odd look on Margot's face, maybe not.

"As nice as it was to win, it wasn't the highlight of the evening." Hank clapped Travis on the shoulder.

Travis rolled his eyes and acted like his father's praise wasn't a big deal, but Loretta knew the truth. Travis King loved his father— admired and respected him. Likely, Hank's praise meant the world to his son. Not that she had much experience with that. The only time her father ever had anything nice to say was when he had an ulterior motive. Namely, money. *It was always about money.*

She allowed herself another quick peek at Travis. He was wearing a cowboy hat. She had a thing for cowboy hats. But *Travis* in a cowboy hat? *Would this ride never end?*

"It was one hell of a performance." Margot nodded. "I was proud of Lori-girl for getting through it. And proud of you, Travis, for giving her a hand when she needed it."

"It was my pleasure." Travis cleared his throat. "She'd have done just fine without me." He was lying through his teeth and they both knew it. It was sweet and irritating. He was so…so frustrating.

The doors opened and, once they realized Hank King was on board, the two waiting executives stepped in. Little things like personal space went out the window in situations like this. A minute alone on an elevator with a big star like Hank? It didn't matter if it meant being packed into an elevator—you took the elevator.

Hank didn't seem bothered by it.

But Loretta was. More so with each passing second. Because of Travis.

He stood right behind her. *Right* behind her. They were all squished together, and she could feel his breath against the back of her neck. Smell the mix of mint and leather that stirred an instant softening deep inside her. Her gaze fixed on the numbers, climbing higher as the elevator rose. *This is the slowest elevator known to man.* She took a deep breath and tried to shut out the warmth rolling off of Travis. The number changed. One level higher. Five to go. *This is why the aliens blew up the building. They'd been stuck in the damn elevator for too long.*

The elevator pinged, the doors opened, and the two executives lingered long enough to take a few selfies with Hank before they left.

Loretta stepped aside, gripping the metal handrail with both hands and pressing herself against the side of the elevator. The space made it easier to breathe. But it also made it easier to see him.

Travis. In his tan cowboy hat. Starched jeans, with a nice crease running down the top of his leg. His leg. His very muscular thigh. Being pressed up against him the night of the awards show had revealed that most of him was muscle. *What are you doing?* This wasn't the time to mentally examine Travis King's attributes. She had way more important things to worry about right now.

Namely, this meeting.

"What brings the Kings into town?" Margot asked. "I'd think folk would come to you by now."

"You think so?" Hank shook his head, a tightness to his jaw. "I'll tell Mr. Powell you said so."

For the first time, Margot's smile slipped. "You two are here to meet with Mr. Powell?"

Travis nodded. "The great man himself."

Loretta didn't like the flicker of alarm his words triggered. Or what this might mean.

"I wish he'd let us know there'd been a change in schedule then." Margot sighed, crossing her arms over her chest.

A schedule change was a logical explanation. But...

"It's not like Loretta or I live down the street." Margot shrugged. "But when the suits call, you come a running."

"Damn inconsiderate of him, though." Hank nodded, frowning. "You two in a hurry to get back home?"

Home. For the moment, Loretta was homeless. There was no way she could stay in the duplex she and Johnny had shared—not after he'd died there. The duplex was identical, a reflection of one another. Which meant every time she walked into her bathroom, she remembered walking into Johnny's... Finding him, in his bath...

"This little miss is heading home with me to Bakersfield and my little golf course side bungalow," Margot offered up. "And since I'm in no hurry to head home, neither is she."

Loretta didn't like where this was headed. Not one bit.

Hank chuckled. "Well, how about we offer you a little Texas hospitality?"

There had to be a way to say no? "Margot, are you sure you're up for this? Shouldn't we get home so you can rest?" She winced, hating herself for using Margot's weakened state to get out of this.

"How about you two come out to the homestead and let us take care of you?" Hank gave Margot a concerned once-over. "But only if you're feeling up to it, of course."

"I'm fine." Margot shook her head. "Damn cancer doesn't know who it's messing with."

"No, it doesn't." Loretta had to smile at that.

"So, we accept your invitation." Margot looked pretty pleased with herself.

Fine. If that's what Margot wanted, Loretta would deal with it. What happened the night of the IMAs had been a fluke and, as long as she kept her distance and curtailed any tantalizing daydreams, nothing would happen. *Not a thing.*

"Barbecue, lemonade, buttermilk pie, watch the sunset off the back porch—slow things down a little." Travis winked at Margot. "Might even get a serenade too."

"Sold." Margot was all smiles. It was almost impossible to resist Travis's flirty side.

*Almost impossible.*

The elevator doors opened and the four of them took the short stroll down the hall to the offices of Ethan Powell. While the outside of the building was all glass and mirrors, the Wheelhouse Records floors stood out. Heavy wooden beams had been installed overhead. The room was outfitted with leather furniture, mounted instruments signed by famous musicians, and a wall of all the gold and platinum albums they'd produced. The wall ran the entire length of the hallway.

*This is why you have to play ball with them.* Loretta scanned the names and albums. Sure, she and Margot could go somewhere else…but this was where she wanted to be. When she and Johnny had started out, it was Wheelhouse that recruited them, honed their sound, and built them up. Right or wrong, loyalty mattered to her—in business and in life.

Her gaze wandered to the Frederic Remington bronze statues of bronc riders and cowboys to the ornately framed Charles Russell painting hanging on the wall behind the reception desk. She got the feeling these weren't reproductions.

Wheelhouse Records could afford to buy originals and install beams that served no structural purpose and put calf-skin leather chairs in their waiting room—and they wanted anyone who stepped foot inside their corporate offices to know that.

The woman behind the desk was pushing sixty, but that didn't stop her from trying to look like she was thirty. Blond hair ratted high and all but lacquered into place with hairspray. Her nail extensions were pointy and tipped with glitter. She wore a shirt that revealed the girls—all hiked up and strapped into a bra with impressive endurance.

She'd been clicking, with her pointer fingers, on her keyboard until she spied Hank King. Then she was up, coming around her desk to give him a hug.

"Good to see you, Hank," she said, pressing a sticky pink

lipstick kiss on his cheek. "Mr. Powell just buzzed to see if you and Travis were here."

"You too, Peggy." Hank kissed her cheek in return. "And here I thought we were early."

"That's what I told him." Peggy waved a dismissive hand. "He's just excited. And you know how he is when he gets excited." She gave Travis a quick hug before turning to them. "Margot, I've been thinking of you every day." She came forward to hug Margot, lowering her voice as she said, "You know my sister had breast cancer. She ended up with a double mastectomy, reconstructive surgery, and a brand-new husband to boot. Now she's healthy as a horse—and she has the boobs of a twenty-year old." She winked.

"I've never had the patience for a husband, but I won't rule anything out." Margot chuckled. "I appreciate you thinking of me, Peggy. Now, I know I've been a little distracted but, did I get my days wrong? I can't see how Mr. Ethan Powell can meet with us and the Kings at the same time."

Peggy smiled. "Don't you worry about that. Hank and Travis. If you two will head in, right there, to that boardroom?" She pointed to a set of doors on the far left, off of the waiting room. "And you and Loretta go in there on the right." She pointed to a different set of doors, at the opposite end of the waiting room.

"We'll see you back here shortly." Hank's voice turned raspy, prompting him to cough and clear his throat.

Loretta had noticed Hank do something similar several times before. And the way Travis glanced his father's way—concerned.

"You better." Margot winked. "I'm already looking forward to the barbecue *and* the serenade."

Peggy corralled Hank and Travis toward the door so she and Margot headed the other way.

"You heard that, didn't you? Hank's cough," Margot murmured. "That doesn't sound too good."

Loretta nodded, pulling open the boardroom door and stepping aside. "I'm sure he'll get it taken care of."

"You better believe it." Margot walked through the door. "That man is about as business savvy as they come—" Margot came to a stop, her mouth hanging open as she stood just inside the door.

"Margot?" Loretta followed. "What's wrong?" But she then she saw exactly what was wrong.

From his seat at the head of the very long conference table, Hank King chuckled. "I bet Peggy got a real kick out of this."

Loretta's faint concern had officially turned into mounting panic.

"Hysterical," Margot said, giving her arm a comforting pat. "Breathe, Loretta," she murmured softly. "I'm sure there is a logical explanation for this." But Margot didn't sound like her usual confident self.

And that was when Ethan Powell walked in, followed by four people Loretta had never seen before. Peggy followed and made her way around the table, passing out folders with a smile on her face.

"Thank you," Margot said, instantly opening the packet.

Loretta couldn't bring herself to look. She knew. Deep down, she knew what was coming. A teeny-tiny part of her clung to the hope that she was not here to discuss some sort of further collaboration with the Kings—namely Travis. But then Margot reached over to rest a hand on her arm and said, "Let's hear this out and think things through before we react."

Loretta nodded, staring blindly down at the packet. The cover read, "The Trail Blazer Tour, North America."

She ran a hand over the glossy cover, the blood in her ears roaring as Ethan Powell and his team of market researchers laid out the where, when, and how of the way they saw things moving forward. They even had a nice PowerPoint presentation complete with bullet points and images from her and Travis's IMA performance.

*That* was what they wanted moving forward.

Loretta, on tour with the Kings. She'd partner up with Travis to sing LoveJoy songs and anything new they came up with—with plans to cut an album in the next year. And, because Mr. Powell knew how much Loretta wanted it, she'd get a couple of solo songs too.

Because *she* wanted it. Not because she was talented enough or that she'd earned the chance to go solo. It was a token—like they were pacifying her...

The words risk and risky were used more than a handful of times too. She understood what they were saying. They were doing them a favor. She and Travis. They were both risks. Her, because her success was tied to LoveJoy. Him, because he was a recovering addict backup singer—who happened to be a King. In a way, she guessed they were doing them a favor. They hadn't dropped her. They'd put together a snazzy PowerPoint to try to sell her on performing with Three Kings. *Three Kings, for crying out loud.* She should be over the moon happy. *Besides, it's not like I have other options.*

But another slide popped up and she couldn't look away. She and Johnny had been LoveJoy. The name they picked for her and Travis... The urge to giggle was unexpected but—come on—really?

*TrueLove.*

# Chapter 6

"IT WASN'T LIKE YOU WEREN'T ALREADY HERE. BAKING," TRAVIS said, standing aside as Krystal pulled the pie from the oven.

"Uh-huh," Krystal said. "I wasn't making buttermilk pie."

Travis shrugged. "Daddy's idea."

"It was?" Krystal smiled up at him and placed the pie on the marble countertop. "Interesting. Here, I thought buttermilk pie was your favorite."

"It might be." Travis shrugged, chuckling when she shot him a look. "Fine. It is. Have I said thank you?" He leaned forward onto the marble countertop and smiled. "Thank you, little sister."

"Whatever." Krystal rolled her eyes. "If you want me to make a buttermilk pie for Loretta Gram, fine. But, nice to Daddy or not, I'm not sure I'm a fan."

"She's been through some shit, Krystal." He shook his head. "Maybe think about cutting her some slack."

Krystal's narrow-eyed assessment was obvious. "Uh-huh." She stared up at him. "You had your meeting this morning?"

"Never miss one, you know that." He winked at her.

"I do." She paused. "I'm proud of you for working so hard. You're in a good place, Trav. You don't need to complicate your life."

Travis didn't bother arguing. If Krystal wanted to read between the lines, there wasn't a thing he could do or say to stop her anyway.

"Stop hiding out in here." Krystal poured lemonade in daisy-covered glasses, put them on a tray, and held the tray out to him. "Here."

He wasn't hiding, exactly. He was giving Loretta space. Hell, he was giving himself space. Ever since he'd climbed into that elevator, he'd been hard-pressed to ignore the pulse between them. If he was too close to her for too long, he was treading water—and she was the undertow. Whatever had been started in the hallway of the MGM Grand Garden Arena, there was no going back.

"Besides, Daddy shouldn't be doing all the talking," Krystal reminded him. "His appointment is tomorrow?"

Travis nodded. It had taken a hell of a lot of strong-arming—including threatening to not go to today's Wheelhouse Record meeting—before his father relented.

"You are going with him, aren't you?" The mix of hope and concern was something they were all feeling.

"I'm going." Travis shook his head, sighing. "He's not happy about it and I wouldn't be surprised if he tried to change his mind but—"

"You won't let him," Krystal finished.

"I won't let him." He wrapped his sister up in a big hug. "But don't worry too much about his voice for now. Knowing Margot Reed, she's doing most of the talking." But he picked up the tray and made his way to the back of the house. After years of constant renovation, the house was a mishmash of style. The entry and formal living room still had the white marble tiles shot through with golden metallic veins, each room sporting an oversized golden chandelier dripping crystals and a multitude of gold chains. The furniture was post-modern—that's what Momma called it. To Travis, that meant boxy and uncomfortable furniture. Every time he walked through the front door, he felt like he was in a confused airport or waiting room.

Travis kept right on going, down the hall, through his father's "man cave" and out the wide-open doors on to the back porch.

Margot was chattering away, sitting opposite his father in one of two large wicker rocking chairs. Loretta was sitting on the edge of the porch, her feet resting on the lower step. She had Krystal's three-legged dog, Clementine, at her side. Loretta was crooning softly to the little dog, earning her a ninety-mile-an-hour tail wag from the internet famous Chinese crested dog.

"Lemonade?" He handed out glasses, saving the last for Loretta.

Loretta eyed the glass but shook her head. "No, thank you. But you can point me in the direction of the washroom." She stood, smoothing the skirt of her lavender polka-dotted dress.

Travis gave her directions and took her spot on the top step.

Clementine burrowed into his side, wiggling.

"I know." He chuckled. "You're getting a whole heap of extra loving today, aren't you?" Clementine promptly dropped onto her side, then rolled so that all three legs stuck up into the air. Travis laughed and gave her a good tummy rub.

"That was some meeting today," Margot was saying. "I tell you, Lori-girl needs a break. Not that she'd ever let on, mind you. Life has made her a little tough."

"She reminds me a little of my Krystal," his father said. "Holding the world at arm's length."

"It can get awfully lonely." Margot sighed. "But sometimes the risk isn't worth it."

There was that word again. Risk. It seemed to be Ethan Powell's—the self-inflated prick—favorite word. And every damn time he'd used it, he'd been looking straight at Travis.

As if he needed to be reminded that he was still considered a wild card. Or that he was damn lucky to be sitting across the table from him. Hell, that he still had a record label at all. One incredible performance with Loretta Gram didn't erase the years of scandals and headaches and fires to be put out—fires he'd caused.

Living life in the public eye meant there was no escaping the past. From photos to fan videos to television interviews, Travis had grown up with the whole world watching. He'd been barely eighteen when Three Kings started drawing serious attention. After that, the world was at his feet. A dangerous thing for a boy that age. Had it taken him a hell of a long time to get his shit together? Yes. There had been nothing subtle about his fall from grace. One minute, he was a charmer with a minor drinking problem, the next he was an alcoholic with rage and control issues. There were videos and countless photos to prove it.

He'd been relieved the whole video nightmare thing hadn't been mentioned. He wasn't naïve enough to think that night would be forgotten, but hopefully that meant they were, all of them, moving on.

Moving on enough to trust him to carry a duo with Loretta Gram. That was damned flattering.

Loretta might want nothing to do with any of this—him included—but Travis hoped she'd take time to think this through. Ethan Powell had worried aloud over where to put Loretta—until they hatched this collaboration. There was doubt Loretta understood the message. This was all Wheelhouse Records had to offer her.

*And what an offer.* Travis sighed, giving Clementine a scratch behind the ear. "I feel for her," he said to the dog.

A recovering alcoholic partner, sharing the spotlight and tour billing, a record with her recovering alcoholic partner and, just to keep her placated, one or two solos. After being half of a fairly high-profile duo, it was a pretty pathetic offer. "It was a damn insult, is what it is."

Clementine's little head cocked to one side, her tail thumping against the wide-planked porch.

Where was Loretta? He'd been sitting here, lost in thought and talking to the dog, for a good ten minutes. She'd be fine. It's a big house, but not so big she'd get lost poking around inside. Still, he felt compelled to check in on her anyway. "I'll go see if Jace is here with the food," Travis said, before heading inside.

He checked the kitchen first. While he knew Krystal wouldn't be out-and-out rude to their guest, he also knew his little sister wasn't the best at schooling her features—or keeping her opinion to herself. And since Krystal had made it clear she was still on the fence about Loretta, he'd rather not leave the two of them alone too long. Lucky for him, Loretta wasn't there and Krystal was too caught up in a phone call with Jace to do more than wave him away.

After searching the living room, his sisters' offices, the media room, and the new home studio, he found her in his father's office—staring at the framed news clipping and photographs decorating the walls.

"You've spent your whole life onstage, haven't you?" she asked, glancing back at him over her shoulder. "I didn't even know they made boots that small."

Travis crossed, shaking his head. "That was Momma. She's always made sure we all looked the part. She's always understood the importance of branding—hell, without her I wonder if Daddy or Three Kings would be where we are today." The admission left a bitter taste in his mouth. He stared at the photo, wishing he could remember times like this. He was maybe three, sitting on his father's lap. Daddy's arms were wrapped around him, placing Travis's pudgy baby fingers on the strings of the guitar Hank was holding. Momma sat on the edge of the stage, smiling and so pretty he didn't wonder why she'd caught his father's eye. "Got to the point where that's all we were doing, though. Onstage and off. Playing a part. Staying on brand." He sighed, turning away from the photo and running his fingers through his hair.

"This one." Loretta didn't comment. She moved on, leaning in to inspect another picture. "You three were adorable."

He, Krystal, and Emmy Lou were all sitting on the back of a massive draft horse. All three in boots and hats. All three grinning from ear to ear. "Past tense? Some would say we still are adorable."

That earned him one of her razor-sharp glares so fast he had to laugh. For a minute, he thought she might smile, maybe even laugh, but she caught herself. Instead, she sighed—all exasperation.

"What do you have against smiling?" he asked, studying her. "Or is it the idea of smiling with me that rubs you the wrong way?"

She faced him. "Or maybe it's that you're not as funny as you think you are."

"That's possible." He shrugged, wishing she'd let her guard down—even a little bit. Then again, her world had been turned upside down and he'd been forced on her, so. He'd hoped, after Las Vegas, things might have changed but... *Apparently not.* "That meeting was something, wasn't it?"

She deflated a little, resting her hip against the massive record player cabinet that took up most of one wall. "It was." Her voice was soft.

"Have any thoughts?" He paused. "Other than Ethan Powell is a prick who was totally getting off on playing God with our future, of course."

"Of course." She smiled then.

Damn but she was beautiful. And her smile? At the sight of that smile, it took effort to gather his wits enough to form a coherent question. "I'm guessing this isn't the way you'd imagined moving forward?"

She shook her head, her attention wandering around the room. "It isn't like they ruined my master plan. I guess I thought—I hoped—I'd be involved in deciding what I'd be doing next. With who. And where."

"That sounds pretty unreasonable to me." Teasing her was taking a risk but, if he kept her smiling, it'd be worth it.

The flash of anger in her eyes cooled when she realized what he was up to. "Ha ha, very funny." But there wasn't a hint of anger to her words.

"See, I can be funny." He winked.

She shook her head, regarding him with amused tolerance. But the longer she looked at him, the more those topaz eyes seemed to laser in on him. "I don't feel like I have all the information. They didn't exactly welcome questions, but there are a few things I'd like to know."

He nodded. "Like?"

"What sort of time-range will this arrangement go on?" She pushed off the cabinet and walked across the room, her gaze returning to the photos on the wall. "Will all marketing be joint? Or will there be individual campaigns too?" She paused in front of his father's first guitar, safely stored inside a glass front display case. The old wooden Martin DXMAE acoustic-electric guitar had many a mile on it. And it showed. Momma had offered to clean it up, but Daddy said he didn't want the wear and tear and stories to be buffed out of something so dear to him.

"I remember wanting a guitar like this when I was younger. I scrimped and saved until I had enough to buy the only one I'd found at a secondhand store." Her whole face softened, her smile warmer—sincere. "As soon as I had the money, I ran there." She shook her head. "It was gone."

Travis frowned, disappointment pressing in on his chest. "That's the saddest damn story I've heard in a while."

Her laugh was husky—and sexy as hell. "It's not, I promise. I was brokenhearted, cried all the way home, to find Johnny sitting on my front steps. He was holding the guitar, a bright green bow on it." She faced him, shrugging. "He did things like that." But her gaze fell away and her voice wavered when she added, "When he wasn't high or drunk, he'd do something special. It was his way of apologizing for letting me down."

Travis swallowed hard, the pressure in his chest increasing by a hundred.

"He was two different people." Loretta wrapped her arms around her waist. "The one whose smile could light up a room. He loved music and writing songs, he loved life and making people happy." She hugged herself. "The other Johnny got stuck in a…a darkness with only one escape route." When her gaze met his, the defeat was staggering. "As much as I loved him, I know how screwed up our relationship was. I don't want to go through that again. I don't want to set myself up for that kind of hurt." Her eyes stayed locked with his. "I don't want my career and my future to be tied to that again." She sucked in a deep breath. "I can't. I won't."

Now he understood. He didn't like it, but he understood. "And you think partnering up with me will do that." It wasn't a question; it was a statement.

She didn't answer him. But she didn't have to.

"I feel certain that you know this, but I am not Johnny." He raked his fingers through his hair. "For one thing, I'm not near as talented as he was." He shook his head. "The rest? I can tell you that it's taken a year to be able to look myself in the eye without hating who I saw. I'm not going to jeopardize that. Recovery isn't about pleasing other people, it's about being honest to myself— and being true to who I am. That's what I'm doing. Every damn day, I get up and recommit to myself." He sighed. "I know I have to live with this for the rest of my life and I will."

Travis had never been afraid of silence. In a family like his, silence had always been a rare gift. Time to think. To listen. To be quiet. But this quiet wasn't like that. The way Loretta was looking at him right now set his nerves on edge. It had nothing to do with today's meeting or the possibility of them working together. This was about her, believing him.

Until that moment, he didn't realize how much that mattered.

"One more question." She smoothed her hair from her shoulder, her gaze bouncing from him to the guitar and back again. "Do you want to be my singing partner, Travis?"

─────────

Her voice wobbled. *Dammit.* Instead of coming across strong, like she'd wanted, she'd sounded…needy and weak. All because he'd been so…so impassioned. Like he meant what he said and he wanted her to believe it. *And he might mean it, right now.* But tomorrow? Or next week?

Words are just that, words, and she'd been fed what she wanted to hear one too many times. This time, she wasn't going to let what she wanted get in the way of what was real.

"I'll be honest, Loretta." The corner of his mouth kicked up enough for her pulse to take notice. "After everything I've put Wheelhouse—hell, everyone—through, I feel pretty damn lucky to still be here." He shook his head, those curls of his falling onto his forehead in a way-too *GQ* model sort of way. "If this happens, working with you will be my privilege."

She had to admit it, he did have a way with words. Wasn't that part of his reputed charm? Being a silver-tongued devil? Rather, the Silver-Tongued King? She'd almost forgotten about that nickname. But now that she'd remembered it, it cast a shadow of doubt over everything he'd just said.

Trust wasn't a concept she had much experience with. Growing up, the only thing she could trust her father to do was say one thing, do the opposite, and leave her to pick up the slack. Before the age of ten, she'd learned to write checks and mail bills, do the grocery shopping, cook dinner, and make coffee—to help sober up her father when he was fall-down drunk.

She'd made gallons of coffee for her father, gallons for Johnny, but she'd be damned if she did the same for Travis.

The only person she could truly rely on was herself. Normally, that is. Around Travis? She was beginning to worry she couldn't trust herself when it came to him. Even now, in the midst of a serious conversation, she was struggling to focus.

"I'm not taking any of this for granted." His gaze hung on a particular picture hanging on the wall, the slight tightening of his jaw grabbing her attention.

It was a family picture—several years old from the looks of it.

It was a publicity still but the smiles, and the affection, were real enough. He, his parents, and his sisters. A momentary glimpse into another time. And since this had been taken well before the current behind-the-scenes drama between Hank and CiCi King, chances are this had been a happier time.

"Here's the thing, Loretta. I know Wheelhouse has turned on the pressure, but this is your life." Travis took a deep breath, his blue-green eyes swiveling her way. "Don't let them strong-arm you into something you'll regret."

Was there a way to avoid regrets? It seemed unlikely. But since she'd already shared way more than she'd planned, she wouldn't give voice to that question. Instead, she waved her hand around the room at all the years and years of Hank King memorabilia. "What about you? I'm guessing this counts as pressure for you?"

"Nah." He was smiling now. "He's Hank King, but he's my dad. I've never wanted to compete with him."

First the eye contact, then the smile...now the rapidly shrinking room. The air seemed to thin, and a rather alarming heat began warming the pit of her stomach. Neither one of them moved—but things seemed to shift nonetheless. She went from being mildly aware of the other occupant in the room, to something else. Something wild and intense and magnetic that twined around her. Around them.

*Just so we're clear, I plan on kissing you Loretta Gram.*

His gaze dipped to her mouth, almost as if he could read her thoughts.

*More likely he can read them on my face.*

"Soup's on." Krystal's voice carried down the hallway. "Come and get it."

Seconds later the click of nails and the jingle of Clementine's collar announced the arrival of Krystal's three-legged dog.

"Hello." Loretta bent to pet the poof on the top of the little dog's head, giving the dog an adoring smile. "Were you sent to come get us?"

"She's here to butter you up so you'll sneak her some food under the table." Travis chuckled. "She loves barbecue."

"Do you?" Loretta asked Clementine.

Clementine's tail wagged so fast, it made her already off-kilter posture more precarious.

"Come on," Travis said, scooping up the dog. "Don't feed her too much sausage. She's not quite as adorable when she gets gassy."

Loretta was so surprised, she laughed. "She does not."

"She does so," he argued, smiling broadly as he led her out of the room and down the hall. "You've been warned."

Loretta tried not to stare at the opulence of the King home. It was so…so over-the-top that she couldn't quite wrap her mind around it. This was their *home*. Considering how busy Hank and Three Kings' tour schedules were like, it was a home they probably didn't spend that much time in.

"It's a lot." Travis nodded, staring around the pristine white entryway. "But it figures. This, all of this, was Momma's doing."

"Oh." While she wasn't a CiCi King fan, she wasn't about to bad-mouth his mother. And her opinion of CiCi had nothing to do with the current state of her marriage and everything to do with a run-in she'd had with her a few years back. It didn't matter how curvy or soft the woman's surgically enhanced body was. To Loretta, CiCi King was coldness and pointy edges. "I see." She did, too. Cold. Impersonal. Intimidating. Glamorous. All words for this room—or CiCi King.

"I'm hoping Dad will let Krystal and Emmy Lou make some changes." Travis shrugged, absentmindedly scratching Clementine behind the ear. "Make it more home for him."

The formal dining room wasn't quite as presumptuous as the front rooms, but it wasn't exactly warm and cheery either. But once they'd all congregated around the fancy table, she didn't worry so much about the room as much as the people in it.

She was having dinner with Hank King. In Hank King's house.

Not to mention Krystal and Jace and Travis...Travis who was laughing at something Margot said.

That laugh jumbled up her insides.

"Emmy Lou and Brock had that wedding thing," Krystal said as she collected two of the place settings.

"Which wedding thing is that?" Travis asked, setting Clementine on the floor and pulling back a chair for Loretta.

He hadn't done it for effect—it was all instinct. It made her smile.

"Some things stick." Hank caught her eye and winked. "I'm taking credit for that one."

"What?" Travis asked, sitting in the chair beside her. "What did I miss?"

Loretta didn't miss the now delectably familiar scent of Travis: mint and leather.

"Something to do with the reception? Lighting maybe?" Krystal scanned the screen of her phone, shrugged, and slid it into her pocket. "The doves or butterflies. Is she still doing that?"

Travis shook his head. "I'm lost."

*You're not the only one.* What was wrong with her? Loretta laughed, surprising herself—and Travis.

"You're hopeless." Krystal shook her head. "Let's eat."

The food was making its way around the table when a man poked his head inside. His gaze bounced from her to Margot and it looked like he'd duck out, but Hank waved him to the table.

"I set you a place." Krystal nodded at the empty place setting.

"Sawyer, this is Margot Reed and Loretta Gram." Travis made the introductions, sucking a drop of barbecue from his thumb, before passing the container to his sister. "Sawyer is the only person who's stuck around who isn't blood related or dating one of my sisters. I'd say it's out of the goodness of his heart but..." Travis scooped some coleslaw onto his plate. "Technically, he's a bodyguard." He used air quotes.

"Technically?" Sawyer asked, sitting between Margot and Jace.

"I am a bodyguard." He thanked Margot for the container of beans. "*Your* bodyguard."

Travis needed a bodyguard? She stole a quick glance his way. The biceps. The shoulders. The chest. Even the neck... *He* needed a bodyguard? Then again, he couldn't work the crowd and keep the more overzealous ones from tearing off his shirt.

The image of Travis, shirtless... She took a long sip of her ice tea.

"And your stand-in, I'm guessing?" Margot asked, taking a roll and handing the basket to Hank. "You could pass for a King, Sawyer. Same bones. Same height."

Margot's comments had all eyes on Travis's bodyguard.

"A love child with one of your roadies, eh, Dad?" Travis tore the corner of his roll, using the rest of it to point between the two men. "He is a couple of years older than me." Travis winked at his father, laughing. "You were young and wild once, I bet."

Hank King shook his head. "Young, maybe. Wild? No."

While Travis and Margot started talking about Hank King's start, Loretta was sidetracked by the tension rising from the opposite end of the table. Specifically, Krystal. From the uneasy way Krystal glanced back and forth between Sawyer and Jace to the pointed gaze all three of them seemed to understand...

But what had them on edge?

She hadn't meant for Sawyer to catch her watching them, but he did. His gaze narrowed, ever so slightly, before his face cleared of all expression and he turned his attention to his food. But, for a second, his jaw clenched tight. When he did that, she could see where Margot was coming from. He did look like a little like Travis.

Loretta took another sip of her tea, studying the man over the rim of her glass.

"I think you should," Margot was saying. "It's your home, Hank. What's that saying about a man's home is his castle? Oh lordy, King? Get it? King? Castle. That is hysterical." She shook her head. "Gut the whole place and start again."

"Except the home studio." Hank held up his tea. "We just finished that and I'm damn proud of the way it turned out. Did you get a chance to look at it?" He turned to Loretta, curious.

"I apologize, I got sidetracked in your office." The confession made her cheeks go hot. "If Travis hadn't found me, I'd probably still be in there."

Hank shook his head. "The door is always open to you."

"Which brings us back around, nicely, doesn't it?" Margot asked, shooting Hank a playful smile.

"Go on." Hank cleared his throat and reached for his tea.

"You sure?" Margot waited for him to nod before saying, "Hank and I were discussing today's meeting and we think it makes sense for you to move in here."

Loretta inhaled the bite of coleslaw she'd been chewing, forcing her to drink her entire glass of tea and accept several sharp pats on the back from Travis before she could answer. Even then, her throat was so tight she only managed to get out one word. "What?"

"Well, darlin', you are homeless. I'd love having you move in with me, you know that. But *everything* is here. The studio. Your singing partner. Your tour collaborators. Wheelhouse Records is right down the road a ways… This makes sense. Flying back and forth from Bakersfield doesn't." She paused. "Unless you're a pilot and I don't know it." She chuckled.

"Brock is," Krystal volunteered, glancing her way. "If you don't want to stay here."

"Brock has a career." Hank King pointed out, reaching over to pat Loretta's hand. "Your call, Loretta. I imagine today has been a lot."

Loretta nodded, numb. Move in. *Here?*

"Can you pass me the ribs?" Jace asked, reaching for the platter—and changing the subject.

Conversation picked up, overlapping one another, with plenty of good-natured teasing thrown into the mix. But no matter how much she tried to engage, Hank's proposition kept circling through her mind.

Assuming, of course, that she agreed to the Wheelhouse Records deal. The thick glossy packet was shoved into the recesses of her oversized bag for airplane reading. Margot always slept through flights, so she'd have plenty of time, alone with her thoughts, to consider all the details. But she was beginning to think the details didn't matter.

What other options did she have? Really?

"Who wants pie?" Krystal asked, standing. "And coffee?" No one turned her down.

Loretta jumped up. "I'll help clear dishes." Better than sitting here, stuck on a hamster wheel, worrying over things she didn't have the answer to. Not yet, anyway.

Her waitressing days came in handy. Between her and Krystal, they had the table cleared in no time. But once they were in the kitchen, Krystal didn't bother with small talk.

"I get the feeling you're not happy about this?" Krystal asked, filling the coffeepot.

Loretta sighed. "Which?"

Krystal's laugh was startled. "Well, all of it, I guess."

"I didn't mean to sound so ungrateful. I do appreciate it—"

"Hello." Emmy Lou swept in. "I'm so sorry we are so late." She hugged Krystal, then hugged Loretta too—as if it was the most normal thing in the world. "But we didn't miss pie. And you know how I love your pie."

"I made three." Krystal smiled. "Just in case."

"That is why you're the best sister *ever*. What did I miss?" Emmy Lou asked, taking inventory of what was still needed. "I'll get plates."

Krystal and Loretta exchanged a look—then smiled at one another.

"Tell me everything," Emmy Lou added. "The meeting?"

It was hard at first. Loretta had never been one to share. Sharing meant letting people in, and she was very selective about who those people were. But, with Krystal and Emmy Lou giving all the appropriate looks of sympathy and support, the words kept coming…until they ran out.

"It's good, isn't it?" Emmy Lou asked. "Not the way Mr. Powell has handled things, of course, but the offer? I mean, I know you have issues with Travis, but I think, over time, you'll see he's a really good, really decent guy."

"He wasn't." Krystal shrugged. "He *was* a partying man-whore who drank like a fish, firmly on the path of self-destruction. I mean, let's just put it out there because we're all thinking it."

"Krystal." Emmy Lou looked and sounded horrified.

Loretta had to smile. Not at what Krystal was saying, but at Emmy Lou. She was truly scandalized by her sister's outspoken assessment of their brother. While Loretta found it…refreshing.

"Was." Krystal didn't have a problem saying what she thought. Or doing what she wanted. And right now, that was giving Loretta a head-to-toe inspection. "And while I can understand why you'd be hesitant to give him a chance, you'll be making a mistake if you don't."

Loretta swallowed.

"You two do sound beautiful together," Emmy Lou said. "And, we're a lot, but, I think, we have fun while we're touring."

"What's the holdup?" Travis pushed through the kitchen door, followed by Brock. "People are getting restless out there." He walked to the counter to stare down at the pies.

From this angle, the way his jeans hugged his thighs and butt did things to her breathing. Loretta tried not to stare at the way he raked his fingers through his hair. Tried. And failed. He glanced at her, surprised to find her eyes on him.

Why was she looking at him? *Stop it.* Not happening.

"Oh, they are?" Krystal asked. "You can take the pies." She nodded at the pies, plates, and utensils ready and waiting. "Loretta, can you help me with the coffee? It's almost ready."

"Sure," she agreed, turning away from the serious kiss Brock was laying on Emmy Lou. It didn't help when, once more, her gaze collided with Travis.

The corner of his mouth cocked up as he shook his head. "It's gross, I know. But you get used to it. Sort of." He grabbed the pies and backed out of the kitchen, calling out, "Come on, lovebirds." Emmy Lou and Brock grabbed the plates and utensils and followed Travis.

"That's part of it, isn't it?" Krystal asked.

"What?" Loretta asked. "Sorry."

"My brother." Krystal paused. "The chemistry, I mean."

Loretta blinked, doing her best to remember where they'd left off before they'd been interrupted. "Yes. That's what Mr. Powell said. Our performance had solid chemistry."

"Oh, Loretta." Krystal had been putting coffee cups on a tray but she stopped now, to look her in the eye. "I'm not talking about onstage." She smiled, almost sad. "Denial won't get you anywhere. Take it from me. Accept it; you have the hots for my brother. Now, what are you going to do about it?" She picked up the tray. "Can you grab the coffee pot?"

# Chapter 7

TRAVIS THREW THE WET TOWEL ON THE BED AND REACHED FOR his pencil, scribbling another note down on the sheet music. He hummed it through, nodded, and pulled on his boxers. Another few notes played through his head, so he added them before he finished sliding on his jeans and a worn, soft rodeo T-shirt.

Sockless, he sat on the side of his bed and ran his fingers down the strings of the acoustic guitar—mentally working through the harmony and rhythm that wasn't quite perfect. He strummed his fingers over the six strings and smiled. His sisters had bought the custom Gibson Hummingbird as a joke, thinking he'd never use it. But he didn't mind the hand-engraved and inlaid artwork. He was man enough to play a guitar with flowers on it. Since it already had flowers, the hummingbird didn't really matter.

What did matter was the deep tones of the guitar and the way it felt beneath his hands. He played through what he'd come up with, nodded, and glanced at the clock. It was just shy of nine o'clock in the morning.

There was no set time for breakfast, but this morning was different. They had company. And even though he'd been up all night, he'd been looking forward to seeing Loretta—to see what she thought of the song he imagined them singing together.

If she was open to it.

He'd worked through the tempo when he'd gone running this morning. As his feet fell, pounding out a beat, his fingers moved along the guitar he could still feel in his hands.

The tune was mostly done. But now, the words began to reveal themselves.

The lyrics were risky. Sexy. Authentic. Raw. He'd tried to go a different way, but the song fell flat and the melody began to fade. He'd made the decision not to force it. Up until now, most of the songs he'd written were collaborations. But this…this one was too loud to ignore. It hadn't been a conscious decision; it had just happened. And it was awesome as hell.

Still barefoot, carrying his Gibson Hummingbird, he headed down the hall and toward the kitchen.

His father and Margot sat at the large farm table, sipping coffee with the morning paper spread out between them.

"Morning," he said, heading straight for the coffee. "Anything new?"

Margot shrugged, but then she saw his guitar. "Whatcha got there?"

"It's called a guitar." He winked, poured himself a large mug of coffee, and leaned against the counter.

"She's on the back porch," his father said, not bothering to look up from his paper as he shifted just enough to reveal a pastry box. "There might be one or two left."

Travis shrugged. "I'll have to come back for one later."

That got his father's attention. "Come again?"

But Travis was already headed out of the kitchen, his pace quickening as he headed through the man cave and onto the porch.

Even with both rocking chairs open, Loretta was perched on the top step. Beside her sat his Molly Harper's #1 Fan mug, steam rising off its contents.

"Good morning." He headed straight for her, nervous and excited all at the same time. He'd shared his music before. But sharing it with his family was different. What if she hated it?

She leaned against the wooden railing, her topaz eyes finding his as she cradled her cup between her hands. There were dark smudges beneath her eyes.

"Or is it?" he asked, sitting on the top step beside her.

She eyed the guitar. "Is that a Gibson Hummingbird?"

He nodded, running his hands over the mother-of-pearl. "The hummingbird is my spirit animal."

She laughed so hard she spilled coffee onto the pair of pajamas she'd borrowed from Emmy Lou.

"Sorry," he said. "I thought you were immune to my humor."

"I am." But she was still smiling. "You caught me un-caffeinated."

"Sure." He shook his head. "No burns?"

She shook her head. "Nope."

He nodded, the guitar resting across his thighs, torn between diving in or waiting for her to ask about—

"I'm guessing there's a reason you brought your guitar to breakfast?" Her gaze shifted from the guitar to his face.

"I was up all night. Wrote something." He swallowed.

Loretta sat her mug down. "You did?" She leaned forward, suddenly alert. "I'm hoping this means you'll play it?"

"Nah." He teased. "I just wanted to show off my Hummingbird."

She shook her head, but she was smiling. And damn, her smile was so damn bright and beautiful he wasn't sure he'd need his coffee after all. "Well, if you change your mind, I'd like to hear—"

"If you insist." He shifted the guitar, ran his fingers along the strings, and started playing.

When her foot started tapping on the step, he began to relax. Her eyes drifted shut and she was swaying along, concentrating on the notes and melody.

Now came the risky part. The lyrics. He cleared his throat and started to sing.

*You've got me where you want me.*
*I can't say that I mind.*
*You tease me but you touch me.*
*One kiss, we're intertwined.*
*It's taken you forever to see me standing here.*

*But now that you do, darlin', let me make this clear.*
*If tonight is all we have, then, girl, tonight you're mine.*
*I'll love you so good, you'll try to slow down time.*
*But you'll miss me, baby, and I'll haunt you in your sleep.*
*My hands, my mouth, on you—you'll want me close and deep.*

His fingers played the final notes and silence fell. A long, awkward silence. He didn't want to look at her, too afraid of what he might see.

"What about the woman's part?" she asked, her voice rough as gravel.

"I thought, maybe, you'd have some ideas?" He leaned back against the railing. "You being a woman and all." He was looking at her now.

She was staring at the guitar, her breathing unsteady and her cheeks flushed. "This would be a duet for us?" She swallowed, hard, before meeting his gaze.

"That's how I'd envisioned it." That wasn't all he'd envisioned. Maybe his subconscious was trying to tell him something. Rather, hit him over the head with something.

She nodded at the guitar. "Can you play it again?"

He'd barely played one note when she started singing. Head thrown back, eyes closed, she was all in. He kept on playing—watching her dark hair dance on the breeze and her pink painted toes tap out the beat on the top porch step. And words that made his head spin and his body stir.

*You've got my body aching now.*
*I can't say that I mind.*
*You tease me but you touch me.*
*One kiss, we're intertwined.*
*It's taken me forever to let you get this close.*
*I see you smile and my craving for you grows.*

*If tonight is all we have, then, boy, tonight you're mine.*
*I'll love you so good, you'll try to slow down time.*
*But you'll miss me, baby, and I'll haunt you in your sleep.*
*My hands, my mouth, on you—you'll want me close and deep.*

She opened her eyes. "So?"

*So?* What the hell was he supposed to say. She got it. She had to sing this song. He was on fire for her.

But the applause from the back door alerted them to their audience.

"Holy shit, Trav." Krystal looked as shocked as she sounded. "That was wow. I mean wow. Am I right?" She turned to Jace.

Jace nodded. "Yep. And I wouldn't mind so much if you handed the song over to me and Krystal."

If Loretta turned down the deal, that's probably what would happen. They'd do it right, of course. His sister and Jace practically melted the stage when they performed together as it was. But, deep down, he'd always know the truth. He'd written the song for Loretta—to sing with Loretta.

"Wow is right." Emmy Lou was wide-eyed. "Forget coffee. I might need some ice water."

"And a fan." Krystal nodded. "When did this gem come to you?"

"Last night." He chuckled. "Didn't get a wink of sleep last night."

"Running on fumes?" Jace asked.

"No. Still on a creative high, I guess." Which wasn't a common thing.

Jace nodded in understanding.

"Last night?" His father's gaze bounced between the two of them. "I'm thinking I wasn't paying enough attention at the IMAs. Because now I get why Wheelhouse is pushing this so hard."

Travis glanced at Loretta. She was reading over the sheet music, her toes silently beating out the rhythm on the steps. It was a good sign, wasn't it? That even now, when they were surrounded by friends and family full of praise, she was more tuned in to the song than anything else. Absentmindedly, her fingers pulled a strand of hair over her shoulder, twining it back and forth as her toes kept on tapping.

There was no denying she got to him. Not just as a woman, but as an artist.

For the first time since Wheelhouse had started their pitch, he realized how much he wanted to do this. All of it. The touring and singing and creating, just like this. This morning had given him a taste of how easy it could be between them. How seamless. How damn good. They could be something.

Sawyer arrived with breakfast tacos, and they all moved inside.

Conversation slowly drifted from the song to music to how his sisters decompressed to a not-so-subtle segue into the real reason his sisters were here this morning.

"We booked a spa day and were hoping you two would join us?" Emmy Lou asked. "We can bring back something for lunch. Brock will be done training by then, and I need a break from all the wedding stuff."

Travis understood. They wanted to be here when their father got home. If it was good news, they'd celebrate. If it wasn't…well, they'd take it one step at a time.

"And Emmy's making me go with her." Krystal's resistance was all pretense. "We made the appointment early, in case you two had to head home today."

"Our flight was scheduled for noon…" Margot's yawn was a production, a sort of see-how-tired-I-am move. "But there's no reason to hurry home, so we could push it back a bit? I think I've earned a little pampering. You too, Loretta. I'd like to stay, if you're all right with that?" She turned, waiting for Loretta's answer.

Travis almost snorted out loud. How could she say no to that?

"Sounds good to me." If Loretta was irritated by this new change of plans, she didn't let on. "Thank you for including us."

Travis inhaled two tacos and was on his third donut when Sawyer nodded at him, then the clock.

Right, Dad's appointment. The next hour was a blur. Austin traffic, finding the highly specialized otolaryngologist they'd had recommended to them, and waiting in the room with a collection of sinister-looking devices and equipment all led up to the arrival of Dr. Anne Hodges.

Thirty minutes of scopes and cameras scanning the inside of his father's throat later, Travis sat by his father, scribbling down notes as Dr. Hodges listed off things his father should or should not do until they had the test results back. The scope had confirmed that his father had trauma on his vocal cords, but until they got the biopsy back, there was no way of knowing if the polyps were cancerous or not.

"If the biopsy comes back benign, I recommend a phonomicrosurgery. I'll make a small incision away from the vibrating edge of the vocal cord and a tiny flap of tissue is lifted so we can remove the polyp or cyst." She paused, in case they had questions. "This technique reduces the risk of scarring and provides the best voice outcome. Though, voice therapy will be required for optimal results."

"Voice therapy?" Travis asked, scribbling away.

"We have three excellent speech pathologists who are familiar with the wear and tear of a singing career on the vocal cords. They have exercises that will help improve your breathing and endurance, Mr. King. And to prevent further complications."

They left the office with a prescription for steroids and strict voice rest. He'd hoped they'd leave with answers and a set plan. And, if the biopsy came back all clear, they did. Surgery. Rest. Avoiding stress. Voice therapy.

The hardest part of that would be the avoiding stress part. Still,

Travis did his best to diffuse things on the elevator ride down to Sawyer and their waiting car.

"I can buy you a little chalkboard to wear around your neck?" Travis teased. "That way if you need anything, you can write it down?"

His father shot him a look.

"I'll take that look as a maybe." Travis chuckled, following his father out of the elevator and into the parking garage.

It was the sudden flash that tipped them off. One, then another—the sudden rapid-fire click of a camera shutter—right before a reporter and cameraman appeared from behind one of the large concrete pillars. "Mr. King," the woman called out, her heels echoing in the garage.

"Shit," Travis hissed, steering his father to the waiting black SUV as quickly as possible.

"Mr. King. Mr. King," the reporter kept calling, her words running together as she asked, "would you care to comment on the rumors about your health? Who were you here to visit today? Should your fans be concerned?"

Travis ignored them until his father was safely inside the SUV.

"I didn't see them," Sawyer said from the passenger's front seat. "They didn't follow us here or I'd have noticed." He was pissed off.

Even after two years of employment, Travis didn't know much about Sawyer—personally. Sawyer was the eat-sleep-breathe-your-job type. He didn't like missing things. For him, it was personal. So this, having press sneak up on them, would chew on Sawyer's insides until he'd learned all the who, what, why, and when's involved.

"It's not your fault," his father managed.

"*Dad.*" Travis sighed. "Keep that shit up and I'm buying the damn chalkboard."

"Chalkboard?" Sawyer asked.

"He's not allowed to talk." Travis nodded at his father. "Not until the doctor gives him the okay. Since he doesn't text—like most normal people these days—we'll be going old school."

His father sighed, frowning.

In the rearview mirror, a furrow cut deep across Sawyer's brow. Was this about the press? Or his father? For a man who made his living off his poker face, it was a significant show of emotion. Very unlike-Sawyer behavior.

"The press back there?" Travis asked, trying to get a read on his bodyguard—and friend. "You think someone in the office tipped them off?"

"Could be." Sawyer shrugged. "A medical center this big? There are cameras all over. The security guards could have called it in. I'll find out." The last three words were gruff.

Travis's phone vibrated. "I've been waiting." He chuckled, pulling his phone out from his pocket.

Emmy Lou had sent a picture of the four of them, draped in white sheets, face down, on massage tables. The text read, Best girls' day ever. Tell Daddy we're thinking of him. Followed by a string of kissy-face emojis.

Another text rolled in seconds later, but Travis was too busy studying the picture to care.

Loretta was laughing. Propped on one elbow. Her long hair hanging over her shoulder. Young. Relaxed. Happy. Too often, she seemed on edge and on the defensive.

*Or does she only feel that way when she's with me?*

═══════════

"X-Y-L-O." Loretta sat back in her chair, peering around the large kitchen table in victory.

"Xylophone." Hank nodded.

A chorus of *shhs* and *hushes* immediately followed.

"Dad." Krystal sighed. "No talking, remember?"

Hank pretended to lock his lips and throw away the key.

Brock sat back, sighing. "Well, that probably just won you the game."

"And that's just eating you up, isn't it?" Emmy Lou giggled. "He's super competitive," she added, smiling at Loretta. "Losing gets him all worked up."

"Sorry..." But Loretta couldn't help but smile. Brock Watson was a mountain of a man, so seeing him pout like a five-year-old was plain adorable.

"She's cheating," Travis said, scooping a massive bite of ice cream into his mouth. Loretta wasn't sure how he made eating ice cream sexy, but he did. For the last fifteen minutes. "Sawyer, use your Special Ops training on her."

Sawyer's deadpan expression didn't waver as he sipped his coffee. "I must have missed Scrabble cheating detection training day."

That had everyone laughing. Again. Loretta couldn't remember the last time she'd laughed this much. It had started this morning with Emmy Lou and Krystal. Together, they were hysterical. The witty back and forth. Krystal's snark tempered by Emmy Lou's sweetness. They weren't just sisters, they were friends. Best friends.

After manicures and pedicures, mud baths and massages and seaweed wraps, they'd come back to the Kings' home. Margot had gone for a nap and Loretta—feeling like a limp noodle after the morning's pampering—found a quiet corner to read over the Wheelhouse Records packet. But thinking about the deal meant thinking about Travis. One went with the other. *It's not a bad thing.* As long as she controlled herself when it came to Travis, things should be fine. It was the controlling herself part that she doubted.

But the quiet didn't last for long. Hank, Travis, and Sawyer showed up within an hour of Brock and Jace's arrival and everyone seemed to be talking at once. It wasn't like they were a small family.

Nope, they were big and loud and opinionated and funny. And when they were all together, all of those things were amplified. For someone who spent a lot of time alone, she found the constant motion and chatter surprisingly enjoyable. And the more time she spent with the Kings, the more she liked them.

Hank's non-diagnosis was taken in stride; Travis had broken out the ice cream, and Jace had located the box of board games. Considering how long it had been since she'd played a board game, she might have come across as competitive.

Not that it had mattered. Brock had won at Risk and Monopoly, so this was pretty satisfying.

"That's nine-hundred-and-ninety-nine points for Loretta." Travis pretended to tally the score. "And four, each, for the rest of us."

Loretta was laughing again. "I guess that means I won?"

Brock sighed, slumped back in his chair, and accepted a bunch of consolatory kisses from Emmy Lou.

"You'll win next time," Emmy Lou said between kisses.

"I don't know. I get the feeling Scrabble is Loretta's game." Jace shook his head at Brock, wearing a big grin. "Might not want to challenge her to a rematch unless you're prepared to lose again."

Brock scowled in Jace's direction.

"We should celebrate." Travis was up, pulling more ice cream from the freezer. "Who's up for another round?"

The game was forgotten as everyone gathered around the marble-topped island in the center of the kitchen.

"Did you buy the store out?" Krystal asked, scooping from several different cartons.

"It was Dad's idea." Travis shrugged. "We didn't know what everyone liked so…"

Brock nodded. "I'm not picky."

"It was very sweet of you, Daddy." Emmy Lou gave her father a hug. "Want some more mint chocolate chip?" At his nod, Emmy Lou piled her father's bowl high with the bright green ice cream.

"Thank you. For the ice cream." Loretta glanced at Brock then said, "And for letting me beat you."

Brock chuckled. "Whatever."

Loretta was smiling as she scooped brownie sundae into her bowl, then added a scoop of coffee.

"I can't believe you posted that picture," Krystal said, staring at her phone. "We were supposed to be relaxing."

"We were relaxing." Emmy Lou pointed her spoon at her sister. "It was my picture for the day. And it's a good one."

Loretta had learned that Emmy Lou was trying to scale back her social media posts. Instead of multiple posts a day, she posted once and set aside a specific time to respond to comments.

"What picture?" Travis asked.

"From the spa." Krystal shook her head. "Your hair looks gorgeous, Loretta. You look all sleek and sexy. I look like I need my hair brushed and someone to tweeze my eyebrows."

Loretta had no idea what Krystal was talking about. By now, she was pretty convinced it was impossible for any of the Kings to look bad. Krystal's eyebrows? On point.

"You're gorgeous." Jace slid his arms around her from behind, pressing a kiss to her cheek. "I like your eyebrows just the way they are."

Travis made a huge deal out of leaning forward and inspecting Krystal's eyebrows. "*Just* like that?" He burst out laughing.

Krystal pinched Travis on the arm, causing her brother to wince and pull away—but he was still laughing.

Travis rubbing his arm had Loretta staring at his arm. His incredibly thick and heavily muscled arm. She swallowed, hard.

There was a momentary lull in conversation as the focus went from conversation to ice cream.

"Oh, I almost forgot." Emmy Lou jumped up. "I have my bridal portrait proofs and I need an opinion on which to give to *Home & Style* magazine."

"I can't." Brock held up his hands. "Bad luck."

"I'm out—in solidarity." Jace nodded at Brock.

"That was a pretty solid excuse." Travis chuckled. "In a chicken shit sort of way."

Jace laughed.

Krystal took the pictures, her green gaze darting toward her sister's face. "Gosh, which one? The one where you look like a fairy-tale princess or the one where you look like a fairy-tale princess?"

"Loretta, help me out." Emmy Lou collected the pictures and offered them to Loretta.

"Really, Em, there's not a bad picture in the bunch." Krystal sighed. "Tell her, Loretta."

Loretta took the stack of photo proofs. "Oh, Emmy Lou." She smiled. "Every bit a fairy-tale princess." She moved on the next one. Then the next. Until she'd looked through the stack. "Krystal has a point. You look perfect in all of them." She offered them to Travis.

"Nope." He held his hand up. "I know you're getting married and I guess Brock is okay, but I'm not ready to see my little sister in a wedding dress. I'll get all damn choked up."

He wasn't teasing. Loretta heard the gruffness to his voice—the way his jaw muscle clenched.

"Land sakes, that was a nap." Margot came in then, her eyes puffy. "What did I miss?"

"Glad you napped." Hank frowned as the kitchen erupted in protests over him using his voice. He held his hands up, crossed her arms over his chest, and sighed.

"Guess I needed it." Margot turned, taking in the puddles of melted ice cream and ice cream scoops on the kitchen island. "An ice cream massacre?"

"Want some?" Travis was up.

"I'd love some plain ol' vanilla, if you have some?" Margot said, her gaze shifting to Loretta. "Can I borrow you for a sec?"

Loretta slipped from her chair and followed her manager from the kitchen. Standing beneath the opulent chandelier on CiCi King's sparkled-infused floor, Loretta asked, "Is everything okay?"

"The label contacted me." Margot shrugged, but the tension around her eyes told her she wasn't as relaxed as she pretended. "They wondered if you had any questions for them. Or if you'd thought about your answer. Basically, what do you want to do, Lori-girl?"

Loretta stared up at the chandelier. "I don't want my career linked to someone unpredictable. Again. And you know how much I loved Johnny." She swallowed against the anger and sadness tightening her throat. "Even if I wanted to, how would this even work? I hate going into this without any sense of certainty."

Margot gave her a long look before she spoke. "If there's one thing I know with absolute certainty, it's that there is nothing certain about life." She took Loretta's hand and gave it a squeeze. "Johnny. Cancer. A deadbeat dad. A damn car crash—whatever. Whatever you decide, don't let things be based on all the ways it could go wrong." She gave it another squeeze. "Don't let fear guide your life choices, Lori-girl. If you do that, you won't do much living. Nothing worth remembering, anyway. You're too young for that. But I'll stand by you, no matter what you decide. And this is entirely your choice." She gave her hand a final squeeze and let go. "If you don't know what you want—"

"I think I do." She blew out a long, slow breath.

"Oh?" Margot was wide-eyed with excitement. "Do tell."

"I think... No, I know I want to do this." There, she'd said it. Admitted it. And it was scary as hell.

Margot hugged her close. "That's my girl." She gave Loretta a pat on the back. "But I'll leave you to tell who you want, when you want. Now, I'm headed back to the kitchen for my ice cream and some one-on-one with Hank King. That man has me all in a tither." She was hurrying back to the kitchen before Loretta could say a word.

"It was melting." Travis's voice.

"Aren't you the sweetest," Margot answered, all high-pitched and breathless. "I'll take it. And, in case you're looking, Loretta is just around the corner."

For a minute, Loretta contemplated making a run for her room. *Stop it.* Now that she'd told Margot she would take the deal with Wheelhouse, she couldn't run away and hide every time Travis King showed up and sent her heart rate skyrocketing.

She stood her ground, pretending to find the chandelier riveting, as the echo of his footsteps drew closer. If she did a mental review of all the things she found…distracting, maybe she wouldn't be overwhelmed when he showed up in person.

The model-perfect hair. Mediterranean-blue eyes. If that wasn't a color, it should be because that was exactly the color of Travis King's eyes. Then there were all the different and equally devastating array of smiles. Plus…the body. The rock-hard, unyielding body she'd been pressed against for far too short a time in the hallway of the MGM Grand Garden Arena. And even though his ass fell under the body category, it was certainly worthy of appreciating on its own. All of those things—together—sort of… *Has me all in a tither.*

But now that she'd dismantled all the things that derailed her, she was prepared. Now that his boots had stopped and he was right beside her, she was perfectly capable of not getting doe-eyed and flustered by him simply…being.

"I don't get it either." He was *right* next to her. "Why does a chandelier need chain mail?"

Chain mail? He surprised her so much that she laughed. "Is that what it is?"

"I have no idea." There was a smile in his voice.

She looked up at him now, one hundred percent prepared…

*Nope. Not at all.* It hadn't worked. Not in the least. Especially not now that he was staring down at her.

"What's wrong?" he asked, his smile fading.

"Why is something wrong?" *Other than the fact that I just snapped at you, of course.*

"Oh, I don't know." His brows rose. "The scowl. The tone. The general fuck-off attitude."

"I told Margot yes—to the Wheelhouse deal." She swallowed, watching him closely.

"You did?" Why did he have to sound so happy about it? Now he was smiling. A smile that lit up his whole face. It gave him a dimple. Crinkled the corners of his eyes. And ignited a throb low down and deep inside of her. "But…you're not at all happy about it."

"I am." *Stop yelling at him.* "I'm very happy."

He laughed. "I see that."

"I do have concerns." She cleared her throat. "And, since we're going to be working together, I think we need to be up front with each other, from the get-go."

"I agree." His gaze swept over her face. "What sort of concerns?"

"You." *And me.* "Me…" *Wanting you.* "I'm concerned…"

"About you and me performing?" His voice lowered. "Or me and you?"

She nodded.

"Which?" He stepped closer.

"Me and you." She swallowed. "And since we're being up front, I'm just going to say it. This tension, between us, is distracting. I…I'm wondering if it wouldn't be easier for the two of us to sleep together." She swallowed again. "Not sleep. Sex. Obviously, I mean sex."

Travis remained silent and still, not so much as an eye blink.

"If we can agree that this is just a one-night sort of thing to clear the air so we can stop fantasizing about each other…and move on."

He hadn't so much as twitched.

"Travis?" Her throat felt tight and her mouth dry. "Please tell me you heard what I said so I don't have to repeat it."

"Mostly." He drew in a ragged breath. "I think. But that last bit? What did you say? Stop something? Before moving on?"

"Stop fantasizing about each other?"

He was smiling then. A totally new smile. The sort that brought her heart to a momentary standstill before jump-starting it straight into the speed-of-light range.

"You heard me the first time?" she whispered.

"I heard you." He closed the gap between them. "But I liked hearing you say it so much I wanted you to say it again."

She was adrift in those Mediterranean-blue eyes—weightless, yearning, floating, and in no need of rescue. When his fingers ran along her lower lip, she shuddered. Rescue was the last thing she wanted.

# Chapter 8

THE THROAT-CLEARING WAS ALMOST DESPERATE. A DEFINITE signal versus a I-need-to-clear-my-throat sort of thing. Until then, Loretta hadn't thought her heart could go any faster. She'd been wrong.

Jumping three feet away from Travis probably didn't make things look any better, but that's exactly what she did.

"I was…" Sawyer broke off, mumbling, before turning on his heel and heading the opposite direction.

"Those were some lightning-fast reflexes," Travis said, looking far too amused.

She tried to glare but ended up smiling. "I live alone. All these people around, all the time, have me on edge." Plus, he'd been touching her. And she'd been reacting. Aching. So much… Surely *this* was something they'd want to keep between them. At least, it was something *she* wanted to keep between them.

"I can imagine." Travis raked his fingers through his hair, but those mesmerizing eyes of his never left her face.

She was having a hard time bringing her heart rate down. "If you're expecting me to be able to go back into the kitchen, you're going to have to not do *that*."

"What?" he asked, his attention wandering to her mouth.

"*That*." The word was harsh and broken.

"I say we don't go back to the kitchen and put all our energy into your plan." The corner of his mouth ticked up, but it was the slight flare of his nostril that made the hollow ache inside warm.

"I appreciate your dedication—"

"I'm a very dedicated man." He smiled. "Especially when it's something I believe in."

"Travis." She wasn't sure what to say, but if he kept going the whole normal heart rate, normal breathing thing wasn't going to happen.

"Loretta?"

"Stop staring at my mouth," she whispered.

"Okay." His gaze didn't move.

"Travis—"

"I'm almost done." He held up his finger, nodded, and scrubbed a hand over his face. "See, I can behave."

She was beginning to doubt that. "Thank you."

He shook his head. "This is going to be one hell of a long night."

Her breath caught as a dozen tantalizing images popped up. All of them more exciting than the last. She was in favor of a very long night. The longer the better.

"In the kitchen. With my family." He chuckled, once more devouring her lips with his eyes. "The place we should get back to before people start wondering where we are." He cleared his throat. "You should go ahead. I'm going to need a minute to calm down. Or go find a bucket of cold water."

*Don't look. Don't look.* But, she looked—her gaze dipping from the way his thin T-shirt skimmed over every edge and contour of his chest and abdomen to the cling of his jeans. If she'd had any doubts about his level of attraction, that was no longer the case. She couldn't look away—she couldn't stop smiling. And she was, smiling. Because that, *all* of that, was for her.

"Loretta." It was a broken groan. Her name had never sounded sexier. Laced with hunger. Gruff and raw and just the right mix of demand and request.

What would happen if they didn't go back to the kitchen? What? This. This was the problem. But she had to believe that ninety percent of this was the anticipation of the unknown. Afterward…afterward things would calm down. And even though there was the tiniest flicker of doubt that this was going to work— she had to try. Didn't she?

*Yes.* Yes, she did.

"I'm going." She forced the words out, forced herself to turn, and forced herself to head back to the kitchen.

Inside, it was as chaotic as ever. A new game was being unpacked and teams were taking shape. They were so excited, it was possible no one had missed them. Except for Sawyer. He sat, a not-so-stoic curve to his mouth as he glanced her way. At the same time, it happened so fast, she might have imagined it. She glanced at the kitchen door, but no Travis. Instead of waiting for his return, she needed to do something. Even though she never drank coffee this late, she made herself a cup—stirring in two teaspoons of sugar and a healthy dollop of cream.

When Travis did show up, he had his guitar, some blank sheet music, and a pencil with him.

If the rest of the room was aware of the current firing back and forth between the two of them, they hid it well. Loretta was hyperaware of Travis is a way that did nothing to calm the thrum of desire between her legs. Every time his blue-green gaze slid her way, she ached a little more. And his smile, just for her? The slow building one that crinkled his eyes just right at the corners? She spilled her too-sweet coffee on her hand and hurried to run it under cold water.

Travis followed, standing too close to her at the sink. "You okay?" he asked, reaching for her wrist. The slide of his fingers against her skin slowly compressed all the air from her chest. He was teasing her, right here in front of his family—in the family kitchen for crying out loud.

*Two can play that game.*

"Yes." Her hand flexed, turning over in his touch before her fingers slid, ever so slowly, between his—and testing her fading control.

But his hiss of indrawn breath was worth it.

"Whose team are you going to be on?" Krystal called out. "Or are you working on something? Since you brought your guitar?"

Charades was a bust. Poor Hank had to write everything down—so the game didn't last long. Long enough, however, for Travis to brush against her twice and run his hand along the back of her calf when he'd dropped the paper with the clue on it.

Settlers of something lasted forever. While she enjoyed the camaraderie of the game, she wasn't all that invested in collecting sheep and wood for her settlements. But she did enjoy Travis making the same play twice in a row because, under the table, she was running her toes along the inside of his thigh.

By then, Loretta was on the breaking point. All it took was one blazing look from him, and she was giddy with anticipation.

Brock almost coerced everyone into a Scrabble rematch but Margot had already turned in, Hank was dozing in his chair, and—as Emmy reminded him—he had training early tomorrow. After that, things started to wrap up fairly quickly.

Krystal and Jace left.

Emmy Lou and Brock left.

Sawyer headed to his apartment over the garage.

Hank, insisting he wasn't tired, convinced Travis to play chess.

Since the kitchen was clean and chess was a two-person game, she tried not to show how disappointed she was as she excused herself and headed to her guest room.

It had a very hotel feel to it—not in the least bit homey but one hundred percent functional. The bed was comfortable. It was definitely the centerpiece of the room. King size. A large, upholstered headboard. Pillows piled high. Some silky soft quilt she'd happily cocooned herself in the night before. She stared at the bed, all the tingles and aches and craving she'd been fighting against crashing in on her.

She pulled her anything-but-seductive pajamas from her travel bag and carried them into the guest bathroom. The glass-enclosed shower had dual waterfall showerheads, a marble bench, and a collection of exfoliators, gels, and moisturizers for use.

She showered, brushed her teeth, paced her room, picked up one of the novels from the stack of artfully arranged books, then paced some more.

Did chess normally take this long?

Was she supposed to go to him?

She grabbed the doorknob, pulled the door open, and stepped into the hallway—and into Travis's chest.

His hands closed on her upper arms, catching her. "You look like a woman on a mission."

She swallowed. "I was just…" *Getting a glass of water. Wondering what the holdup was? Coming after you.* "Getting impatient."

He nodded, his smile teasing. "We can get started right here if you want—"

*Yes, please.* Whatever thoughts she'd had on seduction went out the window. All she wanted was her lips on his. To touch and taste him. She reached up, twining her fingers in his model-perfect curls to tug him down—closer—until his lips sealed with hers.

His broken growl rolled over her, setting every single nerve aflame. With three long steps, he had them in her room—kicking the door shut behind him—and pressing her against the cool wooden surface. She hooked one leg around him, drawing him closer.

"Dammit," he rasped, grabbing her thigh and lifting her against him, fitting her close. So close that his breath was hers and the only thing remaining was the feel of him.

Hard. Solid. Gripping her fiercely. Kissing her softly. The tip of his tongue traced the seam of her mouth, coaxing her lips apart.

She didn't recognize the sound she made; only that the slide of his tongue against hers was the cause. Slow and primal, stroking her in a way that made her body tighten and throb for more.

His fingers slid beneath the edge of her pajama top and up the sides of her spine. A long, slow caress that had her arching into him.

She absorbed every hitch and groan, the spasmic tensing of his grip on her leg as she ground against him, the slight nip of his teeth on her lower lip, and the calloused tips of his fingers tracing along the skin of her side. The higher his fingers traveled, the harder it was to breathe. She was already gasping, already frantic, so the featherlight stroke of her nipple made her wild.

Her head fell back against the door, desperate for air.

His fingers grew more insistent. Stroking until the peaks were tight. Cupping the full weight of her breast and nuzzling the tip through the cotton of her pajamas. His lips brushed against her nipple while one large hand rested between her shoulder blades— holding her in place as his mouth began a true assault on her senses.

His lips traveled up her throat, sucking her earlobe into the hot recesses of his mouth while his fingers worked the buttons of her pajama top free. But the cold air was instantly replaced by his touch. One breast cradled in his hand, the other worked over by his lips and tongue.

The door was replaced by the bed beneath her, and she reveled in the weight of his body, heavy, against her.

She tugged his shirt up and over his head, moaning aloud at the feel of his skin against hers. The slide of his hand over her stomach triggered a series of electric pulses. When he tugged her pajama bottoms down and off, the press of his lips to her hipbone had her hands fisting in the silk-like comforter beneath her.

His fingers were magic, teasing her senseless before his tongue took over.

"Travis," she pleaded, gripping at his shoulders. "Travis, please."

His breath was ragged against her inner thigh. "Tell me what you want."

She propped herself up on her elbows, staring down at him. In her dazed state, she'd no idea she was laying on the edge of the bed or that he knelt between her legs or that her fingers had tangled in his perfect model curls... Her desire was too insistent for her to feel anything else. And now that she saw him, red-cheeked and breathing hard, her craving for this man consumed her. "You," she whispered. "Now." This was new. The desperate ache that only he could fill.

He stood and stared down at her, unbuttoning his jeans. He was solid muscle. His arms. The balls of his shoulder. His hard plane of chest. His contour lines dividing up the muscles of his stomach. The indents along the inside of his hips, cutting deep.

She wanted to explore every ridge and angle of his body. After...

He slid his jeans down and off, kicking aside jeans and boxer shorts and leaving nothing left to the imagination. Even without his hands on her, the heat of his gaze left her panting.

Thankfully, he had a condom. Watching him roll it on was sexy as hell—even more so because he was shaking. As he climbed onto the bed, he pressed kisses along her hip, her stomach, the underside of her breast, her nipple, and the hollow of her throat before he was braced over her.

She reached up, smoothing a curl from his forehead and hooking one leg around his waist.

"Dammit all," he ground out. His hand searched until he'd found hers and threaded their fingers together. And when he arched, slowly easing into her, their hands tightened around each other.

Her lungs were empty, but she didn't mind. She was wonderfully full. Stretched to the point of pure sensation. Gasping, arching, aching for more. They were moving together, straining and arching—those blue eyes of his locked with hers.

They found their rhythm quickly.

The brush of his chest against hers was enough to push her closer to the edge. The fire in his eyes was blinding. She was swept up, wrapped in him, in the way he slid deep, joining their bodies— again and again. The fuse was lit and her insides clamped down. Higher and higher, the harder he thrust, the brighter she burned.

"Loretta," he rasped against her lips, but never slowing.

Her name was what did it. The way he said it. How raw and frantic he was—for her.

Hot and white. Rolling over her, dragging her under. On and on, until she knew she couldn't take anymore. But then it started all over again, harder this time, and oh, so sweet.

Travis stiffened against her, a guttural moan tearing from his throat. It tipped her over the edge again, sending her free falling in bliss as she watched him come apart inside of her.

---

Travis had a hickey on the inside of his thigh. And on his hip. He had a few moon-shaped cuts on his side…and, from the sting, there were probably more on his ass. Marks of last night. Marks of passion. All made by the sexy-as-hell woman sleeping soundly in the bed beside him.

He didn't know what the hell he'd been expecting, but this wasn't it. This was…different. Different enough that he hoped her original plan was up for renegotiating.

He rolled over, spooning around her. It had been one long night. But, damn, he wasn't ready for it to be over. The clock said three—too early and too late. Might as well make the most of the time they had left. His hand smoothed the hair from her shoulder.

She murmured, instinctively arching into him.

He buried his face against her neck and nuzzled her ear.

She arched again, the curve of her ass rubbing against him in invitation.

"You sleeping?" he whispered.

"Yes," she whispered back. "It's my dream so you better make it a good one." He saw her cheek curve from her smile.

He sucked her earlobe into his mouth, smiling at her sharp

indrawn breath. "I'll see what I can do." He ran his hand down her stomach, pulled her hips back just a bit, and thrust deep.

Her moan was the hottest damn thing he had ever heard in his whole damn life. What had it been, five hours? Six? Did it matter? He couldn't wrap his brain around walking away from this—from her. His arm slid around her waist, anchoring her against him as he began to move in earnest. The moment she was clinging to him, her body tightening around him, he came—burying his face in a pillow to muffle his groan.

He rolled onto his back, rubbing his hair from his forehead.

"You're all sweaty," she said, heavy-lidded with sleep.

"We both are." He turned his head, studying her face in the light filtering in from the bathroom. The bathroom, where they'd made good use of the shower—and the bench—and one minty-scented bath gel. "Maybe we need another shower."

She shook her head. "I can't move."

"You just shook you head." He paused. "Now you're smiling." He waited, smiling as she started to laugh. "You can move."

"You know what I mean." She sighed, her eyes drooping shut. "I'm exhausted. You've exhausted me."

"I didn't hear any complaints." He propped himself up on his elbow, smoothing a long dark strand from her face. He liked touching her. "Pretty sure I heard the exact opposite."

"Me?" Her eyes fluttered open but her smile was sleepy. "You're the loud one." She yawned. "I'm sleeping. Remember?"

He bent forward and kissed each of her eyelids. "Then sleep. No more sex."

She laughed again, shifting forward so her head rested next to his on the pillow. As she drifted off to sleep, her features went soft. Beautiful. So damn beautiful.

Tomorrow would be interesting. No doubt about that. Things might have gotten off on the wrong foot but once the whole alcohol-and-pills thing had been cleared up, he and Loretta had been nothing but honest with each other. He wanted to keep it that way—no matter how difficult it might be now that *this* had happened.

He didn't remember dozing off.

"Travis." Loretta was leaning over him, her long hair brushing his bare chest. "Wake up."

He smiled but didn't open his eyes. "Do I have to?"

Her laugh was soft. "Yes." Her hair was soft.

He reached up, running her silky hair between his fingers. With a sigh, he opened one eye. "You're dressed." Both eyes popped open. *What the hell?*

"You sound so...so disappointed?" she managed, laughing.

"I *am* disappointed." He sat up and peered around her. The small digital clock on the bedside table said it was almost eight. "Fuck." He sighed and fell back against the pillows.

"Exactly." She nodded, tucking the hair behind her ear. "It's late. I didn't want you...this...well, it's probably best if this stays between us, don't you think?"

He ran his hands over his face. "Yeah." He wasn't about to volunteer that Sawyer would know. He hadn't missed a day since he'd come home from the Oasis. And after Sawyer'd caught them in the foyer... "I'll go." He sat up, sliding to the edge of her bed.

"Here." She held out his clothes, neatly folded.

He took the clothes, stood, and stared down at her. She hadn't slept more than a couple of hours but she still looked beautiful.

"You're doing it again." Her voice dipped.

"What?" he asked, softly.

"Staring at my mouth." She cleared her throat.

He shook his head. "It's hard not to, now that I know how it tastes...and feels."

Her breath hitched. "You're not playing fair this morning." She pointed at him.

"I'm not?" He chuckled. "You're the one that got up and dressed before I could do what I'd been planning to do."

She shook her head. "You need to go. Before—"

"You start kissing me and I take off that pretty dress?" He finished, smiling.

"You're...you're incredible." Her expression was beyond exasperated.

"Thank you." He reached up, smoothing the hair from her shoulder.

"I didn't mean... You... Oh." She took a deep breath, shook her head, and left the room.

He chuckled, yanking on his boxers, jeans, and T-shirt. He stuck his socks into his boots and carefully, peeked out the door. He made it to his room without discovery. His phone—which he'd intentionally left in his room—was pinging with unread messages.

Archie, his sobriety coach, was checking to see about having lunch later this week.

Two Where are you? messages from Sawyer this morning, followed by a Nevermind.

And a message from Momma. "Shit." He swiped his phone open. "Shit shit shit." He was supposed to meet her in town today for brunch. As much as he loved his mother, there was no doubt that she made things *extra* challenging.

He shaved in the shower, moving as quickly as possible. Brunch with Momma meant spiffing himself up. Freshly pressed button-down, starched jeans, high-shined boots, and his dress tan cowboy hat. He dressed, grabbed his boots, and hurried down the hall, grabbing keys for his prize fully-restored black 1984 Chevrolet short-bed pickup truck.

His phone started ringing five minutes later.

"Travis, here," he answered.

"Where is here?" His father's voice was gruff.

"Dad, what are you doing?" He sighed. "You're not supposed to talk, remember? You can text me—that won't irritate your throat."

"It'll irritate *me*—"

"Dad." He groaned. "Is Sawyer there? Or Loretta? Or Margot?"

There was a general crackle and motion through the receiver.

"Travis?" It was Loretta.

"Well, hi." He smiled. "Miss me already?"

"You'd like that," Loretta said. Her sigh wasn't very convincing; he could hear the smile in her voice.

Travis glanced out the window at the bluebonnets blooming along the interstate. "Have you ever seen a bluebonnet, Loretta?"

"What? No." There was a pause. "Sawyer just walked in. You're having brunch with your mother?"

"On my way now. I forgot all about it. I'm a little tired after last night." He couldn't stop himself from adding, "I'd rather be having brunch with you. Or sitting across the table from you. Or staring at your mouth."

"It's a good thing the phone isn't on speaker," she whispered.

"When I get back, we should go for a drive through the hills so you can see the bluebonnets." It had been a long time since there'd been so many of them. A sea of blue, as far as the eye could see.

"I'm not sure we'll be here when you get back."

He frowned. Just because she'd agreed to the Wheelhouse Records deal didn't mean she'd agreed to staying with them until the tour kicked off.

"All right." She cleared her throat. "It's been fun. Take care." And she hung up.

By the time he reached the country club for brunch, his mood had taken a nosedive. From the sudden downpour that started halfway down I35, Emmy Lou's apology text explaining the latest wedding crisis that was preventing her from coming, to Loretta's cryptic "It's been fun" parting shot—he was done long before he and his mother took their seats in the club dining room.

"I can't shake the feeling you're somewhere else, Travis." His mother sipped her mimosa from the crystal champagne glass.

"I'm right here." He smiled, slathering butter on a biscuit.

COUNTRY MUSIC COWBOY 131

"You know what I mean." Momma shook her head then smoothed her platinum blond hair. "How are you holding up? How are your coaching sessions going with…" She lowered her voice and leaned in. "What's your sobriety coach's name, again?"

"Archie? My sobriety coach's name is Archie." He smiled and took a large bite of his biscuit, not bothering to lower his voice. "We talk every week. Might even get together for lunch this week, if it works out. I'll tell him you said hello."

She sighed. "No setbacks, then? No slips? It's natural, of course. And I'd never judge you on that, Travis. But I'll believe you if you say you're staying…"

"Sober?" He nodded. "I am. No slips or setbacks and no plans to change that, either." It was pretty much the same conversation they'd had at every previous brunch. Part of him wondered if she wanted him to slip just so she could be there for the aftermath.

After another sip of her mimosa, she was leaning in again. "How is everyone else? I talk to Emmy Lou almost every day of course, about the wedding. I was a little surprised to hear she'd agreed to let *Home & Style* magazine take pictures at their wedding. That must have been Brock's choice. Not that I blame them—the money they're getting is nothing to shake your head at."

Did she know Emmy Lou and Brock had agreed to the write-up and photos so they could donate every cent of the money to an anti-drug charity? If she was talking to Emmy Lou daily, shouldn't she know that?

"What do you think about Krystal's new look?" She shrugged. "The whole world knows she and Jace Black are a couple. Was it really necessary for her to ruin her hair with a black stripe in it? Though I suppose it's better than her getting a tattoo like one of his fangirls."

If his sister heard their mother say that, she'd have headed straight to a tattoo parlor just to give their mother the bird. Travis nodded his thanks to the waiter, thankful the food had arrived.

He'd eaten the entire basket of biscuits on the table and he needed to keep his mouth full to stop him from saying anything he'd regret.

"Is your father okay? I've heard rumors—"

"He's fine." If his father wanted her to know about his vocal nodules, his father would tell her.

"That's not what I've heard, Travis." She frowned at him. "I appreciate your loyalty to him and I respect that. Contrary to popular belief, I do care about your father. I always will."

He nodded, cutting into his syrup-drenched French toast. "You know better than to listen to the rumor mill."

Her green eyes narrowed. "I hardly think a close, personal friend qualifies as *the rumor mill*, Travis Wayne." Her perfectly sculpted nails clicked along the tabletop. "I'm glad he's well. Emmy Lou should have a perfect wedding day. I know Hank would never do a thing to jeopardize that but, if he's truly ill, it could complicate things."

*Only Momma would see things that way.* He toyed with the guitar pick in his pocket. This was why Krystal no longer bothered to make up an excuse about coming to brunch. His sister wasn't capable of letting their mother roll off her back. For her, it was easier to avoid their mother altogether. He suspected Momma was okay with that too.

"I'm not just worried about your father's health. He seems to be getting awfully chummy with that Loretta Gram, doesn't he?" Her smile was pinched but her attention was on her eggs Benedict and bowl of fresh fruit. "I know she's been through a lot, poor thing. Loretta Gram is one of those people who has nothing but bad luck."

*If by bad luck, she meant a successful singing career and the ability to do what she loved then sure, Loretta was super unlucky.* He swallowed more French toast. He wasn't going to talk about Loretta with his mother. The whole thing was wrong. From her assumption that her husband would get involved with Loretta to how blasé she seemed about it. Travis speared his French toast, cut off a large bite, and shoved it into his mouth.

"Travis. You weren't raised in a barn." She frowned. "Manners, please."

He kept right on chewing.

"I understand your father has the right to move on, but she's such a sad thing I can't help but wonder if she's using that angle to catch his eye." She took a tiny bite of her breakfast. "Most men, your father included, love getting to ride in on a white horse to save the day. I guess it's a virility boost."

Clearly, Momma knew nothing about Loretta. If she did, she'd know Loretta would ride in on her own white horse—she didn't need rescuing by anyone. The other? His father? Hank King wouldn't move on to another woman as long as he was married. After being married as long as they had, Travis felt confident Momma knew that. But instead of saying a thing, he shoveled in another too-large bite of his French toast.

"It's a bit of cliché, isn't it?" She was leaning forward again. "The May-December rebound romance."

*Cliché?* Travis wiped his mouth and sat back, unable to let that one go. "How old is Kegan Scott, Momma?" He took a sip of his orange juice, already knowing the answer. Every time another photo of Kegan and his mother was printed, their ages were noted within the first line or two of the articles. Kegan was a year older than he was. One year. "Things going well with you two?"

His mother set her silverware down. "I don't think I care much for your tone, Travis."

He tossed his napkin aside. "Momma." He stood, bent forward, and kissed her cheek. "I love you but you keep doing what you're doing and I can't like you." He didn't wait to see her reaction.

Two sleepless nights caught up with him about halfway home. He cranked up the radio, rolled down the windows, and wished he could start the day over. But the farther he got from Austin, the fewer and fewer cars got in his way. The birdsong, bluebonnets, rolling green grass, and the scent of spring in the air eased some of his frustration before he got home.

He was whistling when he headed into the kitchen, drawing his father and Sawyer's attention. "Morning," he said, pulling a mug from the cabinet for a much-needed cup of coffee.

His father pushed a tablet toward him.

Travis turned and read aloud, "How'd it go with your mother?" He shrugged. "No one died." He tapped the paper. "You know, there's this thing you can type out messages on—and then you're not killing trees."

His father pulled the tablet back, scowling.

"Any plans today?" he asked, carrying his mug to the table. "Bachelor living at its finest."

One of Sawyer's brows cocked a half-an-inch higher than the other. "They went to drop off Margot at the airport and do some shopping. She'll be back."

Travis didn't bother pretending he didn't know who *she* was. He knew. What mattered most? She was coming back.

# Chapter 9

Loretta sang, swaying along with the music.

> *Walking by the river,*
> *Moonlight up above.*
> *Hold my hand forever,*
> *Babe, let's fall in love.*

Travis strummed the banjo, plucking a few notes to keep the tone light and carefree. His blue-green eyes met hers and she smiled her approval.

> *So hold my hand forever and, Babe, let's fall in love.*

She stretched out the final note while Travis's fingers flew through the notes and the song ended.

"Yes?" Travis asked, a pencil in one hand.

"I like what you did there." She pointed at the sheet music. "The banjo is better."

"You could say I'm a musical genius." He grinned.

She laughed. She'd been doing that a lot recently, thanks to Travis. And now? That grin was testing her whole "one night" plan. Who was she kidding, *he* was testing her "one night" plan. It would have been completely different if their one night hadn't been so...so...

"Don't you think?" Travis asked, running his fingers through his hair. "If we change the tempo there?"

Since she hadn't been listening to him, she decided teasing

was the best way for her to save face. "As the musical genius, I'll let you decide." There was no way she'd admit her thoughts were distracted. By him. And last night—all the images from last night.

*There were oh so many to choose from.*

Now was not the time for this. She was the one pushing professionalism. Daydreaming about Travis was in no way, shape, or form professional. Calming breaths. Appropriate thoughts. Focus and clarity. She tucked her hands between her legs and concentrated on looking anywhere but him.

Travis had gone through the trouble of digging up some songs he'd been tinkering with on and off for a while. She'd been surprised he hadn't shared these songs with his sisters, knowing how close they were. Not that she was complaining. So far, she'd be more than happy to sing a handful of songs with him. These were more upbeat and playful—unlike the hotter-than-hell duet they'd sung together on the back porch.

"It's a dancing song." Travis nodded, tapping his pencil on the edge of the music stand.

"Dancing songs are always good." Which was true, especially in country music.

"They are." He stood, carrying the banjo back to its stand on the shelf.

Loretta was astonished at the number of instruments Travis could play. Harmonica, bass guitar, pedal steel guitar, banjo, and the dobro—Loretta didn't know anyone who played that anymore. He tinkered on keyboards too. As far as she could tell, he could play—and play well. The new home studio had a wall of cases built specially for the instrument collection.

She watched him carefully consider each instrument before reaching for a wooden Rogue Dreadnought guitar, slipping the strap around his shoulder and tuning it as he carried it back to their stools.

"You like dancing, Loretta Gram?" he asked, sitting on his stool and adjusting the strap.

She couldn't remember the last time she'd been dancing. When was it? With Johnny? And since most dance halls served alcohol, she didn't have many memories that ended well. But he hadn't asked her that. He'd asked her if she *liked* dancing.

"If you have to think about it, maybe we should refresh your memory?" He plucked out a few notes, then turned a tuning peg.

The gruff throat-clearing from the corner of the room reminded her they weren't alone. Sawyer sat in the corner of the studio, his long legs stretched out in front of him as he stared at something on the computer.

"You can come too, if you want, Sawyer. Get you out of the house so you're not hanging around in corners being creepy." Travis shrugged, then lowered his voice. "I have to give him shit. It's what I do. He's been looking at blueprints of the tour venues most of the morning."

"That's very thorough of him." Loretta risked a look at Sawyer, Margot's comments—and Krystal's reaction—springing to mind.

From this angle, he could be Travis's doppelgänger. A doppelgänger bodyguard. There were several differences, obviously. Travis and his hair. Sawyer had dark hair, cut close—not a curl in sight. Sawyer's eyes were dark blue, not nearly as vivid and rich as Travis's. Sawyer was a little taller than Travis, but they were pretty equally matched physically. Both of them were in tip-top physical condition.

"That's Sawyer." Travis nodded. "He doesn't like surprises."

Sawyer's gaze darted their way, lingering on her face—more like judging her. "Why don't you have security, Miss Gram?" he asked.

Travis looked up from his guitar then. "There are plenty of crazy bastards out there."

"I've never had everyday security. I never needed it, I guess. When there's an event, the label hires someone to accompany me. The same on tour." She shrugged. "I'm not as high-profile as the King family. Thankfully."

"You will be," Travis said, his gaze shifting from her to Sawyer. "You're touring with us now. Singing with us. Might be worth looking into." He paused. "You know anyone?"

"I really don't think that's necessary." She waved her hands.

Sawyer's slight headshake was almost imperceptible. Clearly, he disagreed.

"Think about it," Travis said. "It's definitely one of those things you'll appreciate having when you need it. Sawyer's good at what he does. He takes his job seriously." He broke off and whispered, "A little too seriously at times." He sat back, smiling. "He heard about a fan breaking into some actor's house, I don't remember who. Anyway, Sawyer got all fired up about it. He's got this place tricked out with cameras and sensors and tons of high-tech shit. The tour buses too. Drivable Fort Knox. Damn CIA doesn't have anything on the King's Coach I or II." He strummed his fingers along the strings. "Whatever Sawyer thinks we need, my father listens."

The one person she needed protection from wasn't a physical threat. Her father was too smart to try something like that. He'd mastered the art of manipulation with just the right amount of pushing to get what he wanted then pull a Houdini until the next time he was in need. *Pretty sure security can't protect you from parental extortion…*

Travis's gaze locked with hers. "You good?"

She nodded. "Good."

"Tired?" he asked, that grin of his making her insides give and ache. "Didn't sleep well last night?"

That look had her spiraling. And his words? All of a sudden, she could hear the rasp of his breath against her ear. Feel the grip of his hands holding her hips. Taste the salt on his skin. *Maybe I do need protection—from myself.*

She tore her gaze from his. "I'm a little tired. But I shouldn't have any problems sleeping from now on." She started flipping through the pages he had brought with him. *Because we agreed it was a one-night deal.*

Travis's knee pressed against hers, warm and solid. "Guess we'll see about that—"

"Hey, Sawyer," Emmy Lou sing-songed, holding open the studio door. "Look at you two." She headed toward them. "Getting down to business."

"What are you working on?" Krystal followed, carrying a guitar case.

"Hope we're not barging in." Jace paused inside.

Emmy Lou and Krystal both stopped, their movements almost synchronized. Confused expressions. Inspecting her and Travis. Then looking at Jace incredulously.

"Barging in?" Krystal rolled her eyes. "The tour starts in three weeks. Three. Weeks." She held up three fingers.

"Are we barging in?" Emmy Lou asked, dragging a stool over to join them.

Loretta shook her head, thankful for the interruption. "And Krystal is right. I'm the interloper here. I don't want to slow you all down or step on toes."

Emmy Lou shook her head, her blond curls bouncing. "Nope." Her attention shifted to the sheet music. "What is this?"

Travis grabbed for the pages before his sister could. "Nothing."

He didn't want his sisters to know about his songs? *Interesting.*

"I love you to the moon and back big brother, but you just guaranteed we will harass the shit out of you until you hand over the pages." Krystal set down her guitar case and faced her brother.

From the set of Krystal's jaw, Loretta didn't doubt it. Still, she felt for Travis. If he didn't want to share his music, he had his reasons. *But he'd shared his music with me.* The surge of happiness was unexpected delight.

"I'm afraid she's right." Emmy Lou nodded and held out her hand. "We can do this the easy way, or the hard way."

Loretta was laughing then. They all were. Emmy Lou putting her foot down was a sight to see. Somehow, she managed to threaten her big brother while staying all sweetness and light.

"I wish Brock had been here to see that." Travis was still laughing as he shook his head. "Then he'd see what he's getting himself into."

"He knows." Emmy Lou smiled. "And he adores me anyway."

Loretta still hadn't gotten used to this. Any of it. Not the rapid back and forth between the siblings or the devotion between the sisters and their beaus or the open display of affection among them all. It wasn't just the ease with which they teased and laughed. It was the security. There was no denying the love among them. Real love. Unconditional and unwavering... She'd begun to think that sort of love was just a myth. Great for songs and poems and movies but no one had ever truly seen it or experienced it firsthand. *No one in my world, anyway.*

She'd only ever had her father and Johnny and neither of those were healthy relationships.

The older her father got, the less tactful he grew. He used to cajole her, sweet-talk her, do something nice with the end game in mind. When she was little, she'd lie to the principal or CPS so they wouldn't take her away and he wouldn't lose his government support. When LoveJoy entered mainstream music, he swooped in to remind her of how he'd always been there for her—supporting her. Now that he was older and unable to work, he needed her to be a good daughter and help him out from time to time. The thing was, she never remembered her father working long-term. He wasn't a fan of work. He wanted a get-rich scheme, even if the scheme was guilting his daughter into giving him money whenever he wanted it.

Johnny was a different, but the same. He'd moved to Cartwright freshman year of high school. They clicked and, almost immediately, he was spending most of his time at her house. It took a while to figure out why. His stepfather was an addict. An abusive addict. And though she'd tried to help Johnny see that he wasn't the cause of his stepfather's behavior, he never quite believed her. He'd been such a beautiful soul, so gentle and vulnerable, that Loretta had felt fiercely protective of him. She was the one who dragged him to Nashville. She was the one who pushed and pushed until LoveJoy started to get noticed. And once they were noticed, his stepfather—like her own father—reached out to Johnny. He and his stepfather's final conversation had been angry and hostile. So much so that Johnny was certain he'd caused his stepfather to take his life. Johnny was never the same. Johnny's wounds were too big and all-encompassing for her to ever add to his troubles.

Being here, with the Kings, made her wonder what it would be like to have people that you could unburden your soul to. People who wouldn't judge—just listen.

"I remember this song," Emmy Lou said now, snatching one sheet of music. "I loved this one."

Travis hooked an arm around her neck and pressed a kiss to her temple. "Which is the only reason I sang it—for you. It's a bad song."

After spending the morning going over his attempts, Loretta seriously doubted that. He might not want everyone to know it, but he was talented.

"It is not." Emmy Lou cradled the page close. "It's full of happy memories, so be nice."

"Which song?" Krystal asked, smiling.

"Does it have a title?" Emmy Lou asked. "Trav, please sing it. Please. It would mean the world to me."

Loretta was beyond curious now. Not just to hear the song but to see if Travis gave in to his little sister.

"Emmy Lou," Travis groaned. "I wrote this when we were kids."

"Please, please, please." Emmy Lou hugged him tight and smiled up at him. "Please."

He shook his head, placed his fingers on the guitar, and sighed. "You cannot say a word," Travis said to Krystal.

"Cross my heart," Krystal said.

"Remember, you asked for this." Travis gave Emmy Lou a hard look.

Emmy Lou nodded, all smiles. "I did."

Travis glanced at Loretta then, his expression almost apologetic. After a few wavering notes, he started to sing.

> *Don't you cry, I'm right here, listen to my voice.*
> *Stop you tears, take a breath, time to make a choice.*
> *Shut me out, close the door, face the world alone.*
> *Let me in, take my hand, trust what we have sown.*
> *Tried and true, standing tall, I will never bend.*
> *Black and blue, fly or fall, always your best friend.*

All Loretta could do was stare. At Travis. His voice, those words, the notes his fingers set free. Did he not hear himself? Truly?

> *I'll be your knight in shining armor.*
> *I'll be your shelter from the storm.*
> *I'll hold you close when you are frightened.*
> *And I'll protect you from all harm.*

> *You'll be my princess in the tower.*
> *You'll stand beside me through the rain.*
> *You'll let my strength give you power.*
> *You know I'll chase away your pain.*

> *My love is true, never fear. My love for you is here. Never fear.*

Travis played a few more notes, then stopped, resting his hand over the strings to stop the vibrations.

"You wrote that?" Loretta asked, her throat so tight it hurt. "Travis…"

"I know." Travis sighed, running his fingers through his hair. "Are you happy now, Em?" Was he blushing?

Loretta's heart was thumping like crazy. He had no idea how good the song was—how good *he* was. Honest to goodness. She turned to look at the Emmy Lou and Krystal. *Exactly*. She wasn't the only one in shock.

Jace—even Sawyer. All eyes were on him. And *no one* was laughing. At the moment, everyone was pretty speechless.

When Emmy Lou didn't answer, he looked up—braced.

"You have no idea." Loretta shook her head. "Travis, that song is beautiful."

Emmy Lou was crying. "I forgot… How could I forget?"

"Trav." Krystal blew out a slow breath. "I mean. Damn…" She shook her head. "I feel like you've been holding out on us all this time. Why?"

But Travis looked confused. "You're serious?" His blue-green eyes bounced around the room, then sought her out.

"One hundred percent," Loretta said. "This is a showstopper, Travis King." She was happy for him. And proud. "I love every word and note and chord. You *need* to sing this. This needs to be on the radio."

He was smiling—not his usual bone-melting, panties-on-fire sort of smile. This one was sweet and uncertain. Shy, almost. It might be Loretta's favorite Travis smile so far.

---

Travis was glad he'd convinced everyone to get out of the house. Schmitt's Store was a little biergarten off the beaten path that was full of nothing but good memories for them all.

Travis popped another fried pickle into his mouth. "You sure you don't want one?" he asked Loretta.

"A fried pickle?" She frowned. "I'm sure."

"Have you ever had one?" he asked, pushing the basket her way. "You can't judge if you haven't tried them. Besides, *nobody* makes them this good. Nobody. Schmitt's Store has a reputation for their fried pickles."

"I'm pretty sure you're making that up." Loretta's skeptical eyebrow raise aside, she was picking up one of the crispy and golden pickles. "One bite."

"You'll thank me." Travis waited, watching her. "That doesn't count. That's not a bite, that's a…a nibble."

Loretta sighed louder this time and took a large bite.

"Better." He nodded, waiting for her to chew and swallow before asking, "And?"

"Fine. They're delicious." She admitted defeat—not that she was pleased to do so. "Happy, now?" She took another pickle.

"Yep." He slid the bowl of ranch dressing closer. "Dip it in that. Heaven."

She shook her head, but she was smiling. "Anyone else? Before Travis eats them all?" Loretta pushed the basket into the middle of the table.

"Oh, don't you worry." Krystal laughed. "They *know* Travis. For him, it's a bottomless pickle basket." She took a pickle.

"Which is good or he wouldn't share." Emmy Lou nodded. "It has been a long time, though. They might have forgotten."

"Nope." Travis smiled. "Mr. Schmitt saw us—and gave Dad a big ol' hug."

His father smiled. He seemed…relaxed. Everyone was. Everyone, except Sawyer. Hell, he seemed more uptight than ever.

"What's up?" Travis asked. "Expecting a raid or something?"

Sawyer barely acknowledged him.

"We've never brought you out here, have we?" Krystal asked, leaning into Jace. "It *has* been too long since we've been here."

"This is where Daddy cut his teeth." Emmy Lou smiled. "At least, that's what Daddy likes to say, right?"

Their father nodded.

"I think it goes something like…" Travis cleared his throat and did his best Hank King impression. "Long before you all were born—" He broke off, smiling at the laughter his not so good impression caused. "Before your mother or my record contract, I was just some kid with a banged-up guitar and a big dream. I spent most weekends playing on that stage right there." Travis pointed at slightly raised wooden stage on the far side of the wooden-planked dance floor. "Did I cover everything?" Travis asked his father.

His father rolled his eyes and shook his head.

Travis had been teasing, but he knew how much this place meant to his father. There were times he'd still come with his guitar, just to play and sing without all the ruckus that went along with stardom. And since Joseph Schmitt considered Hank near kin, he went out of his way to make sure the Kings were always taken care of. Not just with endless baskets of fried pickles, but privacy. If any patrons started hounding them for autographs or encroaching on their privacy, Joseph had no problems showing folk to the door.

"It had been a long time," Krystal repeated. "The last few years have been…nonstop."

"I like it," Brock said, grabbing the basket of pickles and leaning back in his chair. "Nice to be someplace where you can sit and breathe for a while."

There were murmurs of agreement and nodding heads around the table.

Brock wasn't a musician, but he was one of the most recognizable faces in professional football. Ass, too, since he was the spokesperson for an underwear line. Nothing like seeing your future brother-in-law's ass on a fourteen-by-forty-eight-foot bulletin board along the interstate to make a man proud. Still, endorsements were endorsements and a body couldn't keep taking that sort of abuse forever. If anything, Travis respected Brock's decision to have a backup plan. One that paid pretty damn well too.

"You two should think about having your wedding reception out here." Travis could barely get the words out before he was laughing.

"If you're going to start to pick, I'm going to dance." Emmy Lou stood. "Come on, Daddy." Emmy Lou tugged their father's hand. "Come dance with me."

Their father was up and leading his daughter on the dance floor before she asked twice.

On the other side of the table, Jace, Krystal, and Brock were talking—heads bent together and voices too low to hear. Which was fine by him. Outside of music and earth-shattering sex, he and Loretta hadn't done much to get to know one another. He'd like to change that. Not just because they'd be spending the next couple of months in close quarters but because…he wanted to know her.

Right now, he wanted to know what Loretta was thinking. She sat beside him, her head cocked to one side, watching his father dance with Emmy Lou. There was a ghost of a smile on her lips.

"Are you a daddy's girl too?" Travis asked, smiling.

Loretta's smile vanished. "No." She sat forward, smoothing the red and white checked skirt over her knees before crossing her arms over her chest.

The word was hard and fast. The fidgeting. Her posture. He'd unintentionally hit a nerve and he wasn't sure how to respond. Emmy Lou was the one that stayed clued in on the tabloids and entertainment news. Maybe he needed to find out a little more about Loretta before he started asking about things that clearly bothered her.

He decided humor was the best way to go. "Me neither."

Loretta turned to him, frowning. "You neither, what?"

"I'm not a daddy's girl." He winked at her.

She tried not to smile—she tried hard—but she wound up smiling anyway. "Ha ha."

He chuckled.

"Travis." Joseph Schmitt shuffled toward their table. Travis had no idea how old the man was. From the pictures on the wall—pretty damn old. Mr. Schmitt was mostly bald, stooped over, wore suspenders to keep his pants up, and used a knobby topped cane when he walked. "Pete, here, brought you more of your favorites. Where's your daddy at?"

Pete Schmitt, Joseph's son, shook Travis's hand. "He thought you'd want more of these," Pete said, putting two baskets of fried pickles on the table.

"He's a mind reader." Travis nodded. "Daddy's out there dancing with Emmy Lou."

"Course he is." Mr. Schmitt nodded. "Well you tell him to come round to the bar when he gets a chance. We found a whole trunk of pictures, and there's one or two he might find interesting."

"Anything scandalous?" Krystal asked, raising her voice over the music from the jukebox. "Daddy denies it, but I keep thinking there will be something wild from his past."

Mr. Schmitt chuckled. "I don't know about wild, but I think there's one picture in particular he'll want to see. He and a certain little gal he was sure sweet on. Before your momma, that is."

Travis and Krystal exchanged a look.

Mr. Schmitt started laughing. "Pete. You go on and get that packet for me, will you? I'll rest my bones a bit." Sawyer stood and pulled a chair back for Mr. Schmitt. "Thank you kindly, son," Mr. Schmitt said, using the chair arms to slowly lower himself into the chair. "It's hell getting old. Don't let anyone tell you different."

"This one, Pop?" Pete asked, holding a manila envelope tinged with age.

"That's the one." Mr. Schmitt's knuckles were gnarled with age and his hands shook, but he managed to pull the photos out—even if a couple fell to the floor.

"I got it." Sawyer stooped.

But their father and Emmy Lou had been heading back, so their father beat him to it.

"Damn." Their father's voice was a rusty creak.

"Daddy." Emmy Lou's tone was stern.

But their father wasn't listening. He was staring at the photo, eyes wide, mouth parted, carefully smoothing a bend at the top corner.

"Daddy?" Emmy Lou repeated.

Travis wasn't sure he'd ever seen his father look that way before. The smile was new, that was for sure.

Mr. Schmitt pulled a pair of readers from his pocket. "That the one?" he asked as he looked at their father. "I'd say that's the one." Mr. Schmitt chuckled. "You two singing."

But Daddy didn't respond right away. "Been a long, long time," Daddy's voice rasped, patting Mr. Schmitt's shoulder.

"Don't I know it." Mr. Schmitt nodded. "I wasn't sure but I figured you'd remember Ruby."

*Ruby.* Their father had been sweet on a girl named Ruby. A singer. He risked a glance at his sisters. Likely they were just as focused as he was—making all sorts of mental notes of things they'd overanalyze and talk about later.

His father's smile didn't dim, but his voice cracked when he said, "I remember."

Travis knew he wasn't the only one staring at their father. *Everyone* was.

"Dad." Krystal pointed at her own throat. "Please."

That was the first time their father seemed to remember where he was and who he was with. He nodded.

"You can keep it, if you like," Mr. Schmitt said. "I framed the other one and hung it on the wall of fame over yonder." He cleared his throat. "Whatever happened to her? I remember her momma getting into an accident but, after that, I lost track of her."

Hank shrugged. "Me too," he murmured, holding up a hand to stop any further chastising.

"Damn shame." Mr. Schmitt shook his head. "She had talent. Real talent."

Their father nodded, taking a final look at the photo before handing it back to Mr. Schmitt. Mr. Schmitt seemed just as surprised as the rest of them. The way he'd lit up over the photo, Travis had assumed he'd never let it go.

But his father's smile was gone and he sat, looking worn out all of a sudden.

Travis managed not to snatch the packet of pics from Mr. Schmitt as the old man carefully returned the photos to the manila envelope. Instead, he sat, tapping his fingers against his thighs, until Loretta placed a hand on his knee.

She was smiling ear to ear and shaking her head. *Beautiful.*

He sighed, stopped tapping his fingers, and—on a whim—caught her hand in his. For a brief moment, their fingers explored, his thumb traced the inside of her palm, and a slight shudder raced along her arm. But then she wriggled her hand lose, excused herself, and headed for the jukebox.

And, yes, even dying of curiosity over the photos, his gaze followed her. He liked watching her. The swish of her hair. The flutter of her red and white skirt hanging just above the top of her plain brown leather cowboy boots. The sway of her hips. Those hips. He knew all too well how soft her skin was—how she moaned when he'd lifted her hips just enough to make her fall apart. His fingers bit into his thighs.

He wasn't the only one noticing Loretta, either. One cocksure Ricky Rodeo was sizing her up from his stool at the bar. If he kept staring at Loretta's ass like that, he and Ricky were going to have a serious disagreement. Luckily, Loretta was headed back their way before Travis made an ass of himself by going all territorial on her.

She'd probably be more pissed at him for feeling protective of her than she'd be over the wannabe cowboy checking out her ass. He tore his gaze from hers before she caught him watching her. And that's when he noticed Sawyer.

His bodyguard was normally intimidating. Right now? He looked downright threatening. And even though Sawyer had been around for a couple of years, he was still more of a stranger than not.

All Travis knew was what he'd learned the first month Sawyer had become a member of the King's Guard security team. One, Sawyer was uptight. Two, he was fanatical about working out— Travis regularly regretted asking Sawyer to train with him. And three, Sawyer had an intel military background. So now, when it was obvious that something was weighing on Sawyer, Travis had no way of knowing what or who or why.

Emmy Lou was up, coming around the table. "I'm stealing some of these." She grabbed one of the pickle baskets, then leaned forward. "You should ask her to dance. It's less obvious than you staring at her like that." She pressed a kiss to his cheek and carried the pickles back around the table.

*Why the hell not?* He'd rather dance with Loretta than get caught up in some long-over teen romance of his father's or why the hell Sawyer looked ready to throw a few punches. *Yep. Much rather be dancing.*

She stopped the moment she saw him coming, those eyes of hers flashing and suspicious.

"I come in peace." He grinned. "And hoping you'll dance with me."

"I don't really like dancing."

"Like you don't like fried pickles?" He held his hand out.

"You're awfully cocky, Travis King." She stared at his hand.

"Nope." He argued. "I'm feeling like a damn fool, holding his hand out in front of a room full of folk, all watching to see what happens next."

"You're no fool." She took his hand. "I am."

"How's that?" He led her onto the dance floor.

She shook her head, placing one hand on his shoulder and holding onto the other.

He barely made it five seconds before he said, "I like the feel of you in my arms, Loretta Gram."

She shook her head, laughing. "Is that why you got me out here? To flatter me and sweet-talk me?"

He pulled her a little closer than necessary, spinning her close. "So you're saying I'm not supposed to tell you I think you're beautiful? Or that my hands have been itching to touch you all day?" His voice lowered. "Or that—"

"Stop," she whispered. "Travis." She glanced around the dance floor.

He spun her again, taking care to dodge another couple on the floor. "All I'm doing is telling you how I feel."

She stared up at him, then, stiffening in his hold. "Don't."

He frowned. "Don't what?"

"Don't…don't talk about *feelings* or try to charm me." She swallowed. "Say it. What are you after? And don't tell me nothing because I know that's not true."

He slowed their pace and zeroed in on her. "Maybe I'm just after your smile, because your smile takes my breath away. Ever think of that?" He shrugged. "I won't say I don't want you, Loretta. I won't lie. You are beautiful. I have thought about touching you a dozen or more times today. But right now, all I want is you, in my arms, smiling, while we share a dance."

She blinked, those topaz eyes so intent that they might as well be peering into his soul. Finally, she melted into him and smiled. And, damn, but the feelings that smile stirred up inside him. Beyond the thrum of hunger and the surge of possession was something more, something tender, rooted in his heart.

# Chapter 10

LORETTA SAT ON A BLANKET BENEATH A MASSIVE OAK TREE. She had her phone out, with Margot on FaceTime, so the two of them could watch the filming of the newest Three Kings music video together.

"I can't wrap my head around their budget," Margot said. "This will be your life soon enough."

"I'll be riding around on a horse in a flowing blue evening dress?" Loretta shook her head. "I'll leave that to Emmy Lou. She looks gorgeous. Everyone would be able to tell I'm terrified of horses."

"There's nothing to be afraid of." Travis King flopped down on the blanket beside her.

"Where did you come from?" Loretta asked, inching farther away from him. "Shouldn't you be over there, posing in front of the giant fan?" But it was too late. His gaze met hers and she was instantly, tingling-ly, aware of...*him*. "And not here." With any luck, he hadn't heard the desperation in her voice.

He was studying her, spinning a long piece of dry grass between his fingers. "No."

Three night ago they'd gone to Schmitt's Store and had a wonderful evening. At least, she thought they had. But, ever since then, things were different. For one, they both seemed intent on not being alone with each other. He was still teasing her, still talking to her, still too good-looking for any person to be, but there'd been some shift between them that she didn't understand. Plus, he hadn't touched her. Not the way she wanted or the way she dreamed about, anyway. She was the one who instituted the

Just-One-Night rule. It was a good rule. At least, it had seemed like it at the time.

It would help if she could remember how they were before they slept together. Was there the same sort of friction as they had now—all electric and dynamic and visceral? Had it been less? Had it been more? Not that it mattered. She couldn't go back in time and change what had happened between them.

"You're welcome to share our blanket," Margot said, interrupting her spiraling thoughts. "I'm not sure where Loretta's manners are this afternoon."

"I appreciate that." Travis lay back, propped on one elbow, and tossed the blade of grass over his shoulder.

Loretta did her best not to stare. But, really? How could she not stare?

Up close, he was even more devastatingly manly than he'd been when the giant fan had his curls bouncing and his shirt blown flat against his rock-hard chest. It wasn't like he was wearing anything special. A thin white button-down shirt, sleeves rolled up. Faded blue jeans that accented some of his best features to perfection. Her head-to-toe inspection came to a halt at his feet. Until now, she hadn't noticed his footwear. Rather, his lack of footwear.

"Where are your shoes?" Loretta asked. Was it possible to have handsome feet? *No*. They're feet. Albeit, Travis King's feet. But feet all the same.

"For the video." Travis wiggled his toes. "No boots or shoes. Some artsy thing, I guess."

"It was all very whimsical looking. Emmy Lou looks like part of the sky." Margot's voice was a bit muffled. "At least she was when I wasn't staring at the blanket."

"Sorry." Loretta adjusted the phone stand and made sure the phone was stable. "Better?"

"Yep." Margot's voice was loud and clear. And now that she

was facing the video production, she couldn't see what Travis was doing. Or how he was staring at her ankles.

"What?" she whispered, pulling her legs up and tucking her ankles beneath her skirt.

He looked up at her and smiled.

If he knew the effect his smile had on her, would he still do that? Still smile at her as if he was oh-so-happy to see her? Now that her insides were all wobbly and her heart was in her throat, she was on edge more than ever.

*Stop looking at him.*

She focused on the scene before them. Emmy Lou in an ethereal blue dress. Her long hair in silky smooth ringlets. "She looks like a princess." Loretta smiled. "More than usual."

Travis chuckled.

"I mean that in the nicest way possible," Loretta hurried to explain—without looking at him. "I don't want you to think I was being snide or catty. I honestly think she's one of the most beautiful people I've ever seen. Krystal too, obviously."

"I know." Travis sounded amused. "When it comes to my family, I think the only one you've ever been snide or catty about is me."

"Do tell," Margot—who Loretta was fairly certain they'd both forgotten about—said. "What did you do? What did she say? When was this and why didn't I know about it?"

"It didn't happen." Loretta glared at him.

"I think it was our first rehearsal." Travis was enjoying the way she squirmed. "I think that's right. It was the same day she told me she didn't like me."

"Lori-girl," Margot sounded horrified. "You did *not*?"

Loretta wasn't sure which was greater: the urge to tell him off or the urge to push him back onto the blanket and pretend they were the only two people in this field. She swallowed, tore her gaze from his, and picked up the phone. "Margot, he's picking on me. Travis loves to pick on people."

"It's how I show I care," Travis interrupted, leaning in so he was also on camera. "Hey, Margot."

"Hey, handsome." Margot giggled. "You two are fun. I think I'll leave you two alone so there will be even more to tell when Lori calls me later."

"There is nothing to tell," Loretta was quick to assure her manager.

"Uh-huh." Margot waved. "I can't wait to hear all about it." She disconnected.

"I'm thinking you might not want to tell her all about it." Since Travis hadn't moved back, he was far too close. "There are some things I'd like to keep between us." His gaze wandered to her mouth.

Her already stretched taut nerves were reaching their breaking point. "You are—"

"Thinking about how good we were." He nodded. "I am."

"No. That's not. You have to stop teasing—"

"Or you'll throw me back on the blanket and remind me why I can't help but stare at your mouth." He swallowed, his eyes slowly traveling over her face. "And remember how sweet you taste."

She was speechless then. Speechless and breathless and mindless with need for him.

He was staring right back at her.

"Travis?" a voice called out. "Travis?" A woman's voice.

"Fuck." Travis ran a hand over his face. "Fuck fuck fuck."

Loretta glanced in the direction of the voice. "Is that…"

"My mother?" He groaned, pushing himself off the blanket and dusting himself off. "I'll try to keep her away from you."

"From your mother?" She shielded her eyes and glanced up at him. "I think I can handle myself."

He shook his head, but he was smiling. "You know, you're right. Okay, then, you're on your own."

She frowned. "Watch out for cactus. Or scorpions. Or goat head stickers. Or—"

"Anything else that can damage my poor naked feet?" He

nodded. "I got it. Thanks." With another look her way, he sighed and headed across the waving grass toward CiCi King.

Loretta wasn't one to run away, but one long steel-eyed look from CiCi King made her consider packing up the blanket and heading back to the house. Emmy Lou and Krystal had both wanted her there though neither of them said why. Still, it was better than sitting inside by herself...with far too much time to think about she and Travis in her big, comfy bed.

Not the best time for this. Especially now that Travis and CiCi were done talking and yes, *dammit*, CiCi was headed this way.

"Yoo-hoo." CiCi King was waving. "Can I steal some of your shade?"

*No.* "Of course." Loretta was practically sitting on the edge of the blanket now.

"You are a pretty thing." CiCi paused, hands on hips, to give her an uncomfortably thorough once-over. "So sweet and natural." She knelt on the blanket, looking perfectly at ease in her designer jeans and bright pink wrap-around top. Like she belonged. "Have you ever seen such a spectacle? I can't think of how many of these things they've made, but it never fails to amaze me—the work and talent and time this all takes for something that lasts four or five minutes tops." She smiled at Loretta. "But then you know all about that. Singing is the same I guess."

Loretta had nothing to say to that so she smiled.

CiCi's phone rang. "Oops." She held up a finger. "One sec." She winked. "Hi, darlin'. I'm out at the house. Three Kings are shooting the video for 'Blue Skies.'" There was a pause. "Yes, Emmy's song." She sighed. "Yes, the one she wrote for her fiancé." There was distinct edge to the word "fiancé." "I know. He's good. He's good. I'm proud of him too." Another pause and a laugh a little too brittle to be real. "I think he's turned over a new leaf." This time the pause was longer. CiCi glanced Loretta's way and rolled her eyes—like she was including her. "I'm glad he's staying single. The last thing he needs is to get caught up by some pretty little thing, needing rescue, who will knock him off the wagon." She broke off, nodded, and said, "Yes, you're right. He's all kinds of vulnerable right now, even if he's acting all strong. A mother knows these things." She laughed. "I know, I know. Lunch next week. Yes. Looking forward to it. Bye now." CiCi hung up and placed her phone on the blanket beside them. "One of my bunco friends."

*I've got nothing.* "That's nice," Loretta said, hoping it was a suitable response.

"We've been friends for eons." CiCi ran a hand over her platinum blond hair. "They love my kids, especially Travis. That boy could charm the dew off a honeysuckle. Well, I'm sure you've noticed." CiCi was watching her now.

Loretta couldn't shake the feeling that she wasn't just being watched, she was being catalogued. Mentally dissected and compartmentalized. But it might only feel that way because of the coldness in CiCi's brilliant blue eyes. "He is charming."

"Good thing you're a levelheaded girl. And since you're staying out here, maybe you could do me a teensy little favor?" She paused but didn't wait for an answer. "If you could keep an eye on Travis for me? Most men don't know what's best for them, after all. They need to be kept in line." She laughed.

Loretta glanced toward the cameras and people and commotion and wished there was some way she could find a reason to go there. Now. Immediately.

"I appreciate that." CiCi patted her hand. "I wanted to congratulate you. It's not every day someone gets this sort of opportunity. A new duo, touring with Three Kings, and a record too?"

How did she know this? As far as Loretta knew, the details of the contract weren't common knowledge.

"After everything with poor Johnny and all that trouble with your father, it's about time something good happened for you." CiCi was smiling again—but there was no warmth there. "Ethan

Powell has high hopes for you. He's a smart judge of character so, take it from me, you do what you need to stay in his good graces. He is a man, after all. He needs to be kept in line just like the rest of them. Once you figure out how to do that, there will be nothing stopping you." She turned, giving Loretta another head-to-toe sweep. With a nod, she said, "You just stay focused and keep your eye on the prize and you'll go far, Loretta Gram."

Was she truly offering Loretta career advice? Or was this about something else altogether? And how the hell was she supposed to say anything?

CiCi's phone started ringing again. "Oh, I have to take this one." She picked up her phone and pushed herself up and off the blanket. "I enjoyed our little chat, Loretta. We girls have to stick together now, don't we? I'll see you at the wedding? Take care." She waved, then answered her phone, walking back through the tall grass to the camera crew.

Loretta's phone vibrated.

You lose a limb? Bleeding out? The text read.

Loretta frowned.

You look a little shell-shocked. She has that effect on people. The three little dots kept scrolling. Who was texting her?

Loretta glanced up, her gaze scanning the people gathered round the audio and video equipment. Emmy Lou? Krystal? They had her number.

It's the King you don't like. The one you slept with.

Once the shock wore off, she was smiling. Talk about gall.

Not that there was much sleeping.

Really? Like she didn't know. She knew. And every time she crawled into that big empty bed, he was all she could think about. Him. And that sleepless night. And how, just thinking about it, made her ache. *Your teasing thing is going a little too far, Travis King.* She shook her head and set the phone facedown on the blanket.

But a series of pings had her reaching for the phone and staring at the texts roll in. Each text. One. Word.

We. Should. Talk. About. One. More. Night. Three dots bounced and bounced. Soon.

Loretta stared at the screen, her heart thundering against her ribcage. *What?* If this was a joke, it wasn't funny. If it wasn't a joke, it was a terrible idea. *Terrible.* She turned her phone off.

"We ready?" the director called out. "Places. Cue the music. The fan."

It was quite a production. Emmy Lou walking, her dress blowing out behind her, two white horses trailing behind her. She was singing.

> *One hope, rising inside me, that you'll hear my song.*
> *Each night, I close my eyes, and hope I wasn't wrong.*
> *Cuz losing you, still wanting you, won't leave my mind.*
> *And losing you, yes, loving you has left me color-blind.*

The cameras pivoted to Travis, standing barefoot on a massive rock formation. He was playing a sky-blue guitar, his curls swaying in the fan-engineered wind.

At the top of the rock was Krystal. Her dark blue dress was just as gauzy and ethereal as Emmy Lou's, her long blond locks—plus her signature black stripe—swirling around her as she looked up into the sky. Together, they sang the chorus. Loretta found herself singing along too.

> *All I see is you… All I see is blue.*
> *Blue skies for miles,*
> *Blue birds flying high,*
> *Bright blue like your eyes.*
> *Don't you know oo-hoo—I'm blue when you're gone.*

"Cut!" the director yelled. "Let's reset."

A flurry of activity was happening, but Loretta only saw Travis. He was typing on his phone, then looking her way. It took effort, but she didn't turn on her phone—even if the damn thing felt like it was burning a hole in her pocket. As much as she wanted to deny it, she liked Travis. Liking him and wanting him, together, had the potential to be dangerous all around. And cold smile aside, CiCi King had a point. Travis was vulnerable. Letting things go on with Travis—no matter how much she ached for him—couldn't happen. She couldn't let it.

---

"This is perfect," Emmy Lou said, cutting into the apple pie Krystal had made. "All of it." She smiled at them both. "I know nothing's going to change but—"

"You'll be married," Travis interrupted. "That's a change."

"But not a big one." Krystal frowned. "You're still my sister first. And we're still singing together and going on tour together and you better still come spend the night with me and Jace and we all better still come out here." She stabbed her piece of pie, her breathing accelerating and her tone going higher and higher. "And all the holidays. All of them. They have to be here. All of us together."

Travis wasn't sure whether to laugh or cry. But since Emmy Lou started crying, he had to laugh.

"Come on, now." He put an arm around them both and pulled them in for a big hug. "We like Brock. He's been a part of this family for a long time. There's no reason to get worked up over this. It's not like she's marrying an asshole, leaving the band, and us."

"I *sort* of like Brock," Krystal huffed against his chest.

"Well, I love him," Emmy Lou sniffed.

"That doesn't mean you have to marry him," Krystal said, again. "I love Jace but you don't see the two of us getting hitched, do you?"

Emmy Lou sighed. "I hope you do, someday."

Krystal murmured something that sounded like, "Whatever," then tightened her hold on them both.

They stayed that way for a while, until Emmy Lou stopped sniffing and Krystal didn't sound like she was hyperventilating anymore.

"I love you both." He pressed a kiss against each of their cheeks. "Now, we all good?" he asked, looking them over.

Krystal shrugged. "I'll be better with pie."

Emmy Lou gave them both a final hug and stepped back. "Me too."

"Ice cream?" he asked, opening the freezer. "If there's any left."

The three of them settled around the kitchen table with their warm apple pie and melting vanilla ice cream, enjoying a companionable silence—save the scraping of spoons on the bottom of a bowl.

"It's the first time we've been alone in a while," Emmy Lou said, an odd look on her face.

"It's the first time we've been alone since we learned about Ruby, is what you mean." Krystal smiled.

"How did you get there?" Travis asked, looking back and forth between them.

"Twins," they said in unison.

"Whatever." He laughed. "Why are we worrying about this Ruby person?" His sisters exchanged another odd look—one that made him pause mid-bite to ask, "What now?"

"Not worrying." Krystal shrugged. "Curious."

"I can see that." Travis shook his head. "A little too curious, if you ask me."

"I'm not asking." Krystal smiled sweetly.

Travis chuckled.

"What's wrong with wanting to know more about Ruby?" Krystal asked. "I got the feeling things were left…unfinished."

"Didn't you see Daddy's face?" Emmy Lou asked, scooping some ice cream up with her spoon. "It was some look."

He'd seen it—mostly. Granted, he'd been distracted by Loretta but, unless something more than a look had transpired, he didn't get why they were hung up on this. "A look? You mean nostalgia?" Travis asked. "He was a guy long before he was our father. Let him have his memories without you two poking around in his past. He's an adult and, contrary to what you both seem to think, he can take care of himself. Why does this have to be a big deal?" He watched them, both of them. "I know that look." It wasn't a good look. "Why do I get the feeling there's more to this?"

The fact that they were both struggling to come up with an answer didn't help ease his sudden twinge of anxiety. He thought they'd stopped keeping secrets from each other, but now he wasn't so sure.

The kitchen door opened, breaking the loaded silence. Travis glanced at the door, irritated. He wanted to get to the bottom of this and, unless it was Loretta, he'd rather not be interrupted. But it was Sawyer. Since Sawyer already knew everything, there wasn't any point in keeping things from him.

But Sawyer seemed more interested in the pie and ice cream than the awkward silence.

"There's none left," Travis said.

"Ignore him." Emmy Lou smiled. "Come in. Have some pie." She was up, playing hostess.

"There's another one in the oven," Krystal said, pointing at the oven with her spoon. "I hid it from Travis."

Travis chuckled. It made sense that his sisters had a soft spot for Sawyer—he'd proven himself to them time and time again.

"Since you're here, help me set these two straight." Travis sat back in his chair, holding his bowl close.

"With?" Sawyer asked, smiling his thanks at Emmy Lou for the bowl of ice cream and pie, and taking a seat at the table.

"Travis," Krystal cut in. "Forget it." She waved her hand. "It's nothing."

"How's the pie?" Emmy Lou asked, all smiles.

*What the hell?* One minute, they were going full Nancy Drew and now they didn't want to talk about it. If they were serious about learning more about Ruby, Sawyer was their best chance. Whatever. If they were going to drop it, he wasn't going to bring it up. As far as he was concerned, their father had the right to some privacy.

"Good. As always." Sawyer nodded. "You make it, Krystal?"

"I did, thank you very much." Krystal nodded. "I've never asked what your favorite kind of pie is, Sawyer?"

Travis glanced at his sister. Krystal had a thing about making pies for people—she loved to bake. If she wanted to know what kind of pie Sawyer liked, he'd officially been accepted into the family.

"I'm not picky," Sawyer answered, taking a huge bite.

"You don't have a favorite?" Emmy Lou asked Sawyer. "Or some family recipe or dessert that makes you happy?"

"Not really." Sawyer set his bowl on the table, his expression shuttered. "We never congregated in the kitchen the way you all do."

"I guess we do spend a lot of time in here." Emmy Lou looked around the room, as if seeing it with new eyes.

"Do you have siblings?" Travis asked, alarmed when they all stared at him. "What? She can ask a question but I can't?"

"A brother," Sawyer said. "Younger than me. Ames."

Travis could see that. Sawyer was big brother material—all the way. He had that overprotective vibe thing down, which was one of the reasons he was so good at his job.

"Ames." Emmy Lou smiled. "What's he like?"

"Good kid, mostly." Sawyer shrugged, running a hand along the back of his neck. "Cherry. Cherry pie is my favorite."

"I'll make one next week." Krystal nodded.

"Next week, I'll be a married woman." Emmy Lou shook her head.

"Um, tomorrow night you'll be a married woman." Krystal sighed, irritated. "Unless you change your mind and live in sin like Jace and I."

Emmy Lou laughed. "I know there are hordes of people coming tomorrow, and my dress is big and over-the-top, so are the food and the flowers and the place—and the *Home & Style* deal...but that's not what this is about. Not for me." She took Krystal's hand. "This is about the vow I want to give Brock and the vow he wants to give me—in front of the hordes of people there to witness it."

Krystal sighed.

"Why not make it a double wedding and get it over with?" Travis asked, ducking when Krystal flicked some ice cream at him. "Hey, hey, I'm not cleaning that up."

"Where's Clementine?" Krystal turned. "She'll take care of it."

"Last I saw of her, she was curled up in Loretta's lap, sound asleep." Emmy Lou shook her head. "She's smitten; Loretta I mean. I can't believe she never had a pet growing up."

Travis perked up at the mention of her name.

"I get the feeling she had a difficult childhood," Emmy Lou added.

"Considering what happened to Johnny, I'm not so sure her adulthood is all that rocking, either." Krystal glanced at him then. "So, big brother, what's the deal?"

Travis played dumb. "You know what it is. You saw the Wheelhouse packet, same as I did." They were fishing for info. They didn't know he and Loretta had spent the night together. And he wasn't about to admit he'd sent a chicken shit string of texts hoping to renegotiate their original one-night arrangement. What the hell had he been thinking? *Texting something like that?*

"Yeah, no. That's not what I'm talking about and you know it."

Krystal's sigh was all impatience. "The you-want-to-jump-her and she-wants-to-jump-you thing."

"Jump?" Travis asked. "What are you, fifteen?" Not that she was wrong. He distinctly remembered Loretta jumping into his arms when they were in the shower…right before he'd pressed her against the glass wall… He shook his head. He didn't have the whole poker face thing mastered the way Sawyer did so he needed to change the topic—and soon.

"I think it's more than that." Emmy Lou put her elbows on the table and rested her chin in her hands, watching him. "I think you might be sweet on Loretta Gram."

Travis shoveled a massive bite into his mouth. Sweet on her? *No comment.*

"This reminds me… It wasn't all that long ago we were having a similar conversation about you and Jace." Emmy Lou laughed. "I think there was pie involved then too."

Krystal nodded. "And if I'd listened to you instead of acting like you were wrong, think about all the time and energy I'd have saved everyone."

Travis almost choked on his pie. When Krystal dug in her heels, there was no changing her mind. The more you tried to push her, the harder she pushed back. And everyone sitting around the table had firsthand experience with her stubborn streak.

Her green eyes swiveled his way, narrowing in irritation. "From the look on your face, I don't want to know what you're thinking." One brow rose. "But if you want to be a stubborn ass and repeat the pile of poo you served up last time, fine. Ignore your sisters and how all they want is for you to be happy."

"Will do." Travis nodded.

His sisters' disappointed sighs were in unison, so were the little frowns and the slight pucker between their brows. Even Sawyer laughed then—for a whole five seconds.

Conversation drifted from tomorrow's long agenda to the

upcoming tour schedule and then from Emmy Lou's assurances that Momma was not bringing a date to her concerns over tension between their parents to her repeated nightmare that one of her guests was allergic to shellfish, sat too close to someone eating the lobster, and dropped dead before the cake cutting.

"That's a very specific allergy-related death dream." Travis gave up the fight and started laughing.

It was almost two when they cleaned up the kitchen and went their separate ways.

He'd never say so out loud, but he liked having his sisters home. He'd missed their kitchen counseling sessions. That's what Gramma had called it. Working through the world's problems while cooking dinner—or eating it? *Probably why we spend so much time in the kitchen.* Their family was never short on problems.

He was headed to his room when the jingle of Clementine's collar stopped him. The light from the hall dimly illuminated the interior of the music room—enough that he spied Loretta curled up on the couch with Clem sprawled across her. But once Clementine saw him, she hopped off the couch, ran around him in a circle, and trotted down the hall toward the doggy door in the kitchen.

Loretta jerked awake. "Travis?" Her voice was thick with sleep and sexy as hell.

"Sorry." He cleared his throat. "Didn't mean to wake you." If he were smart, he'd say goodnight and head to his room. He didn't. *Dumbass.*

"I didn't mean to fall asleep." She yawned, pushing herself off the couch and crossing the room to where he stood. "What time is it?"

"Late." His voice was more gravelly than normal. He swallowed. "Too late to be up and about."

She stared up at him, looking more and more awake with each passing second.

"Pie," he said, doing his damndest not to stare at her mouth or reach up to smooth her hair. "I'm sorry about yesterday." He shrugged. "It's hard to tease through text."

Her eyes widened. "You were teasing?"

*Yes. No.* He sighed. He'd told her he'd never lie. Sure, lying would save face and be an easy out but…it was still a lie. "No."

She frowned.

"You want me to lie?" He shook his head. "It'd be a hell of a lot less humiliating to say I was teasing."

"Why are you humiliated?" Her frown grew.

"Rejection's never fun, Loretta." He held his hands up. "But I—"

"We agreed one night." Her voice wavered. "Any more is like… like playing with fire. Fire's not something you can control, Travis."

He swallowed, instantly understanding. She was scared to give in to this. Scared that what was between them would be out of control.

"I need control." She shook her head. "I'm not a risk-taker."

He nodded. "Okay."

"No." She stepped forward, running her hands up his chest. "It's not okay. This time *is* it." Her breathing changed, going husky. "We have to agree. Just this. One more night."

He'd take what he could get. He pulled her close, the feeling of her pressed tight against him tearing a groan from his throat and sending a shock wave down his spine. "Whatever you want," he murmured against her mouth. She might have jumped, he might have lifted her—the end result was the same. He carried her, his lips clinging to hers, to his room and kicked the door closed behind him.

# Chapter 11

LORETTA WOKE TO THE STROKE OF TRAVIS'S HANDS ON HER body. She'd never been this tired in her entire life. Then again, she'd never been this satisfied, either. He was relentless. Almost like he was racing against the clock. Like he knew their time was ticking away and every second had to count.

At the moment, his fingers were doing deliciously wicked things between her legs. And, sore or not, she arched into his touch.

His mouth latched onto her neck. "Good morning."

*Already?* "Is it?" She gasped—his fingers continuing to move. "Travis..."

"I've got you." His lips were featherlight against her jaw and chin but once his lips met hers, he was anything but light. Hot and deep and hungry. His lips took while his fingers gave, and Loretta let go and enjoyed it. It didn't take long for her to tip over the edge. Free falling toward bliss, she cried out—broken and raw—against his shoulder.

Her eyes fluttered open. "It's not fair," she whispered. She was probably all swollen eyelids and blotchy skin, with rats-nest hair. He was all golden and triumphant and gorgeous.

He smoothed her hair from her face. "What's not fair?"

"Nothing." She sighed. "What time is it?"

"Five." He kissed her forehead. "Time enough for one more go around." He kissed the tip of her nose. "Or two."

She laughed. "There is no way twice is physically possible."

"That sounds like a challenge." He pulled her under him.

"No." She pressed her hands against his chest. "It's not.

I promise." She loved the feeling of him. His strength. How incredibly powerful his body was. In his arms, she felt safe—protected. Almost cherished. *That's the sort of thinking that will bring you nothing but trouble.* She didn't need to be cherished. Or protected.

Travis flopped onto the bed at her side, resting his head on the pillow. "But, you're right. I might need a quick nap to reenergize myself." His eyes closed.

"Or ten to twelve hours." She shook her head, watching as his breathing grew deep and steady.

*What did I do?* She stared up at the ceiling. *It's not fair.* There was something about him that rendered her incapable of coherent decision-making. Her pathetic add-on condition that this be the last time was just that—a way to justify doing something she *knew* was wrong.

Travis was, what, a year sober? It had been a long time since she'd gone to an alcoholic's family and friends support group, but she remembered how important that first year was. Avoiding romantic relationships was advised. While she could argue that this was sex and not a relationship, it wasn't that simple. She lived with him. She was singing with him. She was connecting with his family. Soon, they'd be on the road together. Whatever happened in the bedroom, those commitments wouldn't change. They were tangled up in each other for the foreseeable future.

And now that she'd had time to overanalyze every second they'd spent together, and she'd overheard CiCi's phone conversation, she'd begun to question everything. Travis knew her story. He knew Johnny. He knew her career had been on the line. Was that what had prompted all of this?

She pressed her hands to her face. *And this was exactly why all of this was a bad idea.* The sex, the singing, the talking, the spending time, the smiling and laughing. Neither of them needed this sort of complication.

His hand encircled her wrist and pulled her hand away. "What's wrong?"

"Nothing." Her voice said otherwise.

"Loretta." He turned her head. "Talk." He'd been honest with her; he expected her to be honest with him.

She wasn't sure where to start or what, exactly, to say but the first words that came out of her mouth were, "This is just sex."

Travis blue-green gaze held hers.

"That's all." It had to be. "I don't want anything to complicate... *anything*. We both have jobs to do and people that rely on us." He had people—she had Margot. And Margot's cancer treatment... Too much on the line for there to be any confusion. "This is all I have to give."

He propped himself up on his elbow. "Where's this coming from?"

"I want things clear between us." She should stop there. That was all he needed to know. But the words kept coming. "I'm not reliant on you. I don't need you to fix my career or take me in or sleep with me because you think I'm lonely—"

"Hold on. I'd be a fool to think you were reliant on *me*." He paused, his gaze sweeping over her face. "You staying here was practical for business." He shook his head. "I'm sleeping with you because I want you. I hear you and I'll play by whatever rules you set. Okay?"

She nodded, wishing she was hardwired to be defensive. Wishing she could enjoy this—enjoy Travis—without worrying about the consequences or expecting the worst.

His hand cradled her face, the caress of his thumb along her jawline sending a tremor down her spine. "Now, I'm lying here, puzzling over the best way to show you how bad I want you, because it seems to me, you need some convincing."

And just like that, she was back to aching for him. She didn't want to think—she only wanted to feel. Whatever happened tomorrow, she'd deal with it then. But, right now, this was what she needed.

Travis made good on his word. He loved her—face-to-face—until they were both out of their mind and breathless. She was gasping, clinging, but he wouldn't go easy on her. She was the focus of his strength and power and endurance, and she welcomed him with open arms. He only let go after she'd exploded into a million tiny pieces of pure pleasure.

"Sleep," he murmured against her neck, pulling her into the circle of his arms.

She didn't. She couldn't. This was between her and Travis. And since this time *was* the last time, she'd prefer the rest of the household not discover her sneaking from his room. Especially not today—the day of his sister's wedding.

But she'd just stepped outside of Travis's door when Sawyer said, "Morning."

She jumped, dropped her shoes, and came close to hyperventilating.

"Sorry." He didn't look sorry. He looked like he was trying not to smile. "He awake?"

They both knew exactly who he was talking about so she answered truthfully. "No. Will I make it to my room undetected?"

He nodded.

She picked up her shoes and tiptoed, as quickly as she could, down the other hallway to her room. A quick shower later and she fell face-first into the bed. If she was going to Emmy Lou's wedding, she'd need a nap.

Loretta woke up three hours later. Emmy Lou had given her a rundown of the day's events so she knew it was going to be a three-ring circus. And it was, but Emmy Lou's wedding planner seemed to have everything under control.

It wasn't surprising that Emmy Lou's wedding had a fairy-tale theme. The wedding was in one of the historic Painted Churches in the Texas Hill Country. Until today, Loretta had never heard of them. But once she'd stepped foot inside, she was struck by the beauty and intricacy of the walls, arches, and ceiling of the building.

If the architecture and artwork weren't enough, there was the abundance of flowers. The church smelled like a flower shop. Gardenias and peonies and sweet peas an explosion of color and scent—plus hundreds of candles placed throughout.

*Just like a fairy tale.* Loretta couldn't help but smile.

The whole day was like a fairy tale.

Emmy Lou arrived on the arm of a very proud father. From her tulle and lace and crystal-encrusted dress to the mile-long train and gossamer veil, the whimsical fantasy element was complete. But the whole spectacle didn't outshine Emmy Lou's joy. She was so happy it was impossible not to be happy for her. And when her mountain of a professional football player fiancé got a little teary-eyed while she recited her vows, Loretta did too.

That was about the time Travis saw her. But his smile wasn't teasing—it was heartfelt. After all, this was his little sister getting married. He'd want the man marrying his sister to get choked up, wouldn't he? Travis would want to know that the man marrying his sister understood how blessed and lucky he was to have Emmy Lou as his wife.

Brock did.

And while the string quartet and unity candle and butterfly release were lovely, Loretta couldn't stop her attention from wandering back to Travis. Him, in his tuxedo, should be illegal. Didn't he know that a wedding was all about the happy couple? Especially the bride. While no one could outshine Emmy Lou, Loretta was pretty confident Brock came in second in the Most Handsome Man in the room category.

*Or I'm biased because…* Because, why? Because she'd seen him naked? Because she'd been sucked in by his charm? Or because she was developing a huge soft spot for the man she'd sworn to keep at arm's distance. *I need to work on my self-discipline.* When it came to Travis, she had none.

The ceremony was traditional and quick. While the bride and groom were subjected to endless photographs, she and the rest of the guests were shuttled from the church to the reception site. The Gardens was just that, a botanical garden abloom with native and imported colors alike. But, in keeping with the fairy-tale theme, the wedding planner had added *more*.

The small stream that ran through the gardens had floating floral arrangements. Some were simply flowers. Others had tulle and beaded designs. The large oak trees, hundreds of flower pomanders hung in every ethereal and pastel shade available. From large to small, the pomanders and silk ribbons swayed in the spring breeze.

Loretta had never mastered being comfortable in crowds—not that she let on. Johnny had told her confidence was more a state of mind. If she acted confident, even if she didn't feel that way, she'd eventually feel confident. So far, that hadn't been the case. But she kept trying.

When the King family arrived, the cocktail hour under the trees moved inside the massive white tent for dinner and dancing.

"Loretta?" Jace Black waved her down, a young woman at his side. "This is my little sister, Heather."

"Ohmygawd, you're Loretta Gram." Heather had that high-pitched excited fan quality that made Loretta smile. "Hi." She reined it in. "Nice to meet you." She sounded more in control now. "I'll try not to fangirl too hard but no promises." She nudged Jace. "I mean, of course you know Loretta Gram." She shook her head. "Is there anyone you don't know, at this point?"

Jace pretended to think, then shook his head. "I don't think so."

Heather laughed. "You're so full of it."

"Heather." Hank King wrapped Heather in a hug. "How's college? Almost done, aren't you?"

It was like a mini family reunion. Travis scooped her up and spun her around, Heather "oohed" over Krystal's black stripe in her hair, and Jace listed off of Heather's current academic successes. Loretta smiled when Hank took her arm, instantly including her.

She and Hank headed toward their table, trailing behind the others, when CiCi approached.

"Look at you two." She was all smiles, leaning in to give Hank a kiss on the cheek, then Loretta. "Loretta, you look lovely. All sweet and young. But not too young, I guess? Isn't that right, Hank." Her large blue eyes bounced between the two of them.

Her implication wasn't the least bit subtle. But, she couldn't be serious, could she? Travis was always teasing—so was Krystal. Maybe they'd picked up the habit from CiCi?

The idea of her and Hank… Well, it was tabloid fodder. A joke. Hank was a gentleman—a married gentleman. While CiCi had no problem behaving as if she and Hank were no longer married, Hank would never disgrace himself or his family that way. If she knew that, surely CiCi did too?

Hank's voice sounded weak. "CiCi—"

"No, no. You don't owe me any explanation." CiCi sighed. "I guess the no date rule only applied to Kegan and me. But that makes sense, I suppose, since Loretta is already living with you."

Loretta didn't blame Hank for the clenched jaw or the tightening of his mouth. She was having a hard time biting back her temper—but she'd never cause a scene.

"Silly old me thought you were after Travis." CiCi turned the full force of her glare on Loretta. "Boy, did I underestimate you."

After Travis? Like she'd devised some intricate plan to catch one of the Kings? Why? Because she needed the Kings to keep her career? Hadn't she said as much to Travis last night? He'd been quick to dismiss her fears but with CiCi throwing them in her face, Loretta's deep-seated insecurity clashed with her anger.

Hank cleared his throat. "Enjoy yourself," he managed, but the words were raspy. Hank steered Loretta around CiCi and toward their table.

"I'm sorry," Loretta whispered. "If I thought coming here would cause problems—"

"Don't worry." He coughed. "CiCi's being…CiCi." Hank shook his head, taking a glass from a passing waiter. He downed it and said, "I see the way my son's looking at you. You should be here." Hank patted her arm, clearing his throat. "That look, right there." His chuckle ended on a cough.

Travis *was* looking at her. And it was some look. The sort of look that threatened the walls she'd spent years building around her heart. The sort of look that made her wish she could let down her guard and let Travis in. But she couldn't. She wouldn't do that to him.

———————————

Travis was going out of his mind. Every night for the last week, he'd followed where Loretta led. When he said he'd let her set the rules, he meant it. After Emmy Lou's wedding, he'd driven her home and taken her to bed. The following day, they'd rehearsed and eaten donuts and as soon as the house was asleep—she'd turned up outside his bedroom door. Six nights of getting more caught up in Loretta and wishing there were no rules between them.

"Good morning, Romeo." Krystal greeted him as soon as he pushed through the kitchen door.

Their father sat in his chair at the kitchen table, coffee in hand, laughing.

Romeo? Did she know something? Or was she fishing for information? "Good morning?" Travis said, doing his best not to overreact. He ran his fingers through his hair and did a somewhat covert sweep of the room. No Loretta. Not yet.

"Good morning," Jace said, waving his fork. "Radio thing this morning. She's been laughing about it all morning."

"You laughed too." Krystal smiled, her green eyes a little too curious. "I made some scrambled eggs and bacon and pancakes."

"And blueberry muffins," Jace added, shooting Travis a look. "And cinnamon rolls."

"You're welcome." Krystal was chewing on the inside of her lip. *Never a good sign.* "You look a little worn out, big brother."

He tried not to squirm as Jace and his father turned to see for themselves.

"I'm fine." Travis headed to the stovetop where the food was staying warm. "Thank you." He grabbed a plate and served himself a large breakfast before heading to the table. "This is a hell lot of food."

"I was restless." She shrugged. "And, I've got a song bouncing around and there's nothing like cooking to help—"

"You finish it." Travis nodded. Ever since he could remember, Krystal cooking meant a new song was coming. And since she was pulling together ingredients for who-knows-what, she hadn't quite worked the song out yet. "What are we making now?"

"Cherry pie," Krystal said, without looking up. "Sawyer's favorite."

He exchanged a look with Jace, then sighed. "I was going to stop you but…cherry pie sounds really good."

Krystal was smiling again. "How did I know you were going to say that?" She glanced his way then. "You and Sawyer aren't working out together anymore?"

The bite of pancakes got stuck in his throat.

"He was out running when we got here." Krystal started measuring out flour and dumping it into her favorite ceramic bowl. "Alone."

Travis took a sip of coffee, careful to avoid making eye contact. "Not every day maybe, but most days." His nights with Loretta guaranteed one hell of a workout—but he'd keep that to himself. He sat back in his chair. "What's with the Romeo thing?"

"Nonsense is what it is." His father took a sip of his coffee.

Travis grinned.

"Daddy, if Emmy Lou were here, she'd tell you to hush and rest your voice." Krystal sighed. "But since she and Brock won't be back until tomorrow, it's up to me to keep you quiet." She crossed the room, topped off his coffee, and put a plate with a warm, gooey cinnamon roll down on the table. "Here." She kissed their father's cheek then stood, hand on hips, smiling from ear to ear. "It's all sorts of juicy. You and Daddy fighting over Loretta. Good stuff."

Travis glanced at his father. His father shook his head, happily devouring the cinnamon roll.

"Who's winning?" Travis asked.

That earned a chuckle from his father, who pointed at himself with his fork.

"You think so?" Travis asked. "Guess I need to up my game."

"You do. Daddy's has the edge." Krystal nodded. "Did you know Loretta and Daddy were on a date at the IMAs?" She shrugged. "Yeah, me neither. They mentioned Schmitt's Store too—Mr. Schmitt will be so pissed off. Anyway, that was your date, Trav. Drinking and dancing—"

"And fried pickles," Jace added. "Even if Brock did eat most of them."

"I'm guessing the fact that you all were there didn't come up?" Travis asked.

"Um, no. Why would it?" She started cutting the shortening into the flour, shaking her head. "They even put together a series of lovely blurry images from Emmy's wedding that showed you were so distraught by the love triangle that you were drinking again."

Travis sighed. "Did I look like I was having fun?"

Krystal shrugged. "Like I said, they were super blurry."

"Remember when you were trying not to step on Emmy Lou's hundred-thousand-dollar wedding dress and fell into a chair?" Jace asked. "Apparently, you were fall-down drunk."

"Aw, well, there you go." Travis nodded. "Wait, you said blurry pictures. I thought this was on the radio."

"It was." Jace was up, grabbing more food. "*TMN* ran a piece last night. This was a recap."

"Want another one?" Travis asked his father, carrying both plates back to the countertop for seconds. "It's not the worst thing that's ever been said about me. I mean, it's pretty basic soap-opera type shit, but it's laughable."

Krystal decided to find the video of the original interview. She had the television on and was typing in *TMN* when the kitchen door opened and Sawyer came in, holding the door wide for Loretta.

She looked so damn pretty, it was a struggle not to say so. Or to smile or wink or acknowledge the fact that, last night, he'd had her screaming into her pillow. The memory had an immediate impact on the comfort of his jeans.

"Good morning," Jace said.

"Perfect timing." Krystal smiled. "Get some food, please. I made too much and I'll feel bad if it goes to waste."

"You've been busy." Loretta stared at the mountain of food. "Is company coming?"

"Just you two." Travis said, noting the way her cheeks flushed when her topaz gaze met his. "I hope you have an appetite."

Sawyer shot him a look, sighed, and headed for the food. "Since you've slept through workouts this week, you might want to cut back."

Loretta's cheeks went from pink to red, her gaze falling from his.

*Damn Sawyer anyway.*

"Here it is." Krystal stopped, setting the remote on the counter, and returning to her pie-making with one eye on the television. "I'll turn up the volume when it gets to the good stuff."

"Here is… Oh." Loretta stopped in front of the food and stared at the television. "Has something happened?"

"No." Krystal shook her head. "But they're acting like it has."

But Loretta didn't move or get her breakfast. A photo of her and his father the night of the IMAs popped up. He'd almost forgotten how incredible she'd looked in that dress.

"I think we're up," their father said, earning a round of *shhs* from everyone in the room.

*TNM* reporter Delia Youngblood's delivery was almost as over-the-top as her makeup. "The night made an impression on all of us. Not only were we the first to bring you the latest development on the Gram-King love triangle—"

Travis and his father both snorted, causing Krystal to laugh while waving at them for silence.

"But, later this week, we will have an exclusive interview with the man who knows Loretta Gram best." Delia Youngblood turned to her coanchor. "I'm excited to see what insight he'll have."

"I'm looking forward to it," coanchor Caleb Steward said.

A photo of a man wearing a LoveJoy shirt, holding up a LoveJoy album, popped up on-screen. He was tall and thin, handsome in a slightly used-car-salesman sort of way. But the man on-screen wasn't what caught his eye. It was Loretta. She was holding the plate against her chest. From where he sat, she could tell her breathing was rapid and uneven.

"Who is that, Loretta? Do you know him?" Jace asked before he could.

But her answer confirmed his suspicions.

"That's my father." Loretta's voice was flat.

"Up until now, Mr. Donnie Gram has remained silent on his daughter's association with the Kings or how she's been dealing with the tragic loss of her long-time singing partner, Johnny

Hawkins." Caleb Steward paused. "Why do you think he's decided to come forward now, Delia?"

"He said he has some concerns about his daughter. Apparently, he's made several unsuccessful attempts to reach out to her." Delia's pretense at concern completely missed the mark. "He seems to think he might have more luck reaching out this way, publicly."

"I see." But the look on Caleb's face said everything Travis was thinking.

Pretty much: *What the fuck?* Who went on a notoriously inaccurate reality news program to reach out to their daughter?

"Excuse me." Loretta set her plate on the counter, turned, and walked from the kitchen.

Travis hesitated. There was nothing he wanted more than to be there for her. Whatever this was, it wasn't good. Her father had only come up once, and once had been enough. They weren't close. So this? It felt…contrived. A way to reach Loretta, all right. But to what end?

"Are you going to go?" Krystal asked. "Because if you won't, I will."

That was when Travis realized they were all staring at him… And that he'd been staring at the door.

"Son." His father's concern was plain on his face.

Travis was up and out of the kitchen before he'd thought through what to say. By the time he was standing outside her door, he wasn't sure this was the best choice. She was determined to keep distance between them. Not physically. But emotionally? There was no room for emotions between them—she'd said as much.

"Loretta?" He paused just long enough to say her name again, then opened her bedroom door. "Loretta?" There was no sign of her in the bedroom. He glanced into the bathroom. Empty. But he heard her then, her voice muffled, and paused.

"How much does he want?" There was a pause. "I don't know why he's doing this."

Travis turned and frowned. She was in the closet? On the telephone?

"I know. I know. I appreciate it but this is what he does."

Should he leave? Wait? Knock on the closet door?

"I blocked his number. He swore that was it… I know better." There was a slight thump. "I have to pay him. True or not, he'll say what he needs to say to get paid."

Travis couldn't move. He was rooted in place. His blood throbbing in his ears.

"This is why I should never have stayed here, Margot. All of this… I know better."

He was eavesdropping now—something he wasn't comfortable with. He knocked, loud enough that there was no missing it. "Loretta?" he added, his voice gruff.

There was a brief pause. "Just a minute." Another pause. "I'll call you back." And the closet door slowly opened. Loretta was sitting on the floor, pale and wide-eyed and holding her phone in a white-knuckled grip.

Travis dropped down, sitting beside her with his back against the wall. Now wasn't the time to ask the growing list of questions he had for her. She'd likely tell him it wasn't his business anyway. But he hadn't come here to irritate her; he'd come her to offer her comfort. Sitting here beside her, in silence, was the only option.

"My father is an alcoholic. He's gone to rehab, but it was only when he was hungry and we were too broke to put food on the table." She didn't look at him. "He's a gambler. Mostly with my money now, since he's never had much." Her sigh was bone-weary. "But he knows I'll pay it because he'll say whatever he needs to for the money he wants."

Her words cut deep. "Loretta—"

"I'm only telling you this in case he's already done something stupid." She shook her head. "I won't let him drag your family through the dirt for profit, I give you my word."

"What can I do?" he asked, meaning it.

She shook her head.

They sat there for a while. Travis didn't want to push, but he couldn't leave. This wasn't about how strong or capable she was. She was both, he knew that. This was about letting her know she did have someone on her side. Whether she wanted him there or not.

"I've been thinking about your song," Loretta said, surprising him. "The knight song?"

He nodded and turned. "Emmy Lou's song?"

"What if you do the first verse all acoustic only?" she asked. "Then, when the chorus starts, I see strings. Violin, viola, cello, all of it. Go all in with it. Don't laugh but, a harp, even."

"Why would I laugh?" He smiled. "I'm always looking for a new instrument to play."

"I didn't mean you'd play it." Her surprise was evident, but there was a slight smile on her lips.

"You're going to play?" He nodded. "I like it. I can see you playing the harp like a boss."

She laughed then. "Play the harp like a boss? Did you really say that?"

"How else would you play it?" He shrugged. "I think a harp is a good idea. Anything else?"

Her topaz gaze searched his. "I do have an idea for the other song. The dancing song."

After a while, it didn't seem off to be sitting on the floor of her closet. She was caught up in the music and he was caught up in her. That spark she had, the excitement and anticipation of what they were working toward. It wasn't where they were, it was what they were doing. Music was the thing that healed her—that soothed the stress and worry and pain from her heart. It was about creating something beautiful out of the dark. Finding strength in the notes and lyrics that would rise above the noise and chaos of everyday life. Together, they were building a safe harbor to shelter through the storm. And, damn, but he wanted nothing more than to stay right here and be that shelter—if she'd let him.

# Chapter 12

Loretta waved, her arm hooked through Travis's, as they made their way from the side of the stage.

"Welcome, welcome." Late night talk show host, Guy James, met them halfway. He gave her a quick hug, kissed her cheek, shook hands with Travis, and led them to the loveseat opposite Guy James' massive desk. "I am so pleased to have the two of you join me," Guy said once they were all seated.

"Thank you for having us." She smiled.

"It's good to be back." Travis nodded.

"My sincere pleasure to have you both." Guy held a stack of pale blue notecards in his hand. "Before we start with these, I'd like to mention that you're both looking well." He nodded as the audience gave an appropriately enthusiastic applause. "It would seem my audience agrees with me."

Loretta smiled, smoothing her peacock-colored skirt—a color she'd be wearing a lot of thanks to the tour's costumer—over her thighs and sat back.

"Travis." Guy tapped his cards on his desk. "You've been pumping iron, haven't you?" He paused. "Don't deny it. We have this." He pointed at the screen.

It was the first time Loretta had seen a picture of pre-rehab Travis next to post-rehab Travis. The change was incredible.

"You could give Arnold Schwarzenegger a run for his money, I think." Guy shook his head. "Are you working out with your sister's new husband? Mr. Football Star, Brock Watson?"

"I'm flattered but Brock probably wouldn't be." Travis chuckled. "I'd never survive working out with him. But my head of security has been kind enough to whip me into shape. As you can see, there was a lot of work to be done."

Loretta was still processing the change in Travis. It wasn't just the muscles, it was the skin tone and the eyes and the hair. All of him. He'd been handsome before. But now? Handsome didn't cut it.

"What do you think, Miss Gram?" Guy asked.

"Travis King doesn't need any help in the ego department so I'll say, no comment." She smiled.

Guy nodded. "How is this working?" He pointed between the two of them with his cards. "New partners, different dynamics. Have the two of you found your rhythm, shall we say?" He bobbed his eyebrows playfully.

She wasn't sure what to say so she looked at Travis—who was looking at her, looking equally flummoxed.

"We are on the same page, musically," she said. "Wouldn't you say?"

Travis nodded.

"After your incredible performance at the International Music Awards, it came as no surprise that the two of you would be paired up." Guy waited for the applause to die down before continuing. "Loretta, please accept my deepest sympathies about Johnny. You've come on the show a handful of times together and I remember the laughs he brought with him."

Loretta nodded. "Johnny loved to make people laugh."

"Such a shock to lose someone at such a young age," Guy said, letting the silence linger.

"Yes." She agreed. What else could she say? *I can confirm that he did not commit suicide? I can confirm that he committed suicide?* If he was looking for answers, she was sorry to disappoint him. Every day, she wondered the same thing. In time, she hoped she'd come to accept not knowing. "I miss him. I miss his laughter."

"Of course." Guy nodded. If he was disappointed, he hid it well.

"And you, Travis. I'd like to think the muscles and the tan mean you're taking care of yourself?"

"I've been sober for thirteen months, give or take a few days." Travis grinned. "I sort of figured that's what you were asking when you said taking care of myself."

"Yes." Guy smiled. "I wonder if you'd like to share what happened that night? What happened that made you realize things needed to change?"

Loretta stiffened. Was this an ambush? Or had Travis known this was coming?

"You might have heard I had a little bit of a drinking problem?" Travis smiled, his charm working overtime. "And, when I was drinking, I had a bit of a temper problem?"

There was general laughter from the audience.

Loretta forced herself to keep smiling.

"I was at a rodeo and this fellow and I had a…disagreement. I won't go into details because I'm moving on but I made a choice that changed everything." He shrugged. "I was drunk, which was my choice. The rest? I don't know. I left, but I saw the guy's truck and all I could think about was wanting him to understand he was wrong. I got a tire iron from my truck and did some serious damage to his truck. I still don't regret that part. What I regret…" He swallowed, emotion catching him off guard. "I didn't know the kids were filming me. I didn't know until the one fell on the ground behind me and I turned on him." He shook his head. "I didn't hit him. I didn't even think about hitting him. It was his face. This kid who'd been filming me acting like an ass—something I would have done at his age—only to get the sh-stuff scared out of him." He shook his head. "I can be a jerk. I can fight, but I'd never strike out at a kid. Or a woman." He shrugged. "That was it. The next morning it was everywhere. Video. Still shots. The kid, and his friends, phone videos… But the only thing I saw was that kid's face." He shrugged. "I checked in to rehab that day."

"Well done." Guy led the audience in a round of applause that ended with everyone on their feet.

Loretta too.

"We have a video." Guy said, once they'd all returned to their seat. "This is from a woman who was there that night. I'd like to play it now."

Loretta felt Travis stiffen at her side. She resisted the urge to take his hand and hoped that whatever was about to happen wasn't some gimmicky stunt that could ding Travis's steadfast determination.

"Hi, Travis." A woman appeared. "I don't know if you remember me, but I wanted to say how sorry I am about that night." The woman was crying. "We were married then, you see. I was too scared to speak up, too scared of him. It wasn't the first time he'd hit me, but it was the first time anyone had ever stepped in to stop him."

Loretta was staring at Travis then.

"He did love that truck more than he loved me." The woman was still talking. "He never cried over hitting me the way he cried when he saw what you'd done to his truck. For all the heartache this caused you, I'm sorry. I'm glad you're sober and I hope you'll stay that way. I'd like to think he'd never do the things he did if he wasn't always drinking. Not that he's my problem now since we've been divorced a few months now." She waved. "You give your best to your family."

Loretta wasn't sure how to feel. He'd been drunk and lost his cool and made some seriously unacceptable choices… But it hadn't been because he was a horrible person. Drunk, yes. Clouded judgment, definitely. But not such a dick move after all. She'd have likely taken a tire iron to the man's truck sober.

"Did you recognize her?" Guy asked.

"I do." Travis nodded, but he didn't say anything more.

"I hear the two of you have a song for us tonight?" Guy asked.

"Something the two of you will be singing on the tour and the new album you're putting together for next year?"

"Yes." Loretta smiled. "Travis wrote it."

"We wrote it together," Travis argued.

"You wrote it. I only added—"

"It's a joint collaboration," Travis pushed, smiling at her.

"There you have it. The first single from the new duo, TrueLove." Guy smiled, leaning forward to shake their hands.

Loretta and Travis made their way across the stage to the two stools. Travis picked up his Dreadnaught guitar, slid the straps around his shoulder, and faced her.

"Ready?" he asked.

It was the first time they'd performed this song for an audience. A song this hot and sexy was a risky choice but… It was a damn good song.

"I'm ready," she said.

His fingers moved quickly, plucking the first notes forward as he sang.

*You've got me where you want me.*
*I can't say that I mind…*

*Don't stare at him.* Not his eyes or his hair or the way his mouth moved when he said things that made her think of how good it was to be intertwined with him. The ache in the pit of her stomach turned warm as he rounded out the chorus.

*…you'll want me close and deep.*

Now that she knew this was true, the song felt different. More like a conversation between them. One whispered, in the pale light of morning, before life drew them apart.

She took a deep breath, her throat tight as she sang.

*You tease me but you touch me…*

She was aching. And, even though now was not the time to be thinking about it, she wanted his hands on her. His blue-green eyes blazed into hers, filled with the promise of a long night ahead. Her voice wobbled as she sang, but she made it through.

Travis played through the chorus again, his fingers sliding along the strings as his gaze shifted to her mouth. Together, the final lines were loaded with such longing, Loretta struggled to find her voice.

*But you'll miss me, baby, and I'll haunt you in your sleep.*
*My hands, my mouth, you'll want me close and deep.*

The only thing keeping Loretta from launching herself at Travis was the roar of the audience. And knowing that, fifteen minutes from now, they'd be alone—heading for what she hoped would be a sleepless night in their hotel.

"Ladies and gentlemen," Guy James called out, clapping. "Loretta Gram and Travis King. Now known as TrueLove." He fanned himself. "Anyone else needing some ice cold water? Or a cold shower? Is it hot in here?"

Loretta and Travis bowed and smiled and waved their good-byes and headed backstage. Sawyer had their ride waiting, so they headed out through the studio side door and climbed into the backseat of the waiting black SUV.

"Good?" Sawyer asked, climbing into the driver seat.

Travis nodded, staring out the window.

Loretta was acutely aware of the way his hand lay, fisted, against his thigh. If she reached for him, would he lose all control? Was he craving her like she was craving him? Was that why he was staying so quiet and avoiding her gaze?

By the time Sawyer had pulled up to their hotel, Loretta was doubting every look and signal he'd seemed to be giving off.

Sawyer handed off the keys to the additional security the label had hired for the tour, then led them through the back hallways to a clearance-required elevator.

Loretta risked a glance at Travis.

He was waiting. The jolt of connection had her gripping the metal railing that ran the inside of the elevator. The crooked smile had her grip tighten.

Sawyer knew about them but...well, there were some things Sawyer didn't need to know—or see.

When they reached the floor the label had rented, Loretta hurried to her room. She'd give him ten minutes. Maybe fifteen. But five minutes later, she was seriously considering throwing caution to the wind and banging on Travis's hotel room.

It's not like she hadn't spent the last week in his bed. Where had this sudden urgency come from? The song. The song they'd be singing over and over for the next few months. If this was the reaction she had every time they sang it, things were going to get super awkward, super quick.

*Get it together.* She grabbed her pajamas and headed into the bathroom for a cold shower.

But she'd barely set foot under the water when there was a knock at her door. She hurried, grabbing a towel and almost slipping as she skidded across the marble floor, padded across the carpet, and walked down the hall of her suite to the door.

Travis. "I was about ready to kick the damn door down—"

She grabbed the front of his shirt, tugged him inside, and pushed the door closed—propelling him back against the solid surface and twining her arms around his neck.

His lips traveled along her neck. "You're not wearing any clothes."

"You're wearing too many clothes." She was already working the button at his waist free.

"Not for long." He took her hand and headed back the way she'd come, shedding clothes as he went. By the time they'd reached her bathroom, he'd tossed her towel over his shoulder and was busy nuzzling the swell of her left breast.

Loretta was breathing hard but determined. With a good tug, his jeans were gone and her hand wrapped around the long, hard proof of his arousal. At the contact, he groaned—arching into her.

"I want your hands and mouth." She said against his lips. "I want you close and deep."

---

Travis rested his hand on the swell of Loretta's hip, breathing hard against the back of her neck. He liked her ass. He liked her thigh and calf and the spot behind her knee that made her pant... Damn if there wasn't a part of her he didn't like. And, by now, he was feeling mighty comfortable with pretty much every inch of her.

One thing he liked most? The sounds she made. He was the loud one, that was true. But it made every little gasp and moan, every hitch or rasp of her breath that much hotter. He worked hard for those little victories, knowing she couldn't hold back—knowing she wanted him so bad.

She lay on her stomach, panting, all soft and sweat-slicked beneath him.

"Travis?" Her voice was soft. Not sleepy. Wary.

"Loretta?" He leaned forward to press a kiss against her shoulder blade.

She turned her head on the pillow, glancing over her shoulder. "Did you know Guy was going to ask you about that night?"

"I suspected as much." He pressed another kiss against her shoulder blade then rolled onto his back, at her side. "It was the first interview." He stared up at the ceiling and ran his fingers through his hair. "I'm ready for all the firsts to be over. I'm ready to move on."

She was watching him. "And the woman?"

He glanced at her. "The woman from the video? I didn't know about that." He shook his head. "It sort of pissed me off."

"Why?" She turned onto her side, obviously surprised, to face him.

"Because her story makes what I did okay, in a way." He shook his head again. "But there wasn't any justification for scaring the shit out of that boy."

She seemed to be considering his words. "I hear what you're saying about the kid, but… Travis, that could have happened whether you were drunk or not. If that had happened and I'd seen it? I'd have taken a tire iron to the man's truck after that—drunk or sober. Hell, he'd have been glad it was only his truck."

He smiled. "You'd make one hell of an avenging angel."

She shook her head, studying him for a long time before she asked, "Why didn't you ever tell anyone what happened?"

"I didn't want to be let off the hook. It wasn't about the dick or his truck—it was about the kid." He swallowed. "I put that look on his face. That fear. I did that. He was scared of me. In that moment, I might as well have been the asshat beating the shit out of his wife." His throat tightened, so tight he had to force the rest of the words out. "That's the way she'd looked—that's the sort of fear he'd inspired. He was a complete asshole. And so was I."

Part of him wanted her to argue with him. But the other part appreciated that she didn't. She'd listened to him enough to hear what he was trying to say. Maybe that's why he kept talking.

"I'm an alcoholic. I'll always be an alcoholic. But I'd been damn lucky. I found a program that worked for me, SMART. I talk to my coach Archie at least once a week—he's on speed dial on my damn phone. My family goes to weekly meetings. I have nothing but support—I always have." He was studying her, remembering their first interaction. "You weren't wrong about me—that first day in the studio. A year ago, I was that entitled little fuck who didn't stop long enough to see the rest of the world didn't revolve around me. I drank, I partied, and I had everything I could ever want—plus some. I don't have a DUI, I never hurt anyone or had an accident, I never got anyone pregnant or broke the law. I was damn lucky." He shook his head. "What worries me the most? If I hadn't scared the shit out of that kid that night, would I still be that clueless? That willfully self-destructive?"

They went back to staring at each other.

"That was all my shit." He sighed. "I had no right to put that on you."

"I asked."

"You asked if I knew about the video and Guy's questions, not about my lightbulb moment." He tried to tease but it fell flat. Rules or no rules, he didn't want to jeopardize this thing with her. She wasn't ready to consider options beyond sex. He was. But there was no way unloading his past discretions onto her was going to win her over to a lifetime of commitment and unconditional love. "Every day, I'm in a better place. Make peace with my past. Manage my present actions and choices. And am intentional with my future."

"What does that look like? How do you see your future?"

*With you.* He shrugged. "Good."

"Good?" She was smiling then. "Is that your five-year plan?"

He pulled her close. "I'm feeling pretty good right now."

Her smile faded slowly, giving her time to slowly withdraw—about the same time there was a knocking on her bedroom door.

"Expecting someone?" he asked.

"Only you." If she didn't look so panicked, he'd have been pleased with her answer.

"Want me to hide in the closet?" he asked.

She frowned. "Can't we just ignore it? See if they go away?"

He shrugged. "Fine by me." But then his phone started ringing. His phone—which was located somewhere between her hotel room door and the bathroom. Krystal's ringtone.

Seconds later, Loretta's phone was going off. Her phone sat in a charging dock on the bedside table, within reach.

"It's Emmy Lou." Loretta held the phone up. "They want me to come to Krystal's suite? Something about a song Krystal's been working on?"

Travis nodded. "Which means that was probably them knocking on the door." He smiled. "It's only ten fourteen. They'll keep it up for a good two hours." He sat up, running his fingers through his hair. "I should probably go before they come back."

"Does this happen often?" Loretta propped herself up on her elbows, watching as she slipped from the bed.

"Only when she's been struggling." He bent, picked up his grey T-shirt, and pulled it on. "Or when she's excited." He tugged on his boxer shorts. "Or she needs help with music or lyrics." He smiled. "I guess the short answer is yes." He grabbed his jeans off the bathroom floor. "I remember Johnny writing something when we were at the Oasis. He had the same sort of…focus Krystal gets when she's got a song bouncing around inside her head."

Loretta sat up then hugged her knees to her chest. "He did." She tossed back the blankets. "Since it's a pj's party, I guess I need to find some."

That was all it took to have Travis seriously reconsidering his course of action. Why the hell was he leaving again?

"You know, the song will still be there in the morning," he said, making his way around the bed to Loretta—standing naked and damn near perfect.

"You said they wouldn't give up?" Loretta pointed out, rifling through the suitcase that sat on the room's luggage rack. "You should go ahead and I'll meet you there once I find the top." She pulled on a pair of green check pajama pants.

"You could drop those and we could go back to bed," Travis suggested, reaching for her pants.

"I think you need to go support your sister." She tugged her pants away. "If this is what you do, you don't think they'll get suspicious if you don't show up? They might already be suspicious."

He was pretty sure they were all already suspicious.

"Right now, they all like me—I think." Loretta sighed.

"And you think us having amazing sex will make them not like you?" Travis shook his head.

She was laughing. "No. But they might if I get in the way of the way things work. If, for instance, you don't show up when you'd normally show up *because of me*, that might make them not like me."

"Because we're having sex," he added.

"Yes, fine." She was laughing. "Because we're having sex."

"Amazing sex." He pulled her into his arms. "I like it when you laugh."

"You seem to have that effect on me."

"Interesting." He gave her a quick kiss, then let her go. "Now you're saying I *am* funny. Maybe you'll come 'round and decide you like me after all."

She shrugged into a Three Kings T-shirt. The shirt was on the tight side. Hugging her curves—accentuating her curves.

"You're going to have to change." He shook his head. "Otherwise, you're being plain mean."

She stared down at her chest. "This is one of my favorite shirts."

"It's now one of my favorite shirts." He swallowed. "But I'd rather not share all of you with the rest of my family."

"I'll change." She sighed. "Now, go."

He finished dressing—minus a sock—and located his phone. Krystal's text was short and to the point. Get your ass over here.

*Yes, ma'am.* Boots in hand, he headed toward the suite Krystal and Jace were sharing.

Jace sat, a guitar in his lap, a guitar pick tucked between his lips. He nodded in greeting.

"There you are." Krystal looked up when she walked inside. "Where's Loretta?"

He paused, glancing back and forth between his sisters. "I...I don't know."

"Emmy Lou's been trying to call her. And text her." Krystal frowned. "Think she's okay?"

"I'm sure she's fine." He shrugged, flopping onto the couch beside Emmy Lou.

"Daddy called. No cancer," Krystal said. "But they do want to do the vocal node surgery thing."

"That's a huge relief." Travis leaned his head back against the couch. "When is it scheduled?"

"I told him he had to wait until we can all be there." Krystal nodded.

"Good." Until that moment, he hadn't realized just how worried he'd been about his father. It'd suck if he lost his singing voice, but it couldn't compare with Travis losing his father. "Best news in a while." He smiled at his sisters.

Emmy Lou patted his leg. "How did your interview go?"

"Guy James?" Jace asked.

Travis nodded. "He's decent." He shrugged. "He asked. I answered." Except for the video part—that part still bothered him. "I think the duet went well, though."

"I can't wait to see it." Emmy Lou sat, curled up, in the corner of the hotel room couch.

Travis was up as soon as he heard the light knock on the door. "Hey, Loretta. Come on in." He was relieved to see she'd found her pajama top. "I like your pajamas."

"Emmy Lou said pajama party," Loretta said, her hands clasped before her. "So..."

He stepped back. "Come on in."

"We're all here." Krystal clapped her hands. "I know it's late and you probably all had other stuff to do but I think—I hope—this song will be worth it." She handed each of them a copy of her song.

"This was the muffin, pancake, cherry pie song?" Travis asked.

"All of that?" Emmy Lou's eyes were round.

"You lost me." Loretta scanned the sheet music.

"Krystal cooks when she's working on a new song. Bakes, mostly," Jace explained.

"Got it," Loretta said, scanning the sheet music. "Johnny used to clean." She pulled a long strand of hair over her shoulder, twining it around her fingers as she read.

*Damn but she was beautiful.*

"Cleaning? That's a way more productive process." Krystal shrugged.

"And way less delicious," Travis pointed out, sitting back in his chair and turning his attention to the sheet music. He tapped his foot, playing through the song in his head, softly singing the chorus.

*The blood that binds is not enough,*
*It's who stands up and chooses us.*
*You're scarred and broken, that is true.*
*But take my hand, we'll make it through.*

*Time. Time to let go.*
*Time to stand tall.*

*Time. Time to be brave.*
*Time to trust love.*

*All I know is...*
*I lose time when I'm with you.*

Travis glanced at Loretta. There'd been a few times in his life when a song had been so true it nearly knocked him to his knees. This was one of those times.

# Chapter 13

LORETTA'S HEART WAS THUMPING HARD. IT WAS ALL GOOD. Tonight had been…amazing. And standing here, now, holding hands with Three Kings and Jace Black while the packed auditorium roared with approval? She was pretty sure things couldn't get much better than this. She was proud. Of herself, the Kings, the performance—it was one hell of a show. Confetti cannons and strobe lights, costume changes and so much more.

They took another bow, waving and smiling as they left the stage after their third encore.

"I guess that means they liked it," Travis said once they were headed toward their respective dressing rooms.

"It was the song." Krystal winked. "Perfect way to wrap up the show."

Loretta had her doubts. While she loved the song Krystal had presented to them last night, she hadn't realized they'd be performing it tonight. One rehearsal was all they had. One rehearsal to stumble through it—feel out the notes and rhythm—and hope like hell they didn't screw it up in front of thousands of fans.

"Ten minutes and meet here?" Emmy Lou asked.

Loretta nodded, catching Travis's parting wink before heading to her dressing room to freshen up. The record label had arranged meet and greets after every concert along the way. It was her least favorite part of touring, but she'd manage to grin and bear it.

But she hadn't expected to find CiCi King waiting for her.

"That was some show. You'd think they'd try to do a little better than this," CiCi said, surveying Loretta's dressing room. "I thought

I was in Emmy Lou's dressing room but once I saw this, I knew I had the wrong room."

"It works." Loretta shrugged. "Emmy Lou is around the corner." The room with the large gold star taped to it—the large gold star with Emmy Lou King printed on it. There was no way CiCi was here by accident.

"Is she?" CiCi perched on one of the folding chairs. "I'll go find her in a sec. I'm glad I have a minute with you. You go on and do what you need to be ready for the meet and greet, don't mind me."

*Don't mind her?* The woman filled up the room. Loretta was pretty sure there was no nice way to ask CiCi King to leave, but, dammit, she'd had an amazing night. With CiCi King lying in wait for her, she suspected her night was about to take a nosedive.

"I have a friend at *Tabloid News Media*—*TNM*?" CiCi smiled. "She told me that your father canceled his interview? Is that right?"

"I believe so." Loretta tried to be as noncommittal as possible. Yes, her father had called off his interview. Once Margot had made sure her father got the money he wanted, her father retreated.

"Why do I get the feeling he might circle back around, eventually?" CiCi was studying her reflection, almost sympathetic. "From what a friend at *TNM* told me, he'd promised an inside scoop on you and my family too."

"He would say that." Loretta sighed, blotting her cheeks. "It's not true, of course."

"Isn't it?" CiCi frowned. Well, she tried to frown. It was hard for the woman to be expressive due to the amount of Botox or whatever it was injected into her face. "So you don't know anything about what he was planning to say?"

Loretta shook her head. "I haven't spoken to him since…Las Vegas." It had been a little over a month but, for Loretta, it felt like another life. "Even then, we talked about the performance." How he wanted tickets…and money. She'd sent him the money, but not the ticket.

CiCi stood up, reaching for the brush on the counter. "You know, Loretta. I feel for you. The media's exploited all the loss in your life, something fierce. Imagine anyone implying you're bad luck." She shook her head. "I guess they'll say anything to sell a paper, I suppose." She patted Loretta on the shoulder. "I shouldn't have been so hard on you at Emmy Lou's wedding. For that, I'm sorry. If you and Hank are developing a friendship, who am I to stand in the way."

Her mind was swimming with CiCi's words, but she managed to respond to the last part. "It really is a friendship." Loretta met the woman's gaze in the mirror. "Nothing more."

CiCi nodded, turning the brush in her hands. "I see a lot of myself in you, Loretta. The sadness, I guess. We both have lousy fathers. Mine disowned me for following my heart. Yours is emptying your bank account as fast as you can fill it."

An icy coldness settled in Loretta's stomach. How did she know about her father? And the money?

"And we have mothers who deserted us. When my father disowned me for marrying Hank, my mother didn't say or do a thing. Can you imagine a mother doing that?" She shook her head. "But your mother just up and disappeared, didn't she? That must have hurt. To know she left you in the care of a good-for-nothing." She sighed. "Your father. Your mother. Poor Margot fighting cancer. And Johnny."

She was not going to talk about Johnny with this woman. "CiCi, I need—"

"No, Loretta. I need you to listen. I have people watching." CiCi sat the brush back on the counter and looked Loretta square in the eye. "I've heard talk that something's going on between you and Travis—or you and Sawyer. I don't which is true or if they're all true, but fun and games are over. Travis can't risk a run of bad luck, surely you see that? And you, Loretta, are bad luck. And while I feel for you, I do, my family—my son—comes first. You will not screw with his head and send him back to drinking." Her blue eyes never flinched. "Your daddy needs money. I've got money. And if you don't start behaving yourself, I'll make sure your daddy gets a whole lot of money to sing whatever song we can come up with. You, your mother, Johnny… I won't play fair." She paused. "Don't make me end your career, Loretta." With a big sigh, she smiled and headed to the door. "I'll go see Emmy Lou now. It was quite a show."

Loretta didn't know how long she sat there, staring at the door. Should she laugh or cry? It was like she'd been pulled into a soap opera or a Lifetime movie. *But this is real.* All the horrible words and threats… They were real. Did CiCi King have that kind of power?

The whole damn time CiCi had been ranting, she'd been silent, reeling from what was happening. But now words were bubbling up and clogging her throat.

"Loretta?" Sawyer was standing in the door, his face surprisingly concerned. "Was that Mrs. King?"

Loretta nodded. *Yes. That was Mrs. King. She just threatened to destroy my career if I didn't stop sleeping with Travis.* She almost laughed then. Almost. "She…she was looking for Emmy Lou's dressing room."

"Try again." He stepped inside, letting the door swing shut behind him.

She stared at him, willing her heart to slow. "What? Why are you here?"

Sawyer crossed his arms over his chest. "I saw Mrs. King leave your dressing room. She tends to leave quite a wake wherever she goes."

*I have people watching.*

For all she knew, Sawyer was working for CiCi. It made sense. He was closest to Travis—closest to all of them really. They treated him more like family than an employee. She stared at him, long and hard, wishing she was better at reading people. Not that Sawyer was exactly easy to read.

He crossed the room, his eyes on her face, and crouched by her chair. "It's my job to protect the Kings."

*CiCi is a King.* He had to be working for CiCi. Why else would he conveniently show up seconds after CiCi left behind a web of threats? "She was looking for Emmy Lou's dressing room," she repeated.

Sawyer ran a hand over his short-cropped hair, frustrated. It was an unnervingly familiar gesture. Almost like Travis when he ran his fingers through his hair. Sawyer didn't have the same hair but… She couldn't help but study the man. Up close this way, the similarities were more obvious than ever. She'd read that dogs start to look like their owners and married couples start to resemble one another. Was that the case with a bodyguard and his client?

It was a ridiculous idea. But no more ridiculous than the other idea, the one growing louder and stronger the longer she looked at Sawyer.

Who was Sawyer? What was his last name? Could he… Was he Hank King's son? That night, at the dinner table. Krystal and Jace's reaction. Sawyer's too. Margot called him Travis's doppelgänger. *Or brother?*

But if he was Hank's son, he'd be loyal to Hank. He wouldn't be feeding information to CiCi. Things had just become far more complicated.

"Loretta—" Sawyer stared up at her, struggling to say whatever it was he wanted to say.

The dressing room door swung open. "Ready?" Travis paused. "What's up?"

"Nothing." Loretta slipped from the chair, clasping her hands behind her back. "I guess I'm ready." *Breathe. Smile.* And put distance between herself and Travis.

CiCi wasn't the only reason to start putting distance between herself and Travis. It was about self-preservation. Her career. Her reputation. Her heart. She didn't want to admit that, somehow, someway, he'd found a crack to slip in.

*It doesn't matter.*

CiCi had given her the strength to do what she'd been needing to do for some time now: End this. End all the looks and the smiles and the secret touches and the long nights in bed. All of it.

"It looks like something." Travis was frowning, glancing back and forth between them.

"Looks can be deceiving." She took a final glance in the mirror.

She hadn't changed out of her final costume. It was vibrant peacock-colored sleeveless minidress. The fabric was covered in strands of beads and crystals that swayed when she walked. With unsteady hands, she smoothed her hair, added a touch of dark burgundy lipstick, and straightened her shoulders.

Whatever silent standoff was happening between Sawyer and Travis was their problem. She walked between them and out the door, moving as quickly as she could to the hall lined with fans that led to the exclusive meet and greet.

She knew Travis was following her; his boots echoed down the concrete hall of the Staples Center. Not that she turned or looked back. She was too rattled to face him right now. When she faced him, she needed to be calm—firm. Not open for discussion.

The fans were the best part.

So many of the fans lining the hall had LoveJoy posters and shirts for her to sign. She posed for selfies and hugged four different girls who were sobbing over Johnny. They missed him. They'd loved him too. Of course, they were screaming and crying for an entirely different reason when Travis showed up.

She barely glanced his way, wincing as the sound level increased five times over.

He'd smiled. One smile and this was the reaction.

Yeah, she got it. His smile made her pretty damn giddy too.

By the time she entered the meet and greet, she had a steady throb at the base of her neck. She did her best to be charming, make some witty comment or observation, smile and laugh, and move on. Avoiding eye contact with Travis was a challenge because he seemed to be *everywhere*—directly in her line of sight.

When they started taking photos in front of the black Three Kings step and repeat, she was relieved. Now she wouldn't have to see him. But then they were grouped closely together, so close that the scent of mint and leather flooded her nostrils and turned the hard lump in her stomach to something molten and alive.

*And you, Loretta, are bad luck.* CiCi's words.

Over the years, she'd tried to convince herself that wasn't true. That she could make her own luck. But since Margot's diagnosis and Johnny's passing, she wasn't so sure anymore. Maybe CiCi was right. Maybe she was bad luck. Travis had come so far—she didn't want to be the thing that set him back. She couldn't be.

---

Travis sat on the leather couch built into the side of the tour bus. With all the tweaks and improvements to the King's Coach I and II, little things like the hum of the wheels on the interstate were barely detectable. Travis's fingers slid along the neck of the banjo in his lap, playing through the slight changes Krystal had made to the time song. It perked up the tempo and made the whole thing flow more smoothly. Good changes.

"Better?" Krystal asked, a pencil tucked behind her ear.

He nodded.

"All good changes," Travis said, glancing across the bus—at Loretta. *Bad changes...* Whatever the hell was happening between them.

"No surprise there," Jace sounded off, pulling Krystal against his side. "You've got a gift, woman."

"You're just saying that because you have to." Krystal shook her head.

"No, I'm saying that because you're talented." Jace kissed her. "And I love you."

Travis groaned. "You two are on the wrong bus for that."

"It's a kiss." Krystal sighed. "I'm not a fan of this new bad attitude of yours. Since working out isn't mellowing you out, maybe you should look into getting laid."

From across the bus, Loretta choked on her water.

"Are you okay?" Emmy Lou, sitting beside Loretta, began patting her back.

Travis glared at his sister.

"What?" Krystal was all smiles.

He stood and carried his banjo to the back of the bus. His father had several custom cases built in to safely transport some of their favorite instruments. He secured the banjo and checked his watch.

He dialed Archie's number.

"Hey, man," Archie answered, energetic as ever. "How's life on the road?"

"Pretty good." He shrugged. If he was being honest with himself, he felt—confined. "A little cramped."

"Actual space or headspace?"

One of the things Travis appreciated most about Archie was how much the older man got Travis. He was a self-proclaimed hippie, with long hair and a penchant for sandals, but he and Travis clicked. He'd been a jazz guitarist for years, so they could have entire conversations in a form of musical shorthand.

"Both." Travis chuckled.

"What's weighing on you?" His tone was grave now. "I hear it, man. Let it out."

Travis paced the six-foot space in front of the instrument cabinets. "We talked about—"

"Loretta? How's that going?"

"I guess we hit pause." Not that he had any fucking idea how or why or what had happened.

"You're good, though?" Archie asked. "It's been a while since I've been on the road, but I'll pack a bag if you need me."

"I appreciate the offer." Travis chuckled. "I'm good." As far as drinking anyway. He didn't know how to explain it, really. But once he'd made up his mind to cut the drinking out of his life, he had. Nothing had made him question his decision. At least, nothing had made him second-guess that yet.

They went over his Urge Log—something he'd relied on a lot in the beginning. He hadn't needed it in a while, but he understood why Archie was asking him about it. He was worried about Travis.

"You're in the lion's den, Trav," Archie said. "Don't let the fear or the doubt get a hold of you. You've got this."

Travis nodded. "I know my four points, Archie. Motives and goals. Beliefs. Emotions. And behaviors. They might as well be tattooed on my brain."

"You get to thinking you need a meeting, let me know and we'll get you set up with one online." Archie paused. "As a long-married man, I've got a little advice for you. Don't leave things unsaid. You talk, you know. You don't... Well, that's when your brain can have a field day. Especially us creative types."

Talk. Simple. Easy. Since she wouldn't answer his texts, he'd go old-school and do this face-to-face. "Will do."

"All right, man. You keep on being a singing badass. Check in same time next week?"

"Sounds good, Archie. Thanks, man."

"I got your back, man. Peace." Archie hung up.

Travis chuckled. *Peace?* He hadn't felt all that peaceful since he'd walked into Loretta's dressing room last night.

He'd never been a jealous man.

Sawyer wasn't only his bodyguard—he was his friend. As such, he knew Sawyer wouldn't make a move on Loretta.

Dammit. He hated the seed of doubt that had been planted.

Sawyer's face. Loretta's face. She'd been jumpy, eager to put space between them—and keep it that way for the rest of the night.

Loretta had made it clear from the beginning. This was sex. Only sex. He was falling for her—hardcore—but she didn't know that. If she did, she'd probably have kicked his ass to the curb.

What had changed? Something had. And he didn't like it.

Not only had he spent the night alone, she hadn't bothered answering any of his texts. That was the part that knotted his insides. The silence.

He didn't hold with silence. Silence was easy to fill with lies and fears. There wasn't going to be any silence between them. Not if he could help it. It was pretty straightforward stuff. She was done with him—with this... Or she wasn't.

He ran his fingers through his hair, the whisper of a melody floating through his mind.

> *Only one night. Ooh-hoo. Just one more night.*
> *Don't try to fight. Ooh-hoo. You hold me tight.*
> *Only one night. Ooh-hoo. Girl, that ain't right.*

He hummed a few bars then headed back down the hall to the main living area of the bus. Loretta was crooning to Clementine, curled up in her lap. Watson, Emmy Lou's black cat, was doing his best to wedge himself next to Clem. Every time Watson tried to lay down, Clementine would roll over and dislodge the cat altogether.

"I think she's doing it on purpose." Krystal sighed. "She's a jealous little thing and doesn't want to share you with that bad ol' kitty cat."

"Watson is not a bad kitty cat." Emmy Lou picked up the massive black cat. "Are you, baby? Auntie Krystal didn't mean it."

"He's the size of a panther now, you know that, right?" Travis asked. "You can't carry him around like a baby when he weighs almost as much as you do."

"I can carry him around however I want, isn't that right, Watson?" Emmy Lou touched noses with the cat. The cat's purr was so loud they could all hear it.

Loretta was smiling.

"You need a fur baby," Emmy Lou said.

"I'm not sure that's a good idea." Loretta kept rubbing Clementine's stomach. "I'm happy to borrow Clem or Watson. For now."

"I think they're happy with that arrangement too." Travis said, watching as Watson slipped from Emmy Lou's hold to lie on top of Clementine. "That's showing her who's boss, Watson." He chuckled as Clementine's head popped out from under Watson, the white poof on her head more bedraggled than ever.

"What's the word today, Emmy Lou?" Jace asked.

Emmy Lou had purchased an impressive stack of magazines and papers to read on the road. If there were tidbits she found interesting, she'd share.

"You and Krystal are having a baby." Emmy Lou smiled.

"This is the fifth one?" Jace asked.

"At least," Krystal agreed. "Or I'm experiencing one *long* pregnancy."

"Momma is pregnant." Emmy Lou looked horrified.

"The headline actually says, Hank King a father again? Or Kegan Scott's a first-time father?" Emmy Lou said.

Travis was only halfway listening. Watching the color bloom in Loretta's cheeks was far more interesting.

"That's a long headline." Krystal wrinkled her nose. "News must be super slow if we're now including geriatric pregnancies."

Loretta's gaze fell from his, but he saw the way the front of her shirt wavered.

"I'm not sure Momma's geriatric." Emmy Lou shrugged.

"How about we change the subject." Travis held up his hands. "Anything other than our mother's reproductive status."

Emmy Lou flipped through a few pages, stopping to read headlines as well as their horoscopes. "Oh, Loretta, yours is way better than mine." She cleared her throat. "A secret will lead to a deep and abiding love. A person from your past will threaten your happiness but truth will prevail." Emmy Lou looked over the magazine. "Juicy stuff." She sighed. "I miss my husband."

"That is so weird." Krystal shook her head. "Husband. Can't you just say you miss Brock?"

"I miss Brock." Emmy Lou smiled. "My husband."

Travis laughed, running his fingers through his hair. Loretta was laughing too. For a split second, the tension between them melted. Her smile was genuine, fleeting—but sweet. A series of those smiles, tangled in his sheets or held close against him, played rapid-fire through his brain. He wanted that back. Wanted that smile back in his arms where it belonged.

# Chapter 14

TEN DAYS. TEN DAYS OF DODGING AND HIDING AND FIGHTING the urge to track him down and make him love her. Ten days of reminding herself that she was doing the right thing.

The tour convoy consisted of three tour buses and one equipment bus. And while the record label had retrofitted the LoveJoy bus, inside and out, she had a hard time sleeping there. After spending most of her waking hours with the Kings and Jace, the quiet of her bus was...deafening. Without something to distract her, her mind invariably returned to Travis. She knew she was being cowardly. She knew she should face him and offer up some sort of explanation, but she couldn't.

If she tried to look him in the eye, she'd cave. It terrified her.

Once they arrived in Salt Lake City and found their hotel, Loretta headed straight to her room. She wasn't sure what was worse, being on the road with no chance of anyone joining her or being in an executive suite knowing Travis could be her neighbor.

*It doesn't matter.* She stood aside for the bellhop to bring in her bag and smiled her thanks. It didn't matter that she saw Travis and Emmy Lou—or that he saw her.

She pushed her door closed, turned the extra lock, and rested her forehead against the cool surface.

*Way not to overreact.*

Apparently, that was the only reaction she had to Travis. Over-the-top. Highly in tune. Performing with him had been the sweetest sort of torture. If she'd thought she'd craved him before, there was no comparing that to what she was feeling now.

*What you can't feel.*

She unpacked her bag, inventoried her minibar and fridge, scrolled through every channel on her television, and ran herself a steaming bubble bath before she gave up and called Margot.

"Lori-girl?" Margot yawned.

"Did I wake you?" She rested her head on the edge of the tub, the fizz of bubbles echoing in the mostly white marble bathroom. "I'm sorry."

"Don't be." There was a smile in her voice. "You okay? You sound...strung tight."

"I am." She closed her eyes. "Margot...I made a huge mistake."

"Hold on, I'm turning on my bedside lamp." There was some rustling. "Okay, fire away. Just tell me you didn't accidentally kill someone and you're not pregnant."

"Those are the two things that immediately come to mind?" Loretta shook her head, pushing little icebergs of bubbles away. "And in that order?"

"In my book, those are huge mistakes. Stop stalling and tell me what huge mistake you made."

"I slept with Travis." She blew out a slow breath, her lungs aching.

"Well, I figured as much, Lori-girl. It was pretty clear to everyone on the back porch that the two of you were on the way there." Margot paused. "And?"

"And?" She groaned. "That's it. That's the mistake."

"*That's* it?" Margot waited.

"No..." It hurt to draw in breath. "I...I let him in, Margot. And I don't know how to...stop."

"I'm assuming we're talking about that thing you don't like talking about. The 'f' word. *Feelings*." Margot was on the verge of laughter. "And how does he feel about you?"

"It doesn't matter, Margot." She pushed at the bubbles, sending water over the edge and onto the floor. "It's not that simple, and you know it."

"No, I don't know it." Margot sighed. "Why isn't it simple?"

She wanted to tell Margot everything. About CiCi. About being threatened... Even her suspicions about Sawyer. "Because I don't do feelings."

"Lori-girl." Margot sighed again. "You need to take a good long look in the mirror and see why that is. I know your mother's let you down. I know your father's a shit. And, you know I loved him, but Johnny let you down too. Hell, even I've let you down getting sick when you needed me—"

"Stop it. You have never let me down." Never. *And I'll never let you down.*

"It's not you, Loretta, is what I'm getting at. You hear me? You've been dealt a crap hand until now. Now...well, I think you've got all the cards you need to play through."

"You know I don't play cards." But Loretta was laughing.

"I don't either. I doubt what I said made a lick of sense." She giggled. "But you know what I'm getting at."

"I *think* so." She knew exactly what Margot was getting at. She didn't do feelings because she didn't want to be disappointed or hurt again. Or hurt someone else. According to her father, she was very good at both. "How are you feeling?"

Loretta hung up sometime later. Margot was doing well—at least that's what she'd told Loretta. There were times Loretta worried Margot was keeping things from her. *Just like what I'm doing to protect her.* The difference was Loretta was trying to preserve her peace of mind. If Margot was keeping secrets... Well, Loretta didn't want to think about that.

The water was cold and the bubbles were mostly gone by the time she pulled herself out of the massive garden tub. She rinsed off the bubbles, reached for the room service menu, and flopped onto the bed in her favorite pink fluffy robe.

Her phone started ringing.

Unknown caller.

She pressed ignore and hopped up when room service knocked on the door.

"Sawyer?" She frowned. "What are you doing here?"

He handed her a manila envelope. "Travis wanted you to take a look at this."

"He sent you?" She took the envelope and opened it. The first words…

"Sawyer." She didn't make it very far. With a shake of her head, she shoved the pages back into the envelope. "Give it back to him." Her eyes were stinging. *Do not cry.*

"I think he wanted you to keep it." His voice was gruff.

Her eyes were burning now. "I can't." Her voice wavered and she sniffed. "Just, here." She shoved it at him and slammed the door in his face.

But Travis's words were still there. The lyrics their own sort of melody.

> *One night is what you offered,*
> *I said yes, of course.*
> *But let's make that forever, just me loving you.*
> *Rules are meant to be broken.*
> *I'll break them all for you.*

It was a song. *Just a song.*

She headed back to the bedroom and sat on the edge of the bed. Why had she reacted that way? It wasn't the first time bits of real life had spilled over into music. But the forever part? The love? That was pure fiction. *Part of the song.*

She wiped the tear from her cheek and shook her head. *This is why I don't do feelings.* Once they started, she didn't know how to stop them. It was that lack of control part that made her fight so damn hard not to feel.

Her phone beeped. One missed call and voicemail.

She dialed her voicemail.

"Loretta, it's your father." He broke off, his voice thick and slurred. "I'm here. Came all this way to see your show, a proud papa. I came to see you... Where are you? Am I talking to your damn cell phone? After all I've done to get you here and you can't even take a phone call from your daddy?" He sighed. "I need you to come get me, Loretta. I need you now, you hear me? Where am I?" There was another voice, deep and gruff. "I'm at the South Salt Lake City Police Department. South. You hear? You come and bail me out. If you don't, I guess I'll have to call that lady back at *TNM*—let her know you're letting me sit here in a jail cell all night."

Loretta hung up, threw her phone onto the bed, and pulled on some clothes. He was here? After years of phone calls and canceled plans, he was here. If he had an ulterior motive, she'd deal with it later. For now, she'd pretend that he'd come just to see her and her show.

The burning was back—and a solid lump blocking her throat.

She grabbed her purse and hurried out of her room to the elevators.

"Loretta?" It was Sawyer.

"Sawyer." She sniffed. *Damn tears.*

"Is everything okay?" His voice was low and soft.

She nodded.

"Are you going somewhere?"

She nodded, wiping a tear away.

"Do you need a ride?" He was studying her.

A ride? She'd have to get a taxi.

"I'm off the clock." He cleared his throat. "You seem upset, Loretta." He reached out and placed his hand on her arm. "I can help."

"Yes, Sawyer. Thank you." She nodded, breathing a little easier. "I need a ride."

He nodded, guiding her onto the elevator and pressing the

button without another word. He led her through the back hallways and kitchen, then out through the service exit to the vehicles
he and the security team had waiting.

"Backseat," he said, holding the door open. "Just in case there
are cameras waiting."

"Right." She let go of the front passenger door handle. "Of
course." She climbed into the car.

"Where are we going?" he asked, pulling out of the parking
garage and onto the relatively busy streets of downtown Salt Lake
City.

"The South Salt Lake City Police Department." She met his
gaze in the rearview mirror. "My father's been arrested."

---

Travis held the manila envelope in his hands, hoping Loretta
would stop long enough for them to set things straight. Sawyer
said she'd seemed extra emotional when she'd given back the song.
Travis hoped that was a good thing.

But that was before. Now his mind was scrambling to make
sense of what he'd just seen. Sawyer and Loretta. Leaving together.

Then he was back to the night everything changed. The night
he'd walked into Loretta's dressing room and found Sawyer,
crouching by Loretta's chair. Worse, Sawyer's expression. Concern.
Sawyer rarely emoted... Like it or not, that meant something.

Could something be going on between them? He reached into
his pocket, turning the guitar pick over and over.

*Bullshit.* Sawyer wasn't interested in Loretta. Even if he was, he
wouldn't go after her because he knew how Travis felt about her.

Loretta was a different story. She was fighting it, but she still
wanted him. When they were singing onstage, hell—sitting across the
room from each other, the air was alive and electric between them.

But wanting him didn't mean she couldn't want someone else

too. She'd made this clear from the get-go that this was about sex. They'd never talked about being exclusive, either. Technically, she didn't owe him a thing—including monogamy. There could be someone else. Someone like Sawyer.

His lungs compressed so hard and fast his chest hurt. Sure, he'd let himself believe it was more because that's what he wanted to believe. The truth was another story.

What the hell was going on?

*First things first, calm the fuck down.*

If there was ever a time to practice self-management, it was right now. How he reacted to this was his choice.

"I'm choosing to calm the fuck down," he muttered. Clear his head. Get some perspective. Think through what he wanted and what steps he could take to get there. Since he had zero experience with this sort of thing, he could sit here and spin his wheels or he could get some help.

He walked down the hall to Emmy Lou's room, hoping like hell she was still awake. He adored both of his sisters, but tonight he needed less sarcasm and more support. She and Krystal wanted to do the whole family breakfast thing in the morning, so he had a key card to her room. With any luck, she'd still be up. If not... well, maybe he'd check out the hotel gym and see if he could sweat some of this shit out.

He swiped the card and opened the door. Emmy Lou's suite was large, large enough that he could hear his sister talking before he could see her.

"But Sawyer's mother?" Emmy Lou was talking. "Are you sure that Ruby is Sawyer's mother?"

*Ruby?* The name was familiar. Travis slowed. Ruby as in Daddy's ex-girlfriend... Sawyer, what? *What did she just say?*

"That's what the private eye said." Krystal's voice. "He couldn't find anything that shows Daddy knows Sawyer is his son, though. Which we'd basically figured out."

Travis froze. *Daddy knows Sawyer is his son.*

"I have so many questions. Why wouldn't Ruby tell Daddy about Sawyer? No matter what happened between them, Daddy had the right to know he had a son." Emmy Lou was upset.

*What the hell?* He braced a hand against the wall. *What the fucking hell?*

"We don't know, Em. Sawyer's a couple of years older than Trav. For all we know Ruby tried to reach out to Daddy and Momma did what Momma does." Krystal's tone was sharp. "We just don't know."

"What do we do now?" Emmy Lou asked.

"Like I know? It was one thing when we thought he was Daddy's. Now we know." Krystal paused. "I don't want to hurt anyone, Em, but I can't take the secrets. It's not right. Daddy should know. Travis should know."

Travis shook his head, leaning into the wall. *Then why didn't you tell me?*

"I know. I know." Emmy Lou's voice was tight. "What about Sawyer? Is this our news to tell? I keep thinking about Daddy. And Trav... Travis is doing so well. I want everyone to stay okay."

He couldn't do this—not now. He'd come here looking for a refuge. Not this. He pushed off the wall. If he went in there, he'd say things he'd regret.

Better to do what he'd set out to do. Clear his head. Get some perspective. He almost laughed then.

But none of this was funny. *Fuck this.* He left the way he'd come in. He didn't head to his room; being alone right now wasn't smart. He knew that. Instead, he pulled open the door to the stairs and jogged down the twenty-two flights of stairs to the lobby. He'd broken a light sweat by the time he'd reached the ground floor, but he was still on edge. The lobby was mostly empty. The restaurant was closed but the bar was open.

*Fuck it.*

He headed for the bar.

The bartender nodded a greeting. "What can I get you?"

"Sprite and cranberry." Travis sat on one of the empty stools and scanned the menu. "And two orders of cheesy fries."

A quick sweep of the bar told him he'd been noticed. But he wasn't exactly giving off welcoming vibes so, hopefully, everyone would keep their distance. Right now, he needed distance.

How did he wrap his head around this? All of it. For the first time in his life, he was in love. That, alone, was enough. But, no, why stop there?

He stared into the non-cocktail the bartender slid his way, wishing it was something stronger. Not because he wanted it—he never *wanted* it. He just wanted the numb it could give. It'd be a hell of a lot easier to deal with all of this if he wasn't so twisted up over it.

Not only was the woman he loved possibly involved with his best friend. Come to find out his best friend and bodyguard, Sawyer, was his fucking half brother? A half brother his sisters knew about? His sisters knew. But they worried about what he'd do if he found out.

Then again, there was video proof of how well he handled himself when things didn't work out so well. *When I was drinking.* But he wasn't drinking.

He'd made a commitment to himself. He wasn't going to break it.

Just like they'd made a commitment to him. No lies. No matter what.

"Travis?" Sawyer was standing beside him.

*Sawyer.*

"I could use some space right now," Travis said, his grip tightening on his cranberry and Sprite.

Sawyer's eyes darted from Travis's face to the drink and back again. "You sure that's the best idea?"

He wasn't sure of a damn thing. Travis ran both hands through his hair. "What do you want from my family, Sawyer?"

Sawyer's brow creased, then smoothed. "What I was hired to do, Travis—"

"No." Travis shook his head. "I know." He stared at him, watching closely. "I know who you are."

Sawyer ran a hand over his head, his jaw clenching tight.

"My sisters know." He was still watching him. "You know that?"

"I suspected." He cleared his throat.

"So you three haven't had some heart-to-heart talk about how to spring this on my father?" He sipped his drink. "Our father."

Sawyer sat on the stool beside him. "No."

"Cheesy fries." The bartender slid the piled-high plate across the bar. "Can I get you anything?" he asked Sawyer.

"The same." Sawyer pointed at Travis's glass.

*Because he thinks I'm drinking?* Travis shook his head and finished his drink.

Sawyer picked up the drink the bartender offered, sniffed it, then took a sip.

"It's cranberry juice and soda." Travis grinned at the look on Sawyer's face. "I'm not going to undo a year of hard work just because of…this." He pointed at him. "Everyone's walking around on eggshells, like I'm some ticking time bomb or something. *That's* what pisses me off more than anything. That my perceived vulnerability is an excuse for their behavior. I call bullshit." He grabbed a cheesy fry. "The three of us agreed, no more secrets, no more lies, period. But, no, Travis might fall off the wagon so we *have* to keep this a secret?"

Sawyer stared into his drink. "If it makes you feel any better, you're not special. I'm keeping secrets from…everyone."

"Everyone as in my family?" He paused. "You've been here for almost three years and, until a couple of weeks ago, I didn't even know you had a brother."

"I try to keep my personal and professional life separate—"

"That's why you're working security for your father and half-siblings." He looked Sawyer square in the eye. "Makes perfect sense."

Thankfully, Sawyer didn't argue.

"Can we cut the shit?" Travis said.

Sawyer nodded.

"You knew who we were when you got this job." It wasn't a question. "You've had a hundred opportunities to speak up but you've stayed quiet."

Sawyer's jaw muscle flexed.

"I'm asking again. What do you want from my family?" He knew he was staring the man down but, dammit, he couldn't help it. He was done with secrets. Done with lies.

"Honestly?" Sawyer cleared his throat. "I came here to hurt you all. Hank, most of all."

"He knows about you?" Travis asked, angry all over again. His father had made some mistakes in his life—but setting aside a son? That was above and beyond a mistake. That was an inexcusable dick move. He spun his new drink slowly, hoping like hell his father was just as in the dark as Travis had been.

"I was sure he did. How could he not know?" Sawyer's jaw was working overtime now. "But my mother kept it from me so why wouldn't she keep it from him too?" He shrugged. "My dad died—the man I thought was my father, anyway—and Mom was selling the house. I found a box of her things, put two and two together, and headed to Austin to find out for myself."

"And what, you took one look at our dysfunctional family and couldn't leave?" Travis's laugh was bitter.

But Sawyer shrugged and cleared his throat. "I couldn't leave."

How would this have played out if Sawyer had walked up to his father and told him the truth? Would he have been welcomed with open arms? How did a man do that, anyway? Walk up to a stranger knowing he was your father? *A father that had no idea he existed?*

"What did your mom say?" Travis asked.

"I didn't tell her." Sawyer's lips pressed flat. "I just left."

"Fucking secrets." Anger damn near choked Travis. "I guess we have more in common than just our father." He held his glass up.

Sawyer tapped his glass to his. "A messed-up family and a lying mother?" He nodded.

They sat in companionable silence, devouring the food and finishing off their drinks.

"There's something I need to tell you," Sawyer said, looking pained.

"Let me guess? About Loretta?" Travis ran a hand over his face. His heart already hurt; might as well rip it open and let it bleed out. "I'm pretty sure I already know."

"She hasn't come right out and said it yet, but I know why she's holding back. I'm hoping, in time, she'll come clean so we can fix things."

Travis frowned, a flickering hope returning. "If she hasn't told you how she feels, I'm not throwing in the towel. She's worth fighting for."

"I know." Sawyer nodded. "Why do you think I'm doing this? I'll figure out the truth soon enough."

"What if the truth is she doesn't know?" Travis wiped his fingers on a napkin. "I don't have much experience with this sort of thing, but I'm pretty sure you're supposed to lead with your heart and, sometimes, the heart isn't as forthcoming as you'd like."

Sawyer was frowning now. "What are we talking about?"

"Loretta," he snapped.

"And what your mother has on her?" Sawyer asked, his gaze narrowing.

"No…" He paused. "Wait. What?" He shook his head. "My mother?"

"That night, in her dressing room?" Sawyer waited for him to nod. "CiCi had just left. From the look on Loretta's face, I knew something had happened, but she wouldn't tell me anything."

That night... The night everything had changed. His *mother* was the reason?

"Are you fucking kidding me?" Just when he thought he had a hold of his temper... Why was he surprised. This was his mother. His mother who seemed hell-bent and determined to make everyone as miserable as she was. "What did she do tonight?"

Sawyer glanced at him from the corner of his eye. "Tonight?"

"I was headed to her room when I saw the two of you leave." He waited.

"CiCi wasn't involved." Sawyer reached for a cheesy fry. "Donnie Gram is in town. He was arrested for public intoxication and called Loretta to bail him out, then caused a scene on the steps of the jail and got hauled back inside."

"She's back in her room?" Travis asked, debating whether or not to check on her. He wanted to—more than anything. Sawyer, his sisters, his mother, his father... They could all wait.

# Chapter 15

LORETTA WOKE UP WITH A HEADACHE AND FELT NAUSEOUS. She hadn't slept much—she couldn't. Every time she closed her eyes, the whole horrible mess at the police station was waiting to replay in her head. She rolled onto her back and pressed her hands to her eyes. She'd crawled on top of her bed, fully dressed, and fallen into a restless sleep.

She had a handful of text messages and two voice mails but before she could face the fallout from last night, she needed a shower and some coffee. Lots of coffee.

The shower helped.

The coffee did too.

But the voice message from her father had her pouring more coffee and taking some pain medicine too.

"I don't want your tickets or your backstage passes. You think that's going to make up for last night? For embarrassing me that way? I'm ashamed of you, Loretta. Ashamed that you're my daughter."

Margot's message was next. "Hey Lori-girl, give me a call. This mess with Donnie is all over the place and we need to come up with a press release. Call me when you're up and moving."

Loretta picked at her biscuit then gave up, calling Margot on FaceTime.

"Morning. You're looking a bit rough, Lori-girl." Margot looked all wide awake and energized. "Have you turned on the news this morning?"

"No. I'm still downing coffee." She might even order another pot before the morning was through.

"The good news is, he hasn't commented." Margot paused. "All we have is the mugshot, the two of you on the front steps of the police station, and how he was released this morning."

That was it? That didn't sound like her father, at all. He never passed up the opportunity to earn a dollar—or a moment in the spotlight. Unless he had something waiting in the wings. "I'm... surprised." She made a face at Margot.

"Let's just count our blessings," Margot said. "What do you think of this?" Margot read out the very short and concise statement she'd come up with. "Donnie Gram was arrested for public drunkenness. His daughter, Loretta Gram, paid his bail." She broke off.

"What about the fact that he was taken back inside after yelling at me then heckling one of the police officers?" Loretta asked, sipping her coffee.

"There were no additional charges filed." Margot shrugged. "I see no reason to mention it."

"You're the boss." Loretta nodded.

"Am I?" Margot laughed. "How's everything there?"

"Everything?"

"Travis?" Margot sighed.

"Things got a little complicated last night so..." Loretta shook her head.

"Today is a new day. You make the most of it. And try not to let this thing with Donnie get you down." She waved. "Break a leg tonight."

"Will do." Loretta blew kisses and hung up her phone.

Today *is* a new day. But nothing had changed—not really. They'd do a rehearsal and sound check around three. Have time for dinner. Hair and makeup and getting ready for the show at nine. She and Travis would sing their four songs together and she'd act like she wasn't falling for him—because being in love with Travis King was the stupidest thing she could do. Not just for her, but for him too. After the final ensemble encore, they'd climb into their buses and make the overnight ride to Phoenix. A lonely, too quiet bus ride that would lead her back around to all the reasons she was bad for Travis, why they'd never work out, and why she couldn't love him—even if she wanted to.

She eyed her bed, still made up and tidy except for the pillow she'd used. If she wanted to, she could take a nap. She should take a nap. It was going to be a long day and, even though the thing with her father wasn't as cataclysmic as she'd anticipated, the day was still young. But, even with the black-out curtains pulled and the REM-inducing sounds playing on her phone, she couldn't stop tossing and turning.

When she threw back the covers, she turned on her favorite baking show, dug out some bright red glitter nail polish, and drew herself a bubble bath. It wasn't as glamorous as the spa day she, Margot, Emmy Lou, and Krystal had, but it provided a few hours of distraction.

The Vivint Smart Home Arena was already buzzing with pre-show activity. It was one of Loretta's favorite times to poke around. Right now, the anticipation was high. All sorts of positive energy to draw from.

*Exactly what I need.*

"Hey, Loretta." Emmy Lou was sitting on the edge of the stage. It didn't matter that they were just rehearsing; Emmy Lou always looked ready to walk onstage. Her hair was perfect. Long, golden curls that fell down her back with no hint of frizz. She went with light makeup, almost an au naturel look. If her makeup was au naturel, her style was extra girly-girl. A pink V-neck shirt with puff sleeves, white fitted jeans, a hand-tooled belt with her and Brock's pet name "Bremmy" cut into the belt band, and tan and pink leather boots that had just enough sparkle to catch the eye.

"Hi." Loretta smiled, feeling way underdressed next to Emmy Lou. Hair done, makeup, nails newly painted and shiny, and a favorite navy blue belted shirtdress and broken-in brown leather boots. It was only since this tour had started that she'd put much effort into her rehearsal attire. Not to compete with Emmy Lou, there was no competing with Emmy Lou, but to look nice. For herself. And, maybe, for Travis.

She sighed, doing as covert a sweep of the stage as possible.

"They're not here." Krystal walked onto the stage, holding her guitar. She wore black and purple leggings, an oversized black sweatshirt that hung off one shoulder, and her hair was in a barely holding bun. "Travis or Sawyer. Oh, hey, Loretta. Have you heard from Travis?"

"No." Not today. She might have ignored his text and his phone call last night after the whole disaster with her father, but she'd had to. Her father yelling, "You're a coldhearted bitch I'm ashamed to call my daughter," had felt like a slap in the face. She'd wanted comfort so much it hurt. And Travis… Well, Travis was Travis. If she'd answered him, she'd have gotten comfort and so much more. It would have totally invalidated the last few weeks of distance she'd put between them.

"They're not answering my calls." Krystal was frowning. "Or my texts."

"It'll be okay." Jace slid his arm around her waist. "They'll be okay."

But even Loretta could tell he was worried.

"Did something happen?" she asked, then backtracked. "Does this… I mean, I'm sorry about my father. If this—"

"No, no." Emmy Lou shook her head. "Oh, Loretta. I'm so sorry. I'm a terrible person. I should have checked on you first thing this morning." She stood. "Are you all right?"

Loretta nodded. "I'm fine. But if this has caused a problem—"

"It didn't." Krystal shook her head, cradling her guitar close. "I think, maybe, Travis overheard something last night. Something Emmy Lou and I were talking about." She glanced at Jace. "Something that would have really, really upset him."

Loretta's heart dropped. Travis... "But Sawyer is with him?" Sawyer was levelheaded. He might not be the most emotive man on the planet but, in a crisis, he'd remained calm. Last night, she'd appreciated that.

"I don't know." Emmy Lou shrugged.

It wasn't the first time Loretta felt that prick of unease along her spine. Whatever had the three of them worked up, they knew more than they were letting on. Whether she had the right to it or not, it angered her.

"If Travis... If you're worried about him drinking, shouldn't we call his sponsor?" Loretta asked. "That's what he's there for. And, if Travis needs help, then we should get it for him, shouldn't we?"

Jace nodded. "Yeah. I'll call Archie." Phone in hand, he walked off the stage.

Loretta forced herself to breathe. She'd been here before. With her father. With Johnny. Teetering on that line of despair and anger and hope. Despair that all they'd worked toward was gone. Anger that they'd let themselves slip. And hope that there was still time to step in and stop this before it got out of hand.

But, dammit, Travis wasn't her father. It had taken her a while to accept that Travis King wanted to get sober. He'd had that a-ha lightbulb moment. He was all about owning his decisions and choices. He wouldn't do this.

He wasn't Johnny either. Travis had a strength Johnny never had. Johnny's light wavered long before his death. But Travis? She'd never know a person to burn as bright as he did. He was too alive, too vital and determined—stubborn even.

"He won't drink," she said. She said it and she meant it. "He won't."

Krystal and Emmy Lou looked at her then, uncertain.

"Loretta, you don't know—"

"I don't need to." She interrupted Emmy Lou. "I trust him. That's what he needs. You to trust him."

Emmy Lou reached out, her lower lip trembling. "How can you be so sure?"

Loretta took her hand. "I just…am." She squeezed her hand. "He's so damn stubborn. After all the gossip and radio and trash-talk, he won't drink just to prove the whole damn world they're wrong about him."

Krystal's smile was reluctant. "She's got a point."

Jace returned. "I called. He said he'll call him, but he's not worried."

"Well if his sponsor isn't worried and Loretta's not worried, maybe we should trust that he's doing something important and we should rehearse?" Krystal asked.

As far as rehearsals went, they sounded terrible, but Loretta appreciated the effort they all made. They had dinner together in one of the greenrooms, sharing cartons of Peking duck, chow mein, kung pao chicken, and spring rolls while helping Jace solve a celebrity crossword puzzle.

By the time they split up and headed for their dressing rooms, Loretta was on edge. It wasn't that she'd changed her mind about Travis; she hadn't. But what if something had happened to him? What if something was wrong—something that had nothing to do with his recovery?

*He's fine.* She looked her reflection in the eye. *He is fine.*

Wardrobe was first. The costumer had designed matching dresses for all three women. Skin-tight and suede, with small cutouts of stars and hearts. But tonight, her peacock dress felt too hot and extra tight. Her hair was smoothed and ironed and sprayed while color and foundation, cream and powders were dusted and sponged and blended until her reflection was bright and shiny and technicolor.

*He is fine.*

Final touches like the black choker necklace with the peacock stone heart and shimmering peacock earrings signaled the end of all the prep work.

She almost fell out of her director's chair when her phone vibrated.

He's here, Emmy Lou texted, followed by a string of thumbs-up, smiling, and clapping hands emojis.

She hurried down the hall to wait in the wings of the stage for her entrance, for her and Travis's first song, "Close and Deep." When the lights dimmed, she maneuvered her way across the cords and tape, light stands and support poles, until his broad back was in sight.

*Travis.* She could breathe and the fear that had a vise-grip on her heart slowly began to fade.

He turned right about the time she reached his side. The opening song had a lot of flash. Drums and confetti, a guitar solo, and a whole lot of Travis stirring up the crowd. The lights came up and Loretta drank him in. Travis. Those blue-green eyes. Right here. He was breathing fast and there was a hint of sweat on his brow, but it was his smile that did her in. That smile reached into her chest and decimated the walls she'd spent years reinforcing to protect her heart. One smile.

*I love you.* Dammit. *I'm a damn fool.* But it was true. She reached out, grabbed the front of his shirt, and held on.

His hand caught hers, holding it against his chest.

The roar of the crowd was deafening, a sea of flashes rippled across the auditorium, and with a shake of his head, Travis let go of her hand to play first few notes of the next song.

He sang each word like he meant them. Like he was singing for her alone. And when he reached the chorus, Loretta was spellbound by the hunger in his eyes.

―――――――――

Travis wasn't sure he'd ever wanted a woman more than he wanted Loretta Gram. *Right now.* He stalked off the stage and headed toward her dressing room, a man damn near possessed. He knew he had two songs. Two. And he'd have to be back onstage. But between then and now, he needed Loretta. If he couldn't touch her, he'd damn well look his fill.

He'd spent the whole damn day chasing down the worst of her life, looking for any threat or wound or person that Momma could dredge up and use against Loretta. If he needed to hold her close and know that she was okay, he had good reason.

He'd deal with his mother soon enough.

But now that he was standing outside of her dressing room, he wasn't sure what to do. Loretta Gram was the first woman his heart had wholly committed to. He'd had no choice in it. It was done. Immovable. Permanent. And he was more than okay with it.

Would Loretta want a recovering alcoholic with a womanizing past and a family worthy of their own reality television show? She sure as hell deserved better.

When the door opened, he wasn't sure who was more surprised—him or her.

"Travis?" She stepped back, her voice soft and husky.

"You…" He cleared his throat. *I love you.*

"Come in?" She stepped aside for him. But once he was inside and the door clicked shut, she grabbed his shirt front, her hand twisting the starched pale blue cowboy-cut button-up.

She was mad? Upset? He couldn't tell—the roll of emotions kept going. He'd never meant to hurt her. She'd been hurt too much already. If it was up to him, he'd stop her from ever hurting again. Or, at the least, shouldering the hurt with her so it wasn't her burden alone. *If* she'd let him love her, that is. Because, damn, when it came to this woman? There was no end to the amount of love he had to give. "Loretta?"

She shook her head, her hold tightening so that two of the snaps on his shirt popped open. Her gaze zeroed in on the exposed patch of his stomach and a switch was flipped. The heat from her topaz eyes incinerating any protest his brain conjured.

Her fingers slid across his skin, his hand tangled in her hair, and there was no stopping either of them. The taste of her was like a match to gasoline. The touch of her tongue. The rake of her nails. Her gasp when he spun her around and pressed her back against the door.

There wasn't enough time.

His lips trailed along her neck, sucking and clinging until she was all but panting.

When his mouth covered hers, he pulled her in close. If he couldn't love her body, he'd love her mouth. Explore the heat and softness and taste that inflamed him until there was nothing but her.

Like now.

Fitted against him.

Soft and warm.

He tore his mouth from hers, groaning. "I have to go."

"I know." She wasn't touching him now.

"I don't want to go." He needed her to know that.

"I know," she whispered, her gaze locked with his. "I don't want you to go."

"Good." He had to smile then. "Remember that later. When this is over and I come looking for you." He pressed a kiss to her temple, cradled her head in his hand, and sighed again. "Dammit, woman, you make it hard for me to do the right thing."

She turned into his hand and pressed a kiss against his palm. "You better go. I think you'd be missed by, oh, several thousand screaming fans."

If he didn't look at her, it'd be easier for him to leave. Not that there was anything easy about leaving. He took comfort in knowing they'd have more time later. After Phoenix, they had a lot more time. Three days. Granted, his father's surgery had been scheduled so they could all be there, but there was a whole hell of a lot of them to share the load. He and Loretta would have the time to hash things out—without concerts or tour buses or the lack of privacy to interrupt them.

Knowing that buoyed him through the rest of the concert and gave him something to hold on to.

It didn't make it any easier to look his sisters in the eye. Or Jace, for that matter. The only reason he'd managed to set aside his frustration with Sawyer was because of Loretta. Sawyer was adamant he wanted to help. He had the connections and the know-how to find all the information his mother had tracked down for later use. If Travis tried to go it alone, who knew how long it would have taken him. It didn't mean they were good—he'd even said as much to Sawyer—but their common goal put all the rest on hold. For now.

He sang his heart out and made damn sure his fans were getting their money's worth. This was why he was here. They put him there. And this was his way of thanking them. All five of them were on tonight, bringing up the energy level until the roar of the audience was constant and booming. They took turns, alternating lines, until they got to the end.

The big finish never failed to impress. Strobe lights and confetti cannons coordinated for a literal explosion of sound and color. They grabbed hands and took a bow. Then another. The noise level of the crowd was ear-splitting—exactly how he wanted to leave their audience.

A stage assistant was waiting with water bottles for them all. "You guys were amazing. Now hydrate."

Travis grabbed a water bottle when Sawyer caught his eye.

Sawyer didn't look happy. That's what that tension around the eyes meant… Their father looked the same way when he was grappling with something unpleasant.

Travis shoved that little revelation aside as he reached Sawyer. "What?"

"Her father." Sawyer shook his head. "He gave *TNM* one hell of an exclusive."

"Fuck." He ran his fingers through his hair. "Bad?"

"You could say that." Sawyer's jaw muscle flexed.

"Wheelhouse is aware?" he asked, noting the uptick in Sawyer's overall tension. "Damage control?"

"Your father wants us to call from the bus," Sawyer said, "after the meet and greet. I'll tell Emmy Lou and Krystal. Get them on the Kings Coach II."

"We'll be there." Travis saw a flash of peacock from the corner of his eye. Loretta, heading for her dressing room. He jogged after her. If he couldn't be the one to tell her, he'd sure as hell be there when she found out.

He caught up with her about the time she was answering her phone.

"Hey, Margot. Yes, just finished." Loretta said, smiling up at him. "I think it went well." She paused. "Sure." She kept walking, but her steps got slower and slower. "When?" She glanced at him then. "It's out there?"

He nodded.

Her eyes closed. "Dammit." Another pause. "I'm so sorry, Margot. I should have known. I should have known…" She shook her head. "Right. Of course…Hank? Now?"

"Sawyer will get someone to take care of your stuff," Travis murmured.

Loretta nodded, her attention split between what he was saying and whatever Margot was telling her. Whatever it was, it didn't look good. They reached her dressing room and Loretta was red-faced and shaking.

"I know. I know." She sucked in a deep breath. "I'll call you in a bit. I am sorry, Margot." Carefully, she set her phone down on the counter.

"Loretta." He stepped forward, ready and willing to be what she needed.

"Travis." She held up her hand. "I can't do this right now." She swallowed, her hands gripping the edge of the makeup counter.

He didn't argue. He didn't say a thing. He didn't know what to say. "I'm here."

She glanced at him. "I'm fine."

"I know. You're fine. You're strong." He shoved his hands into his pockets so he wouldn't reach for her. "But you don't have to be."

She stared at her phone for a long time. A very long time. "Travis. I apologize if I gave off the wrong impression." She cleared her throat once, then again. "I like having sex with you. I like it a lot. But that's all this is. And, honestly, I thought we'd moved on until…well, earlier. I think it's best if we just don't do this." She swallowed. "I know it's best." Her knuckles were white. "I can't worry about you. This is my career. My life. It's *all* I have. I know that sounds harsh but, I can't be responsible for…you."

As far as words went, these were fucking brutal. "Why the hell would I want that?" This was how she felt?

"Okay." She nodded. "Good."

"Sure," he ground out, hating how this felt. "No problem." He shrugged. "Sex only. Done. Moving on."

Her gaze narrowed. "Then let's just forget about earlier so I can focus on whatever backlash my father has caused." She looked at him then—the way she'd looked at him that first day. With contempt and impatience. "Because that's what really matters right now, don't you think? Not getting laid?"

Something gave in his chest. A fluid pop that injected tiny shards of pain into his bloodstream. Beyond the pain, he felt… hollow. It had been a long time since he lashed out in anger, but instinct kicked in. "I was sort of hoping to get laid tonight."

She was shooting daggers at him now. "I'm sure you'll find someone at the meet and greet who'd be happy to accommodate."

More words were ready, verbal weapons ready to fire. But he

swallowed them down and shrugged. "I'll see you in there." He cleared his throat. "Afterward, Kings Coach II. Some damage control thing." He didn't wait for her answer, and he sure as hell didn't make the mistake of looking at her again.

At the moment, she didn't know she'd basically ripped his insides out. He'd rather that wasn't common knowledge.

He went into automaton mode. Pictures with the fans. Doling out autographs. Being charming. He could do it, all of it, in his sleep. His smile never faltered, but that didn't mean he wasn't bleeding out.

The meet and greet was a blur. From the looks Emmy Lou and Krystal kept shooting him, he wasn't fooling them. But he wasn't trying to fool them. The only people that mattered were the fans. An hour and thirty-seven photos clustered in front of the Three Kings' step and repeat later, he was shaking hands and heading for the service exit.

How many times had he given Emmy Lou shit for being naïve? Too many times to remember. Suddenly, he meets Loretta and drinks the Kool-Aid? Was it because she was the first girl he'd slept with since recovery? Because she was inaccessible, he'd looked forward to the challenge? Because the attraction he had for her was…like breathing?

But he couldn't do that. That's not who he was anymore. He loved her. He loved her and he'd survive a broken heart.

He sat on the bus, pulled out his phone, and scrolled through the top stories. There was a string of hashtags that made him wince. #LorettaGramIsABitch was the first one. #LorettaGramHasNoSoul, #WhatTheHellLoveJoy, and #NoLoveInLoveJoy #NoTrueLove were also at the top of the list.

The link to the video was there. But Travis couldn't bring himself to click on it. After all the digging he'd done today, he doubted there'd be any surprises. Somehow, some way, Donnie Gram had managed to turn Loretta into the villain. Considering his current volatile state of mind, Travis wasn't sure watching the interview was a good idea.

Things got increasingly crowded when his sisters, Jace, Loretta, Brock, and Sawyer were all sitting on the bus. He was so agitated, he gave up his seat on the built-in leather sectional and paced the small space behind it, his guitar pick in his hand.

Loretta, for her part, remained mostly quiet. She stared at her bright red nail polish, her hair pulled over one shoulder—almost hiding. "I'm sorry for this," she said once they'd put their father on speaker phone.

"I don't want to hear you say that again." Their father's voice was raspy. "It's a simple matter of he said, she said. When you all come home, we'll set the record straight. I've already had our people contact Molly Harper at *Good Morning USA*. She's been good to us—I know she'll treat us fairly."

*Good.* Travis approved of his father's plan. Molly Harper was to daytime news programs what Emmy Lou was to country music. There was an inherent likability about her that made people trust her. Once that interview released, Donnie Gram's credibility would be forever tarnished.

He hoped.

It didn't seem to matter that she'd shredded his heart fifteen minutes ago, Travis was worried about Loretta. He knew how hard it was to love and hate a parent. His mother managed to justify her actions so that they were for a greater good, even if she was the only one who could see that *greater good*. But Donnie Gram was only in it for himself. This was about money, plain and simple. Donnie Gram was willing to exploit his only child for money; there was nothing else Travis needed to know about the man.

But the question was, who paid him? Was it *TNM* or had his mother stepped in? And who, exactly, was his mother trying to protect this time? What sort of greater good was she aiming for this time? He'd find out soon enough. He'd invited her to lunch the day they got back to Austin. One big happy family.

Travis was done with all the lies and secrets and manipulations. He wanted it all out and in the open. If that helped remove the target his mother had placed on Loretta, then he'd be happy. Not as happy as if Loretta loved him. But happy enough to know he'd given her some small sense of peace.

# Chapter 16

LORETTA WAS EATING CHEESY FRIES ON HER BED WHEN THE pounding started on her door. She'd turned off her phone and was pretending to sleep but, really, all she wanted was time to herself. The drive to Phoenix had frayed her nerves down to nothing. Not just the riding in the bus with Travis and everyone else. But the video.

The inescapable video.

The edited, grainy, heartless video.

The audio had been so warped that she could barely make out the words let alone recognize the voices. Instead of her father calling her a coldhearted bitch, he was asking her how she could be so coldhearted toward him. They'd also managed to make it sound like he was apologizing that she was ashamed of him and changed the whole sequence around so that it looked like the cop was defending her father against Loretta—not that the cop stepped in to defend her.

It should have been laughable. But it wasn't.

He was her father. Her father, who was slated for a primetime follow-up live tomorrow night on *TNM*. Because he hadn't made things bad enough?

The pounding continued.

"We know you're awake." It was Emmy Lou.

"Come on, Loretta," Krystal added. "We can make Sawyer break down the door. It wouldn't be the first time we'd owe a hotel property damages."

Loretta frowned at the door.

"That was when I was drinking," Travis explained. "But thanks for letting that go."

Loretta didn't want to smile. She didn't want to see him or ache for him to put his big, strong, warm arms around her. She didn't *want* to want to apologize for the horribly cruel things she'd said to him.

*I am a coldhearted bitch.* She sniffed.

Her phone vibrated.

She swiped the home screen and laughed. A picture of Emmy Lou and Krystal making sad puppy faces while Jace and Travis looked appropriately put upon by the whole selfie thing.

"We heard you laugh," Krystal said.

She sighed, sat up, and set her cheesy fries on the bedside table. She tugged her robe more tightly around her and padded across the carpet to the door. She flipped the handle, opened the door, and headed back to her bed.

"It's so dark," Emmy Lou said.

Loretta flipped on the bedside lamp, rapidly blinking as her eyes adjusted.

"If you're going to really embrace self-pity, absolute darkness is the best way to go." Krystal kicked off her flip-flops and jumped onto her bed. "Ooh, cheesy fries." She smiled. "I brought Red Vines. The world's best candy."

"If you like eating red wax." Travis sat on the floor beside the bed, his gaze fixing on her bare ankle and calf.

Loretta shifted, crossing her legs. "You all just happened to be roaming the halls at two in the morning?"

"No." Emmy Lou laughed. "We came to cheer you up." She tossed her purse onto the bed. "We weren't sure what your favorite was so we basically bought one of every sugary thing they sell in the gift shop."

"Meaning, the candy bars cost at least nine dollars each so make sure you chew and savor every bite." Travis nodded. "And, if you don't want it, throw me the peanut nougat chocolate thing."

Loretta eyed the stash of candy. "I'm not sure what that is."

Travis rose onto his knees and leaned against the side of the bed for the candy—which was *right* beside her. Unless she was going to climb into Emmy Lou's lap, she had no escape. She'd just have to act like Travis being in her personal space didn't bother her. Luckily, the thundering of her heart was muffled by the crinkle and rustle of candy wrappers as Travis hunted down his peanut nougat chocolate thing.

"Found it." He held up the candy bar and smiled.

He knew what he was doing. He knew he was close enough that all he'd have to do was lean a couple of inches to the right and he could kiss her. *He knows* and *he's enjoying it.*

"We bought that for her," Emmy Lou reminded him, sighing with disappointment.

Loretta tore gaze from that devilish grin. "Honestly, I can't eat all of this."

"Oh, we'll help you. Toss me the taffy things." Jace sat on the floor, catching the bag Travis threw his way, then leaning against the foot of the bed. "What are we watching?"

"Porn." Travis started laughing the minute Emmy Lou launched a pillow his way.

"It's not porn." But Loretta was smiling. As far as distractions went, this was working.

"Travis is totally teasing you, but this was all his idea," Krystal said, sliding off the bed and onto the floor by Jace. "He was worried about you."

"We all were," Emmy Lou added.

"I wasn't." Krystal raised her hand. "I figured you might relish a little privacy, but I was overruled."

"You didn't have to come," Travis pointed out.

"Well I didn't want to miss out." Krystal winked at her. "I mean, I'll give you privacy but I'm also completely content talking trash about Donnie Gram. I'm calling him Donnie Gram because calling him your father assigns some sort of blame to you. Which is bullshit. So, from now on, the asshole is Donnie Gram."

"I can't argue with that." Loretta nodded.

"Does that mean I should start referring to Momma as CiCi?" Travis asked.

"I do." Krystal shrugged. "Most of the time. I just feel gross calling her Momma. She's not a nice person. All her secrets and lies and maneuverings… Mom or mother or Momma is a title—a revered title. And a good mother won't do any of those things."

Jace slipped his arm around Krystal's shoulders and pulled her against him. Loretta watched as Krystal's head rested on Jace's shoulders.

Loretta glanced at Travis. Travis was staring at the candy bar, the boyish smile gone.

"I know," Krystal said from her place on the floor. "There's the shark octopus thing on the science fiction channel on demand."

"You want to watch a shark octopus movie?" Jace asked, chuckling.

"Me? No. But I promised Heather I'd watch it and I want to keep my cool sister status."

"Heather is Jace's little sister," Emmy Lou said. "She's at college. The sweetest thing ever."

"We met at your wedding." Loretta smiled and handed Krystal the remote. "Far be it from me from taking away your cool sister status."

"Thank you," Krystal said, flipping through the channels.

Loretta sat back against the padded headboard, a pile of candy in her lap. "This was really nice of you," she said. "I know it's just a crappy video but…"

"He's your dad." Travis almost sounded angry. "And he's letting the media tear your character apart?"

Loretta couldn't help but look his way again.

He looked perfect, as usual, but in a tired way. Almost as if he could rest his head against the edge of the mattress and he'd drift off to sleep… And she could run her fingers through those curls of his. She flexed her hand, pressing her fingers flat on top of the comforter.

His eyes narrowed, watching her hand.

"How's your father?" She sounded weird. Probably because of the lump in her throat. "Is he nervous about the surgery?"

Travis shrugged. "He's real good at keeping his feelings hidden." He was staring at her. "Self-preservation, I guess."

Loretta swallowed, acutely aware of just how closely he was watching her. "There's nothing wrong with that. Especially if you've been burned. Why set yourself up for more of the same?"

His jaw muscle clenched. "Because he knows we love him. It's safe to be vulnerable with the people you love." Travis cleared his throat.

"But people throw that word around all the time. Aren't some people…unlovable?" She knew the answer to that. She was one of those people. Loretta sat forward, twisting a long candy rope. "How do you know when it's real?"

Travis went back to studying her. But this time it wasn't a stare down; it was gentler than that. "You *know*. And once you know, you have to trust it."

*I want to.* "Or not," she countered. She knew, deep down in her bones, that she loved him. "People use love as this universal answer. It makes things better, makes you happy, makes you whole… But it can do the opposite. Nothing hurts worse or strips away your dignity or makes you believe a lie or leaves a hole you'd never realized you had before. Love sucks."

That was when she realized the television had been paused and her and Travis's conversation had become the center of attention.

"At least, in my experience, love sucks," she tried to tease. Her gaze darted to Emmy Lou. "I'm sorry. You just got married. I'm so sorry."

"I'm sorry, Loretta." Emmy Lou took her hand. "It took Brock and me ages to find our way back to each other. And there was a lot of hurt along the way. But now? I don't want to think about my life without him. I hope one day you'll find someone who makes you feel that way. Until then, my heart hurts for you."

Loretta swallowed hard, staring at the candy in her lap. "Let's just chalk up my emotional outburst as a sleep-deprived rant and forget it ever happened."

"Okay." Krystal paused. "But I feel like I need to say this much. I get where you're coming from. I do. And there are days when I look at Jace and I know it's going to fall apart because, honestly, why would he stay with *me*? I'm rude and bossy and opinionated and I don't admit when I'm wrong—"

"All things I love," Jace interrupted. "Especially getting you to admit when you're wrong."

"Which isn't very often." Krystal shook her head. "But then he looks at me and it makes sense. I breathe easier when he's around. He's…gravity. I know that I'd rather go through hell with him than without."

This was why she didn't do feelings. It got awkward. How could you have a conversation based on something so insubstantial and subjective? To Emmy Lou and Krystal, love was good and purposeful.

"Shark octopus time," Krystal squealed, pressing play.

Loretta fluffed up the pillows and stared at the absolute mess of a movie they were watching. Around the time the thing had walked onto land to go after the girl in the bikini, Loretta drifted off.

She stirred the moment the light clicked off. She sat up, her heart slamming against her chest.

"Loretta?" Travis sank onto the bed. "I didn't mean to wake you," he murmured, his scent—mint and leather—flooding her still sleepy senses. "I'm getting my peanut nougat chocolate thing and I'll be on my way."

She laughed. "I'm pretty sure that's not the name."

"No?" He chuckled. "Guess it would be a little hard to fit on the wrapper."

She smiled into the dark.

"It was my idea." Travis cleared his throat. "Coming tonight."

She held her breath, waiting.

"If it was a bad call, I'm sorry."

Her hand moved across the blanket until she found what she was looking for. His hand. Warm. Solid. "It wasn't." There was a fragile intimacy between them—held together by the safety of the dark and their hushed voices.

His hand turned over, his fingers threading with hers.

"I've been thinking about what you said." He swallowed. "I know how you feel about honesty—we're on the same page there."

*Except I lied to you.* She hated herself a little then. She had lied to him.

"What about respect? And loyalty. My father said those are the three things that support a relationship. Instead of worrying about the 'L' word, maybe give a chance to the man willing to give you those three things—that inspires those feelings in you." His fingers slid from hers. "You deserve that, Loretta."

She managed to hold back her tears until after the door clicked closed behind Travis. All this time she'd fought to hold on to her heart, he'd never once said anything about having feelings for her. She'd been thankful for that. It was easier and safer to keep things the way they were. That's what she wanted, wasn't it? No risks. No pain. No more loss…

She didn't want to lose Travis. He was…worth the risk. If he cared—even the slightest bit—and she was too scared to speak up, she'd lose him anyway.

Travis was glad he'd had a meeting with Archie that morning. He'd cleared his head, worked through the goal, come up with a plan—generally made himself believe that he could do this and, somehow, it'd be okay. Not right away, but eventually. *Maybe*. He had set three spots at the kitchen table. Himself, Momma, and Daddy. At this point, he couldn't bear to keep his father in the dark. He hadn't quite figured if or how he should be the one to tell his father about Sawyer—but that was none of Momma's business.

"What's cooking?" Krystal asked, pushing through the kitchen door, a bouquet of flowers in her arms.

"Lasagna." He barely spared her a glance. He'd played nice the night they'd converged on Loretta's room because he didn't have the nerve to go alone. But after that, he'd been keeping his distance. By now, he had no doubt that his sisters knew something was up. And since neither of them had dared to bring it up, he began to think they might know what he was upset about. Until one of the three of them stepped up, there was no hope of easing the tension between them.

"Lasagna?" Her brows rose.

"Don't get too excited." Travis sighed. "It's frozen."

Krystal smiled as she pulled a blue glass vase from the cabinet. "Who's coming?"

He saw her glance at the table. "Momma."

She almost dropped the vase. "Here?"

He nodded.

"And?"

"Daddy." He rearranged the silverware but they still didn't look right.

"Why?" She was frowning. "Do you think that's smart? I mean, Daddy has his surgery tomorrow morning—"

"I'm not sure how lunch today will affect his surgery tomorrow?" He glanced at his sister.

"No." She shook her head.

"Ooh, what smells so good?" Emmy Lou asked, breezing into the kitchen with a grocery sack. "Garlic?"

"Lasagna," Travis repeated.

"Who is coming?" Just like Krystal, Emmy Lou gave the table a quick look.

He turned. "Momma is coming. Daddy is joining us so I don't do or say something I'll regret." He ran his fingers through his hair, his agitation mounting.

"What's happened?" Emmy Lou asked, crossing to him. "Is everything okay?"

"This isn't about Sawyer." Travis frowned, watching them both turn red. "This is about Loretta. And Momma."

Krystal recovered first. "What about Loretta and Momma?"

Travis walked across the room, opened the far drawer, and pulled out the manila folder Sawyer had handed him after their morning run. "This is everything Momma's using against Loretta."

"For what?" Emmy Lou asked, sinking into one of the kitchen chairs.

"That's what we're going to find out." He shrugged.

Krystal opened the cabinet and pulled out two more plates.

"I don't need you two to stay," he argued.

Emmy Lou looked ready to cry but Krystal rolled her eyes and ignored him, setting two extra places and fixing the silverware all the way around the table.

Krystal made biscuits, Emmy Lou cut up fruit for dessert and mixed fresh lemonade, and Travis tried not to overthink what needed to be said.

When the tap-tap of Momma's stilettos echoed down the hall, the three of them paused long enough to exchange a look. She burst in, all smiles and perfume.

Travis couldn't remember a time when he hadn't considered his mother dazzling. She'd always had this magnetic quality about her. She liked to say you could draw more flies with honey than vinegar. That wasn't true. Not when it came to Momma, anyway. She made her mark through fear. Sure, in the beginning she was sugar-coated enough. That's how she lured folks in—it was only afterward that they realized it was all a trap.

"I didn't know I'd get to see you all." Momma's bright blue eyes barely touched on Krystal.

"We'd stopped by to leave flowers and crosswords for Daddy." Emmy Lou smiled. "It smells so good we invited ourselves to stay."

"I'm glad you did," Momma said. "Where is that handsome husband of yours?"

Emmy Lou kept Momma distracted with wedding photo proofs, updates on the tour, and Watson stories. Emmy Lou ignored the fact that Momma couldn't stand the cat.

"Afternoon," Daddy said, his voice scratchy.

"Oh Hank, you sound rough." Momma frowned. "Nothing too serious, I hope?"

Daddy shook his head. "Nothing to fret over."

"Good. Good. I know the kids will take good care of you until you're through this." Travis couldn't detect anything but sincerity in his mother's tone.

Food was passed, drinks were poured, and Travis was trying to remember his original opener. Lucky for him, Momma got things started.

"And where is your pretty little house guest?" she asked, cutting the lasagna into tiny bites.

"Margot's here. She and Loretta are on a conference call with the Wheelhouse people." Travis took a long sip of lemonade and dove in. "Speaking of Loretta, I was wondering what you think of her, Momma?"

"She's a sweet, sad thing." Momma set her fork down. "I can't say I'm not worried a bit. The last thing you need is getting involved with someone who has that sort of history."

*History.*

"What history?" Hank asked, frowning.

"Well, Hank honey, the poor girl doesn't exactly have the best luck, now does she?" Momma smiled. "Her father, her mother, poor Johnny…"

"What about them?" Krystal asked.

Momma cleared her throat. "Johnny's not the only one who's struggled with drugs and alcohol." She shook her head, picking up her lemonade. "Does she drink or do drugs? I only ask because I don't want that sort of thing around you, Travis." She smiled. "And now this mess with her father. I hope it won't make things harder on her."

"I'm trying to figure out what it is you object to about her, Momma." Travis sat back in his chair.

"I have no problem with her," Momma assured him. "I just want what's best for you."

"And what if Loretta's best for me?" he asked.

"This is what I was worried about." Momma dropped her napkin on her plate. "You are in no place to be thinking about a relationship, Travis. And not with someone like Loretta Gram, for goodness sake. She'd bring you down, son. And when that happens, how long do you think it will be before you start drinking?" She shook her head. "Look at her life, Travis. You can't deny there's a pattern."

"Is that why you went to see her?" Travis asked. He stood, headed to the drawer for the manila envelope he'd stored minutes before. "Sawyer saw you leaving."

"Oh he did, did he?" his mother snapped. "How convenient. And where is he? I'd love to hear what he thinks he saw."

"Sawyer's taking some time off." Time he'd more than earned off. But, with all that had come out, would Sawyer come back? If he didn't, were he and Emmy Lou and Krystal supposed to pretend he didn't exist? That was a whole other can of worms they'd deal with. Later.

"Travis?" His mother waved a hand in front of his face. "Sawyer said what, exactly?"

"He said you left and Loretta was very upset." He placed the envelope on the table. "He also put this together for me. A copy of all the information you collected on Loretta."

"I won't apologize for trying to learn more about the woman you and your father have brought into our home." She folded her arms over her chest. "I'm your mother. I can't help that I worry about you."

"Momma." Travis shook his head, momentarily dumbfounded. "Worrying means a talk or a card or a text message. Worrying does not mean compiling a file complete with sealed childhood court records. Why do you need this information? Why would anyone need this information? Unless you're going to work for the CIA or FBI."

But his mother didn't budge.

"A couple of days after your visit with Loretta, her father is in town, drunk, and causing a scene."

His mother's eyes narrowed.

"It didn't take too long to see who bought Donnie Gram his airplane ticket and his hotel room. Even if I could find a way to rationalize you digging through her past, I can't get past this. You brought her father there." He swallowed hard. "You set this up, for what, as a warning? Some sort of power trip? Why?"

"Why?" she snapped. "I wanted her to stay away from you, Travis. Because she's not good enough for you. Because she's the sort of woman who preys on men like you—"

"Men like me?" Travis shook his head. "Weak? Vulnerable? About to fall off the wagon? In need of protection? Someone who needs looking after?" He shot a look at his sisters then. "I can't tell you how much that pisses me off. I've busted my ass to get sober, busted my ass to stay sober. I don't miss meetings, I check in, and I take care of myself. I do that. I've committed to that. I don't need looking after and I sure as hell don't need you to tell me what's best for me." He was staring at his mother. "Every week Daddy, Em, and Krystal call or go online for the family support session. You don't even know my sponsor's name. Part of my recovery is surrounding myself with people who believe in my success and my ability to get there." He sighed. "You don't fall into that category. This proves that." He tapped the file.

She stood then, no traces of her calm facade in place. "I can't keep being the bad guy here. Not for you or your sisters or your father. I can't do it. I won't do it. All I've ever done is love you the only way I know how. But I don't think there's a place for me here anymore." She broke off, waiting—as if they'd stop her or ask her to stay.

He held his breath, half expecting Emmy Lou to do just that.

But the silence held.

"I think maybe you're right, CiCi." His father finally spoke up. "I think it's time we all move on. I'll get those divorce papers drawn up and we'll go from there."

Travis knew it was the right thing, but it didn't stop it from hurting. All of them. Messed up or not, they'd been a family. Now that was ending and they'd all have to find a way to come to terms with it.

From there, it was all slow motion. Momma leaving. Daddy staring straight ahead. Emmy Lou crying. Krystal cleaning up.

It was done.

But none of them felt good about it.

At the moment, he felt like shit. "Dad?" His voice was low. "That, a divorce, is between you and Momma. I never intended this to happen. I wanted you to know what she'd done because I...I don't want there to be any more secrets between us."

His father looked him in the eye. "I think that's a damn fine idea." His voice was unsteady. "I hate to think about all the secrets that have slowly chipped away at our family."

Travis glanced at his sisters again.

"But I need you to know that I know you've got yourself sorted. There was a change in you the day you came home, but it was Johnny's death that clinched it. The morning we all heard about it? I remember your face. I knew then, you'd never go back." His father took his hand. "Ever since you were little, you set your mind on something and that was that. You wanted to learn to ride a bike, you did it. You wanted to learn the banjo, you did it. You want Loretta Gram, you go after her." He cleared his throat. "She's not the sort of woman to drive you to drink. She's the sort who will whip your ass if you even think about it."

Travis chuckled.

"I need to tell you more often that I'm proud of you." He squeezed Travis's hand. "I am. I'm proud of how you've weathered this storm. Proud that you're my son." By now, his voice was weakening. "And I love you."

"I love you too." Travis squeezed his hand in answer. "But you need to rest your voice now."

His father nodded.

"You want anything, Daddy?" Krystal asked. "Some fruit? Emmy Lou cut up a fruit salad."

"Sounds good," their father wheezed.

"Dad," Emmy Lou said. "How about we bring it to you on the back porch, if you'd like?"

Their father gave a thumbs-up and headed from the kitchen.

Travis didn't move. He couldn't.

"You did the right thing." Emmy Lou's hand rested on his shoulder. "Travis... I—we—can't bear this. Please, please forgive us."

Travis ran his hands over his face.

"You've made your point." Krystal sat across the table, her green eyes pinned on him. "You're right. We were horrible, micromanaging sisters—"

"Who can't lose you, Trav. We can't," Emmy Lou said. "It was stupid and wrong not to trust that you could handle it but...I was scared."

"You're going to have to give me some time." He stood. "I love you both and I know you meant well but what you did means you don't trust me to stay sober and take care of myself." He shook his head. "Worse, I hate knowing this and keeping it from Daddy. It's not okay."

"Is Sawyer coming back?" Emmy Lou asked. "He is, isn't he?"

Krystal was chewing on the inside of her lip. "If I were him, I wouldn't. We've been nothing but trouble for him from day one."

"He said he'd let me know." Travis ran a hand over his face again. "He's got some decisions to make. I told him he'd have to tell Daddy the truth if he was going to stay. If he's leaving, I'm telling Daddy. Either way, the truth is coming out."

Emmy Lou and Krystal stared at him, surprised.

"Daddy deserves to know." Travis shook his head, beyond frustrated. "How can you think otherwise?"

Emmy Lou shook her head. "You're right."

"One more thing, Trav." Krystal paused. "The day you disappeared with Sawyer?"

The day Sawyer had been a badass and helped track down the incredibly thorough information his mother had collected on Loretta.

"We were all freaking out." Krystal sighed. "Jace even called Archie. You don't just disappear like that."

He nodded. "Okay." He didn't like it, but it made sense.

"Loretta said you wouldn't drink. She was adamant about it."

"She was." Emmy Lou agreed. "You might want to consider keeping her around because she believes in you."

He smiled. It felt good knowing Loretta believed in him.

It was only later, when they were sitting on the back porch, that Travis went back through the conversation with his mother. With any luck, there'd be some big reveal that gave him hope about

Loretta but that hadn't happened. Yes, she'd stayed away from him after Momma had threatened her but it had everything to do with protecting her career—and nothing to do with protecting him. But then she'd been honest with him since the beginning. And, as much as his heart wanted more, he respected that.

# Chapter 17

THERE WAS AN ODD SENSE OF DÉJÀ VU WHEN LORETTA WALKED into the original Kings Music Studio. Now, of course, it belonged to Wheelhouse. But the walls were still lined with gold and silver and platinum records, tour posters, and framed photos of performers and industry bigshots. The only difference now was all the albums, posters, and photographs weren't strictly Hank King or Three Kings. Now, it was a variety of Wheelhouse's chart-toppers.

Just like that first day, she headed down the hall and into the recording booth.

But today wasn't about rehearsing or recording a song. Today was about setting the record straight. Just her, Travis, Molly Harper, and several million viewers.

And when that was over, she was going to try this whole honesty, respect, and loyalty thing with Travis. She had some honesty to take care of. That didn't mean he'd suddenly have feelings for her. It could be all about the sex—the sex was incredible. But if there was even the slightest chance the two of them could be more…well, she was willing to give it a try. Maybe it had been Emmy Lou's comment about Brock making it easier for her to breathe. Or maybe it was Krystal saying she could face anything with Jace. But Loretta got it. It was big and scary and way outside her comfort zone, but the whole certainty thing was real. All of it. For her, that was Travis.

Margot walked with her, arm in arm. "You holding up?"

Loretta nodded. Which was worse? Her nerves over her interview or her nerves over taking a blind leap of faith and hoping Travis didn't laugh in her face. No. He wouldn't do that. Even if he wasn't interested in her, he'd never laugh at her. He was too decent a guy.

"You haven't said much all morning." Margot patted her hand.

In a few minutes, she'd be expected to say a lot. "I guess I'm saving my energy."

"Go get 'em," Margot said, releasing her and taking a seat next to Hank against the far wall.

"Loretta." Molly Harper shook her hand. "It's so nice to see you again. I really appreciate you and Mr. King coming to me to set the record straight."

"I appreciate the opportunity." Did she? Did she really want to get on national television to do this? But if she didn't, people would have no choice but to believe the lies he'd spread.

"You look a little green." Travis smiled down at her. Was it her imagination or did he seem nervous? "Beautiful. But green."

Molly laughed. "I'll give you two a couple of minutes and then we'll get you set up with mics."

"You ready?" he asked.

For the interview? The sooner they started, the sooner it was over and done with. To tell him she loved him? *No. But I'm doing it anyway.* "Honestly? I'm a little queasy." She tried to smile. "It's different when you're performing or doing a promotional interview. This is about *me*. My father."

"I know. I'm damn sorry he's put you in this situation." His gaze swept over her face. "But you have the right to stand up for yourself, Loretta. You've done nothing wrong."

The ferocity of his voice tugged at her heart. It sounded like he cared. Then again, she really, *really* wanted him to care.

His voice dipped to almost a whisper. "I had lunch with my mother."

"Oh?" Was that the appropriate response? She hoped so; it was about the only thing she could come up with. She felt confident insulting his mother wasn't professional behavior.

"You came up in conversation." His gaze narrowed. "I didn't know she'd threatened you. Sawyer mentioned her leaving your dressing room?"

"Oh." She'd decided leaving CiCi King out of it was for the best. "I told Sawyer it was nothing."

"And he didn't buy it. My mother has quite a history, you see. And Sawyer knows all about what she's capable of." He sounded bitter.

"Sawyer cares about you all." She paused. "He's more than just your bodyguard; he's your best friend, isn't he?"

"Best friend." He nodded, the muscle in his jaw working. "And my brother."

"What?" Loretta was openly staring now.

"We don't have time for that right now. Just another chapter in the King family saga." His crooked grin had a direct impact on her pulse. "That's one thing you can count on. Drama. Though I'm doing my damndest to change that." His gaze lingered on the curl resting over her shoulder. "You didn't tell Sawyer what my mother had said. Why?"

"I...I panicked." Which was true. "It was sort of a warning, for me to stay away from you." She swallowed, watching the surprise on his face.

"To stay away from me?" he repeated.

"She said she had people watching." Loretta shrugged. "At first, I thought she was teasing because—you know—*you* tease a lot in your family. But then I realized she was serious, and I didn't know what to do. She was worried about you and, as far as she's concerned, I'm trouble."

"You? No." He frowned. "I can't say the same thing about her. Whatever her excuse was, she had no right to threaten your career."

"It wasn't my career I was worried about." She swallowed, meeting his gaze. "Everything's changed, Travis. I have some things to apologize for."

Those blue-green eyes were intent now. The mix of mint and leather grew just the slightest bit stronger as he stepped closer. "You do?"

"I lied to you," she whispered.

He was frowning now, a deep V marring his forehead. "Loretta—"

"Wait, please wait. I'm not proud of it. I was wrong, I know it. But, at the time, I didn't feel like I had a choice." *Say it.* "Not without hurting the people I care about. I let fear kick in and cloud my judgment and for that, I'm so sorry."

His jaw muscle clenched.

"Let's get you ready for filming." An especially perky film assistant approached, mic in hand. "Is it easier to thread this through? Or do you want to clip it on your waist?"

Loretta was tempted to tell the assistant to wait but, with a film crew and Molly Harper standing by, she was the one who would have to wait.

"We'll talk? Afterward?" Travis asked, his expression and voice unreadable.

She nodded again.

One of *Good Morning USA*'s crew clipped a mic on the front of her pale-yellow sundress. They dusted powder on her nose, straightened the black choker necklace with the peacock-colored heart, and smoothed her hair with a light spray.

Travis, on the other hand, was ready to go. Perfect hair. Devilish grin. Those eyes.

It was no wonder Molly Harper was all smiles. Travis seemed to have that effect on people.

"We're not live so we can cut and edit this later," Molly said, offering an encouraging smile. "Let's get started?"

Molly eased them into the interview. First they discussed the scope of the tour, then Molly asked some questions fans had sent in, before changing course and getting to the heart of the interview.

"This tour has brought some big changes with it," Molly said.

"Loretta, you've always worked with Johnny. Travis, you're a member of Three Kings. How has it been working together?"

"After you," Travis said, propping his elbow on the arm of his chair and smiling at Loretta.

Loretta smiled. "As you can see, Travis is charming."

"I do see." Molly laughed. "He does have a reputation for being quite the charmer. Some would even say he's a lady's man. Is there any truth to that?"

"No." Loretta shook her head. "I don't mean he isn't a lady's man—just that I haven't observed him in action." *Thankfully.* "To answer your original question, *I* think we work well together. The music comes easily between us… That might sound weird."

"No." Travis shook his head. "I'd say that about sums it up. We do work well together. I think it helps that we both want this relationship to succeed. And, I like her." He smiled at her, that eye-crinkling smile that had her gripping the arms of her chair. "We have a lot in common. We both value honesty and respect and loyalty. I think, if you have those things going for you, you can make it through just about anything." He paused. "Right?"

Loretta couldn't help but stare at him then. He's talking about TrueLove. *He's talking about work.* But he said relationship… And, dammit, her fool heart was thumping like a drum. "Right." She swallowed.

"Then I guess the video released by Donnie Gram was difficult." Molly Harper's smile was sympathetic.

"It was hard, yes," Loretta agreed, ignoring the pang in her heart. "It's hard to see someone you love struggle like that."

"Your father struggles with alcoholism?" Molly asked.

Loretta nodded.

"Is this a new development?" Molly asked, glancing back and forth between the two of them.

"No." Loretta took a deep breath. "It's not new." It was who he was. The only version of her father she could remember.

"This is hard, Molly," Travis said. "The guy we're talking about is her father." He glanced at Loretta. "She doesn't want to speak ill of her father."

Loretta nodded. Her stomach hurt over all of this. He was her father. Not much of one, but the only one she had.

"No, of course not." Molly nodded.

"But I can't stand by and see Loretta torn apart by headlines." Travis shrugged. "I feel for Donnie Gram, I do. I know how hard it is to stop drinking and stick with it. But if there was ever a reason to try, with every damn thing you had, it would be for her."

Loretta turned to stare then. What had he said? Could they hear her heart racing with the mic clipped to the front of her dress?

"For his daughter?" Molly clarified, leaning forward for his answer.

"Sure." Travis smiled. "If he's smart enough to figure out how to get paid to show up, cause a scene, get arrested, and cause another scene, he's smart enough to stick to a recovery program. But the motivation isn't there. He won't get paid to get sober. He'll get paid to keep throwing dirt on his daughter's name."

"Paid by who?" Molly asked.

"The highest bidder, I imagine." He shook his head. "I know it's hard to imagine, but not all news outlets are as ethical as you and *Good Morning USA*, Molly."

"It's not just for money. I mean it is, but it isn't." Loretta scrambled to explain. "He has a gambling problem; when he needs money, he needs it right away." Which didn't make her father sound as sympathetic as she'd hoped. Why was she still trying to get him sympathy? Because that's what she'd grown up doing. Making excuses for him.

Molly blinked. "Interestingly enough, we received a video this morning. An unedited version of the video *TNM* released. It paints a slightly different story about the events of that evening."

Which was news to Loretta.

"The truth has a way of coming out." Travis nodded.

Why didn't Travis seem surprised? But she knew... Deep down she knew. Travis had done this. Why?

"Considering everything that had come to light this morning, is there something you'd like to say to your father, Loretta?" Molly asked.

"I'm not sure." Where to start? In the end, whatever she said or didn't say wouldn't matter. He only heard what he wanted to hear. "I want to say I'd never turn my back on my father. I worry about him every day. I hope he'll find the strength to take care of himself and get healthy." She swallowed. "I've sent him money before but I always worry I'm supporting his habits—the drinking and the gambling. It's terrifying to think I could be sending him what he needs to keep making himself sick. And if I stop? He finds someone else to send him the money—at my expense."

Travis held her hand. "Damned if you do and damned, publicly, if you don't."

Molly shook her head. "That's quite a dilemma."

"But I can't do it anymore." Loretta sighed. "I can't keep worrying about what he'll do next or what skeleton he'll pull out or what he'll make up to get money. I'm not going to live in fear anymore." She glanced at Travis then.

"People think being a celebrity is all fame and money and parties." Travis shook his head. "That's not bad but there's a darker side to it all. Everyone wants a piece of you. You don't know who's after what or what they're willing to do to get it. Until you find out and get your legs knocked out from under you. Even then, it's not over—not if the press gets a hold of it." He glanced her way. "Really it's about finding the people who help keep you grounded. The ones who believe in you, no matter what."

Loretta couldn't look away. His words resonated. *I believe in you.*

"On that note, Travis, you said you had a new song you wanted to share?" Molly asked.

Travis nodded, taking the guitar one of the assistants handed him. "I do."

"You do?" Loretta asked, smiling. "You're full of surprises."

Travis winked. "Always."

―――――――――――

His heart was in his throat, but he sang through.

> I heard your heart is guarded, that you're cold as ice.
> But one look told me different, I think I'll roll the dice.
> One night is what you offered, I said yes to your rules.
> But now I want forever, it's up to you to choose.

He gave himself permission to look at her, to study her—to sing just for her.

> What I'm saying, baby, is let's break all the rules.
> Let's hold on to each other and act like damn fools.
> All I'm asking, baby, is trust what's in your heart.
> Let's face this world together and never be apart.

Those topaz eyes were blazing now, drawing him in. But he couldn't get lost yet. He still had things to say. He pulled his gaze from hers to finish the song.

> Loving you is breathing and sleeping at your side.
> Loving you is freedom with nothing left to hide.
> And loving you is gravity that holds me on the ground.
> Love me too and, baby, we'll be heaven-bound.

His fingers moved quickly, letting each note take shape before moving on to the next. It was a ballad. Not as melancholy as one

Krystal would write, but it wasn't meant to be melancholy. He was reaching out to Loretta—reaching out with hope. The last note still hung in the air when he opened his eyes.

The studio was quiet.

Beyond the camera man, his father was watching. His father, Hank King, was proud. And, dammit all, it got him choked up.

"That was some song," Molly said, her hand pressed to her chest.

But Travis wasn't worried about Molly's reaction or the camera crew or Margot. He'd poured his heart out for Loretta. Hell, she was his heart. He hadn't expected tears. She wasn't crying; she was fighting against them. But she'd heard his song and, from the looks of it, she'd felt it too.

*Damn but I hope so.* He tore his gaze from hers. There were things to say, but first they had to get through the rest of the interview.

"How did you come up with this song?" Molly asked, ever the professional.

*She's sitting right beside me.* Travis almost chuckled. "Every song is different."

Molly nodded, asking about other songs and how his writing process differed from his sisters'. In time, Loretta snapped out of it too, answering questions and laughing at a photo Emmy Lou had posted of Travis with Watson and Clementine sleeping on top of him.

"She has no respect for privacy." Travis smiled.

"It's an adorable picture, Travis," Loretta argued. "There should be more adorable stuff on the internet. It makes people happy."

"Are we talking about Watson or Clementine?" He smiled. "Or me?"

Loretta's smile was a thing of beauty. "Watson and Clementine, of course."

By the time the interview had wrapped up, Travis was out of patience. Loretta was right here, so close he could take her hand if he wanted. And he wanted to. But he still didn't know how she felt.

Even if she did love him, Loretta was gun-shy about feelings. There was no way she'd open herself up to him in front of an audience. Like it or not, he'd have to wait until they were home and there was no audience. Once the camera was turned off, they handed back their mics and stepped out of the way for the crew to clean up, but Loretta grabbed his hand.

"Thank you." Her eyes searched his. "Thank you for knowing I wasn't capable of that. With my father and the video, I mean. It means a lot, Travis."

"I know." He cradled her hand in his. "I felt the same way when I heard you were so damn confident I hadn't fallen off the wagon." He smiled. "Krystal and Emmy Lou made sure I knew all about it."

She stared at their hands.

"You, believing in me, means something." He cleared his throat. "*You* mean something to me."

"Travis…" She broke off, her voice lowering. "I know how important honesty is and I lied." She took a deep breath. "I was mean, more than mean, to hurt you. I was so scared and I thought, if I did, things would end between us and CiCi wouldn't pay my dad to cause problems for you and your family and me—"

"Back up." His hold tightened. "What were you scared of?"

Her gaze fell.

"Don't shut down on me now, Loretta."

"Travis…" She tried to tug her hand from his. "This isn't easy for me—"

"I get that." He shook his head. "You're not the only one who doesn't do feelings. I've spent my whole life toying with them. You've done your damnedest to avoid having them. But here we are. Having feelings." He smiled.

"I don't have the best track record with feelings." Worry edged her voice.

"Me neither. Something else we've got in common, besides shitty parents."

"Your dad—"

"Is excluded. Don't change the subject." He pulled her close.

"There are people watching," she whispered.

"I'm fine letting them watch," he whispered in return. "But, if you're not, I can let you go."

She shook her head, gripping the front of his shirt.

He smiled then, the panic and uncertainty fading. "I know how I feel but we can focus on honesty and respect and loyalty instead of feelings. If that makes it easier, we can start there. If you're willing to try?"

She stared up at him. "What about love?" It was a whisper.

"You'll never have to ask if I love you, Loretta. I do. I always will." His heart hammered away.

"You do?"

"That song was for you, Loretta. From me, to you." He swallowed. "I love your spirit and your smile and the music inside of you. I love that you accept me and believe in me as I am."

A wavering sigh slipped between her lips, encouraging him to pull her a little closer.

"If you can find it in your heart to love a self-centered, spoiled pretty boy with fair to middling talent, a penchant for donuts and staring at your mouth, then I'm the one for you. I'm hoping you can because it'll be one hell of a challenge to pretend like I'm not crazy in love with you every second of every day and every damn time I look at you."

"You're the one for me, Travis King." She rested her hand against his chest. She stared up at him, the look on her face flooding him with love. "As long as you promise to always look at me like you're crazy in love with me."

"Do I have a choice?" he asked, resting his forehead against hers. "Look at you."

She pressed her hand against his jaw. "Really? You with the model hair and the smile and the eyes."

He grinned. "Don't forget all the muscles I have from working out."

"How can I forget?" She ran her fingers through his hair. "I love you."

He was grinning like a damn fool. "You're right. I won't let you forget." He pulled her close and kissed her softly. "About how fine you think I am or that you love me." He kissed her again. "And since everyone here, including the *Good Morning USA* staff, has been listening to the entire conversation, I have witnesses." He looked up, doing a quick sweep of the room. "Yep, everyone."

Loretta buried her face against his chest. "Everyone?" she whispered.

"Everyone." He pressed a kiss to the top of her head. "And while I appreciate the witnesses, this is about me and you. Me and you and *feelings*."

She looked up at him. "You do make me have all sort of feelings." She laughed at the way he was now staring at her lips. "Feelings as in I love you." She smoothed his curls. "I really love you, Travis King."

He stared down at her, all too happy to stay just as they were— wrapped up in each other. And happy. *So damn happy.* "Then I'm the luckiest man alive."

"ARE YOU KIDDING ME?" THEY COULD NOT BE SERIOUS. KRYSTAL glared at her daddy, country music legend Hank King, in pure disbelief. "Why would this be *great* news? For me, anyway." Blood roared in her ears and a throb took up residence at the base of her neck. She slipped the leather strap of her favorite Taylor spruce acoustic guitar from around her neck and placed the instrument tenderly on its stand. "It's great news for what's his name—"

"Jace Black," her manager, Steve Zamora, said.

"Whatever," she snapped, shooting a lethal gaze at the balding little man. "I'm sure he's ecstatic. He gets to sing my song, my *best* song. With the one and only Emmy Lou King." She downed a water bottle, parched from singing for almost two hours straight.

"Come on now, Krystal. They're singing one of *your* songs," her father soothed. But she wasn't ready to forgive him. Or see any good in this. And when he added "You know Emmy will do it up right. She always does," it stung.

*Unlike me.* Her spine stiffened and her fists tightened. She and her twin, Emmy, were different as night and day. A point her momma was all too happy to point out at every opportunity.

"Don't get your feathers ruffled, now. You know I didn't mean anything by that." Her daddy tipped his favorite tan cowboy hat back on his forehead, crossed his arms over his chest, and frowned.

*Poor Daddy.* He said the women in his life were the reason he was getting so grey. It wasn't intentional. She didn't like disappointing him—he was her hero. But, dammit, he couldn't pull the rug out from under her and expect her to smile and thank him. She wasn't a saint. She wasn't Emmy.

Steve tried again. "This is a win all around, Krystal."

"No, it's not. Not for me," she argued. Blowing up wasn't going to change their minds, but maybe reminding her daddy how special this song was. "Daddy, you know this song means something to me, that it's…important. I'm connected to it, deep down in my bones. I can sing it and do it justice." She hated that her voice wavered, that sentiment seeped in. This was business. And while the business loved raw emotion and drama in its music and lyrics, they weren't fans of it from their performers.

"Now, darlin', you know how it works. It's all about timing." Steve used his soft voice, the please-don't-let-her-start-screaming-and-throwing-things voice. Like lemon juice in a paper cut.

"Timing?" she asked. The only thing Steve Zamora cared about was kissing her legendary father's ass and managing Emmy Lou's career. "It's been my sister's time for ten years now."

Not that she begrudged her sister an iota of her fame. It wasn't Emmy Lou's fault that she was the favorite. She had that *thing*, a megastar quality—that universally appealing sweetness that the world adored. Krystal had a real hard time with sweetness.

Why the media, fans, even the record company labeled Krystal the rebel, a black sheep, the wild child of the King family was a mystery. Marketing, maybe? The good twin, bad twin thing? Whatever. She had her days. And her very public breakup with Mickey Graham hadn't helped. To hear him tell it, she was a selfish prima donna who'd broken his heart. It'd hurt like hell that everyone was so willing to believe the worst of her. But her pride had stopped her from telling the truth—the real truth, not Mickey's version of it. His tall tales cemented her bad-girl image, so she'd embraced some of the freedom it gave her.

"I get you're disappointed, Krystal, but there will be other songs." Daddy's hand cupped her cheek, his smile genuine and sympathetic.

*He did not just say that.* His easy dismissal cut deep. Yes, there would be other songs, but this one *mattered*. People might chalk it up to her breakup with Mickey. She knew better. The song had come from a wound that wouldn't heal. A wound that haunted her dreams and reminded her to guard her heart, to never let anyone in. Every scribbled note, tweaked word, chord change, or key finagle had led her to both love and hate the finished product. But it made her proud.

Her daddy had said he was proud, too. Just not enough. While she'd never asked her father to plead her case at their label, Wheelhouse Records, she realized, deep down, she'd hoped he would—for this song—without her having to ask. But if he had championed her, she'd be cutting the single, not Emmy and some new music reality TV star.

"You good?" her father asked.

*No.* She glared.

He sighed. "Breathe, baby girl. Don't want you spitting fire at folk for the rest of the night."

She didn't need to be reminded of the Three Kings fans lined up outside. This had been her life for the past ten years. It was more than singing side by side with her twin sister and older brother, playing her guitar until her fingertips hurt, or waking up humming a new melody, new lyrics already taking shape. It was making people *feel*. The only thing that mattered was the fans. Was she upset? Yes. Hurt? Most definitely. But when she left her dressing room, a dazzling smile would be on her face—for them. After the meet and greet would be another story.

Her father let out a long, pained sigh. "Might as well go ahead and send him in."

Send who in? Her dressing room was entirely too crowded

already. Not that protesting would make a bit of difference. She flopped into the chair before her illuminated makeup mirror, all but choking on frustration, and rubbed lotion into her fingers and hands. Hands that were shaking.

Steve leaned out her dressing room door, calling, "Come on in, Jace. She's looking forward to meeting you."

Jace. She froze. As in Jace-the-song-stealer Black? She was not looking forward to meeting him. Some wannabe singer from a no-count TV talent show. *American Voice*? Or *Next Top Musician*? Or something else gimmicky and stupid?

In the mirror, she shot daggers her father's way. He was pushing it—pushing her. She applied a stroke of bloodred color to her mouth, jammed the lipstick lid back on, and pressed her hands against her thighs before risking a glance in the mirror at the man who'd stolen her dreams.

He was big. *Big* big. He had to stoop to get through the door of her dressing room.

"Mr. King, sir." Jace's voice was deep and smooth and impossible to ignore. But that didn't mean he could sing. "It's a real honor." He extended a hand to her father. Polite. That was something.

"Good to meet you, son," her father answered, shaking his hand and clapping Jace on the shoulder.

Tall *and* broad-shouldered. A weathered black leather jacket hugged the breadth of his shoulders and upper arms. As he pivoted on the heel of his boot, her gaze wandered south, revealing a perfect ass gloved in faded denim. She blew out a long, slow breath. Very nice packaging. *But* a great body didn't mean diddly when you were performing live, in front of an audience of thousands.

He glanced her way then. It was a glance, nothing really, but it was enough.

*Oh hell.*

Of course he was drop-dead gorgeous. Thick black hair, strong jaw, and a wicked, tempting grin on very nice lips. *Dammit.* He shook hands with her weasel manager, Steve, before giving her his full attention. A jolt of pure appreciation raced down her spine to the tips of her crystal-encrusted boots. *It's not fair. None of this is fair.* She fiddled with her heavy silver Tiffany charm bracelet and tucked a strand of hair behind her ear, too agitated to sit still.

Talented or not, it wouldn't matter. Not when he looked like that. Which was exactly why he was here. That face. That body. Jace Black and Emmy Lou King? His dark, dangerous good looks and her sister's golden sweetness? They'd make quite a pair onstage, singing her song…

*Her* song.

Her temper flared, quick and hot. She didn't give a damn what he looked like. Or if he had manners. He hadn't earned the right to her words, not by a long shot. And since he was a big boy, she'd take it upon herself to show him how tough this industry could be. Starting right here, right now.

His gaze locked with her reflection. "I can't tell you how… amazing it is to meet you, Miss King." That velvet voice was far too yummy. "I know every word to every song you've written." He needed to stop looking at her so she could stay pissed off and feisty.

But he didn't. And the longer he looked, the harder it was to overlook the way he was looking at her. Admiring her as a singer and songwriter was one thing. But right now, something told her he was appreciating more than her music.

Too bad she couldn't like him. At all.

She ignored her daddy's warning look and stood, turning to face Jace. Her momma raised her daughters with a deep under-standing of female charm and the power it could wield. With a dazzling smile, she shook the hand he offered, fully intending to use her powers for evil. But the brush of his calloused fingers against her palm threw off her concentration. It had been a long time since she'd been even slightly attracted to a man. But this time, there was nothing slight about what she was feeling. *No, no, no. Stay mad.* "Oh, I doubt that, *Chase*."

"Jace," he said, grinning.

*Oh hell, this is bad.* That smile. She knew his name, but still… "Right." She bit into her lower lip, drawing his attention to her mouth.

His nostrils flared just enough to make her insides soften. Not the reaction she was hoping for. He cleared his throat and tore his eyes away, that square jaw of his clenched. Tight. That was a weakness of hers—a man's jaw muscle. Only two things made a man's jaw tick like that: anger or desire. And, right now, she was pretty sure Jace Black didn't have a thing in the world to be angry about. But she did. Big-time. The slow, liquid burn taking up residence deep in her stomach was beyond inconvenient.

Steve said something original like, "What did you think of the show?"

"Incredible. Y'all are even better live, I think, if that's possible," Jace said. "I'm a little starstruck—guess you can tell."

Was he? She couldn't tell—his hotness was getting in the way. No way she was going to let a pretty face and tingles lead her astray, not this time. "That's always nice to hear." If it was true.

"I want to thank you," Jace said to her father—of course. Only someone like Hank King could get a nobody reality star this sort of break. "I know how lucky I am to get this opportunity." He had *no* idea. His luck was her loss. Not that he could know or understand how much his words stung. His gaze returned to her when he said, "Your music has always meant a lot to me—a lot of folk, I'm sure. But your new song—"

"*My* song?" She couldn't take it anymore. His reminder lodged a sharp spike in her throat. "From what I hear, it's yours now." She ignored her daddy's disapproving frown and the panic on Steve's face. Like her temper was totally unexpected? They should have thought about that before bringing *him* in here seconds after crushing her hopes and dreams. The sting of tears infuriated her further. None of them would ever see her cry, dammit. Ever.

"It's a good song." From Jace's expression, he knew something wasn't right. But he kept right on talking. "It's one of the best things you've written. When I read it—" He broke off, shaking his head. "I'm still in shock I get to sing it."

"That makes two of us," she whispered. But at least he got it, about the song, anyway.

He hesitated, then stepped closer. If she'd had room, she'd have stepped back. Because Jace Black up close was even better—worse—than Jace Black at a distance. Good skin. Even, white teeth. And a holy-hell amazing scent that had her toes curling in her blinged-out ostrich-skin boots.

"I'm guessing I wasn't your first pick?" His gaze never left her face, waiting for an explanation.

She shrugged, wondering why she'd suddenly lost her ability to fire off something quick and biting.

"And you're not happy about it." He swallowed, the muscles in his throat working.

She heard him—she did. But the air between them was crackling something fierce and it was taking total concentration not to get lost in those light brown eyes. After spending the last two years avoiding men, she wasn't sure what, exactly, was happening. Only that she needed to keep her guard up and as much space as possible between them. Pretty words and even prettier packaging might have made it easier for him to worm his way in with other people, but it wouldn't work on her.

What did he want? Beyond singing her song, of course. She studied him openly, exploring his face and searching his gaze for some nervous flutter or guilty flush. Mickey's eyes tightened when he was hiding something. Just a little, mind you, but when she saw it now, she knew it was a red flag. And Uncle Tig... *No.* She swept thoughts of him aside.

But Jace?

The flash of pure, unfiltered male appreciation in those incredible eyes had her insides fluid and hot. If only they'd met under other circumstances...then it would be okay to get tangled up in bed somewhere—and have one hell of a time wearing each other out.

She swallowed, the images all too tempting. Too bad she had to hate him. "Don't you worry over me, *Jason*. I'm tough."

She wasn't feeling very tough at the moment. The sooner today was over, the sooner she was done with Jace Black. Which was better for his career, anyway. Even though she was pissed he'd taken her song, it wasn't in her to intentionally sink his career just to spite him. No, that was more her momma's MO—and she was nothing, *nothing*, like her momma.

Enough. She was tired and irritable and on the verge of coming undone. Her fans were waiting and they deserved the best her she could muster. She turned, glancing at her reflection and smoothing a wayward strand of long blond hair into place. Crystal chandelier earrings and a beyond-blinding crystal necklace—Momma was all about the bling—accented the plunging neckline of the concert's final costume change. The ultrafine black suede fringed dress felt like silk and was cut to perfection, clinging in all the right places.

From the tightness of Jace Black's jaw, he noticed.

Maybe she could muster up the energy to mess with him a little, for the hell of it. "Time to go meet the fans." A dazzling smile just for him. Yep, that floored him. "You are planning on tagging along, aren't you?"

His gaze narrowed—confused. Maybe even a little nervous.

"We weren't staying—" a man in the corner said.

"Well, that doesn't make any sense." She hooked her arm through Jace's. A warm, very thickly muscled arm. Not that muscles mattered. "And who are you, anyway?"

"My manager. Luke Samuels," Jace said.

A weasel—like Steve. He had hair and was dressed better, but there was no denying the similarities: too eager to please and dewy with anxious sweat. "Miss King, it's an honor, a real honor—".

"Sure. But since you're here and all, might as well come meet some fans. Since our fans will be your fans soon enough." She beamed up at Jace again, but this time around, he looked down-right suspicious. So he was smart, too?

"If you want—" Luke began.

"I do," she said, tugging Jace along. "Besides, you should meet Emmy, maybe get a few pics of the two of you." She didn't know why she was torturing herself. Seeing her sister and Jace together, paired up to sing her creation, wasn't going to improve her mood. But there was no going back now.

Smile in place, she walked into the hall to the sound of those fans that paid extra money for the backstage passes and meet and greet. "You know how to work the crowd, *Jake*?" she asked, empha-sizing the name. His delicious grin told her he hadn't missed it. "Now's a good time to get some practice."

Now that she'd led him into the lion's den, he could fend for himself. With a wink, she let him go—but he followed closely—his scent still teasing her nostrils. Best to ignore him and focus on doing her job.

She enjoyed this part of it. This was what it was about—these people loved their music, loved them. Their enthusiasm was con-tagious and reassuring. As much as she'd like to deny it, she wanted to be liked, maybe even a little bit adored, the way her sister and brother were.

And Jace Black? Apparently, people knew who he was and, from the way they screamed his name, liked him.

If he wasn't stealing her song, she'd have considered being a fan, too. But he was, so she wasn't. Still, from that wicked grin to those beautiful eyes, there was a whole lot about Jace Black to like.

*Don't screw this up.* Jace tore his gaze from Krystal King.

If he was smart, he'd hang back and watch the Kings work the room. He could only hope to handle a crowd like this with half their composure. When someone recognized him from *Next Top American Voice*, he got red-faced and tongue-tied. He wasn't sure why he'd gone along with Krystal—he just had. And now? He sure as hell hadn't expected to be recognized. Women were screaming his name, waving their cameras at him—some of them were *crying*. Crying?

It made him uncomfortable as hell. Here he was, blushing and stumbling over what to say, and these people knew his name, thought he was talented, wanted to touch him and get his autograph.

"Smile and wave," his little sister, Heather, had told him. "Pretend like you're having fun. Like you're going fishing." He wished she were here, poking fun at him, keeping him grounded. Since she wasn't, he'd follow her advice. He leaned into the crowd and smiled at the dozens of phones snapping pictures.

He didn't know if he'd ever get used to this. To him, it was overwhelming. Crazy. And "*part of the job*"—the Wheelhouse Records PR department had assured him.

Krystal's husky laughter set the hair on the back of his neck upright. Out of the corner of his eye, he saw her hugging a fan. The tenderness on her face was unexpected—and oh so real. He'd been warned about Krystal King. She was guarded. Check. Had a bit of a temper. Check. The spark in her green eyes confirmed that, too. No one had to tell him she was sexy as hell—he'd always known that. But nothing, *nothing*, had prepared him for how fiercely he'd respond to her.

To say he was attracted to the rebel King was an understatement. But there was more to Krystal King than what the media,

Wheelhouse Records, and his manager had to say. Anyone who could write the lyrics she did or create music that made him ache was more than cold and angry. Her music was her voice—weighted with real passion. The sort of emotion that had him wearing out Three Kings CDs in his old truck and singing along whenever one of their songs was on the radio. His favorite songs? The ones she wrote. Not only did he admire her music, but he admired how she handled the bad-girl persona and public character-bashing she was regularly subjected to. He never believed the tabloid headlines or talk show gossip, but if she was angry and guarded, she had plenty of reasons.

Was he one of them now?

The way she'd looked at him…he hadn't been prepared for that. He couldn't tell if she was all angry fire or sizzling from of a different kind of flame. Wishful thinking. There was no way someone like Krystal King was interested in him. All he knew was looking at her too long had him burning in a way that set warning flares off in his brain. Watching her now, blond hair hanging down her back and the fringes of her black minidress swinging around a pair of long, toned golden legs, had him wishing. Hard.

*Bad idea. Don't screw this up.*

"Jace." A woman grabbed his hand. "I love you. Your voice is perfect." Her cheeks were flushed. "You're perfect. I voted for you every night."

"I appreciate that. But I'm not perfect," he said, smiling. "I can promise you that."

"You are. You are. And I love you," the woman insisted, her grip tightening.

"And he loves you, too. You have to share him with the rest of us," Travis King, the only male member of the Three Kings, gently pried the woman's hand loose. "But he's real glad you came out to meet him. Got something for him to sign?"

The woman nodded and offered him a poster of the Three

Kings. He glanced at Travis and signed the corner, feeling like a fraud. He handed it back, smiled, and moved on. "Thanks," he murmured to Travis.

"Clingers are hard," Travis said, signing and talking and not missing a step. "One woman jumped over the tape and into my arms. She was no lightweight, either. Pulled a muscle in my back and had to get one of them to help her back onto the other side of the tape."

Jace looked in the direction of Travis's nod. Three men and one woman wearing "King's Guard" shirts. *Clever.* "Security?" he asked, smiling in spite of himself.

"Always," he said. "I hear my sister roped you into sticking around?"

"Not sure how it happened," Jace confessed.

"Krystal has a way of getting what she wants." Travis laughed. "Come on, take a break in the greenroom. Then it's time for group pics and hanging with the money." He led Jace down the hall, all the while smiling and waving.

Krystal joined them, no sign of her earlier tension present. She sort of…glowed, happy and excited. "You two stand together too long and we might have a riot on our hands."

Was that a compliment? It sure as hell sounded like one.

"Just own it, man. Own it and enjoy every minute." Travis grinned. "You'll never have to sleep alone again."

"Travis, there are times I'm ashamed to call you my brother." Clearly, she didn't appreciate her brother's attitude. By the time they entered what resembled a small conference room, Krystal was back to being tense and quiet.

One wall was lined with mirrors and floor-to-ceiling folding screens. Jace was blindsided by the photographs hanging on the wall just inside. He wandered, reading autographs and shaking his head at the impressive display of talent that had visited the Chesapeake Energy Arena before him. Willie Nelson. John

Connelly. Loretta Lynn. And a smiling, younger Hank King. Here he was, a west Texas roughneck, surrounded by reminders of everything he wasn't. Sooner or later, the rest of the world would snap out of it and he'd be back on the grasshoppers, drilling for oil from dawn till dusk.

*Might as well enjoy it.*

On the opposite wall, a long table was covered with trays of pastries, fruit, and cheese. He almost took pictures for Heather—almost. She'd love to see this—the fancy sparkling water bottles in large glass bowls full of ice. Above that, three large televisions played, muted. The room and its occupants seemed to be on fast-forward, while he was stuck in slow motion.

He shook his hands out and did his best not to stand out.

His manager, Luke, was waiting with Mr. Zamora, looking almost as nervous as he felt. Jace had taken a gamble hiring him, but Luke had grown up in the business and knew all the right people. Like CiCi King. He had no idea Luke's mother and Hank King's wife played bunco together, but he suspected that was how he'd ended up here. His voice was only part of it—having the right connections sealed the deal. Still, standing against the wall as the room filled with the chart-breaking, award-winning King family and the entourage that cared for them had his insecurities kicking in. Sure he sang some, for himself—or at the bar in town. But he had nothing, *nothing*, like the talent in this room.

Sure, they talked and laughed just like normal folk—but there was nothing normal about these people. He didn't belong here. This was not his life. This wasn't real; it couldn't be.

It didn't help that Krystal kept glancing his way. Even standing there, talking to her brother, she radiated a sort of defiance that was hard to ignore. Hell, if he was honest with himself, he didn't want to ignore her. He'd prop himself up right here, against the wall, and look his fill if he could. No woman should look this beautiful in real life. But she was.

# Acknowledgments

This series has been an emotional roller coaster. In order to challenge the Kings with real-life issues, I had to dig deep into some difficult topics—some more difficult than others. It helped having my Romance Besties there with me every step of the way. Allison Collins, Teri Wilson, Jolene Navarro, Julia London, Patricia W. Fisher, Frances Trilone, Molly Mirren, Makenna Less, K.L White, and Storm Navarro—you guys are the best cheerleaders and friends anyone could want.

Thank you to Susie Benton for being so sweet and supportive when I needed it most. Pets are family too—you totally got that.

To my family, I know it can't be easy living with me, but you have to admit it's never boring.

And thank you to the readers for letting me share my stories with you.

# About the Author

*USA Today* bestselling author Sasha Summers grew up surrounded by books. Her passions have always been storytelling, romance, and travel—passions she uses when writing. Now a bestselling and award-winning author, Sasha continues to fall a little in love with each hero she writes. From easy-on-the-eyes cowboys, to sexy alpha-male werewolves, to heroes of truly mythic proportions, she believes that everyone should have their happy ending—in fiction and real life.

Sasha lives in the suburbs of the Texas Hill Country with her amazing and supportive family and her beloved grumpy cat, Gerard, The Feline Overlord. She looks forward to hearing from fans and hopes you'll visit her online. Facebook: Sasha Summers Author, Twitter: @sashawrites, or her website: sashasummers.com.